THE SHADOW AND THE SUN

MONICA ENDERLE PIERCE

GOLDEN
FLOWER

Developmental Editor: Maia Driver
Copy editor: Colleen Vanderlinden
Cover and Interior Illustrations: Qistina Khalidah
Cover Design: Scott Pierce

Published in the United States by Stalking Fiction
print ISBN-13: 978-0-9859761-4-9

THE
SHADOW
AND
THE SUN

GOLDEN FLOWER

STORIES THAT STAY WITH YOU

SEATTLE, WA

MONICAENDERLEPIERCE.COM

DEDICATION

For Emeline
May you find the beauty in shadows

KALIX
NORTHERN WASTES
TELEYANSK
SCHORVALA
Yasan Khot
Chono Khot
Beach Camp
Lake Fera
Garrison
Ballard River
The Thumb
North Selga River
Floria
Tatlis
URSINTUM
Drevya
The Fist
NALVIKA
Lake Tatlis
Kharaton
Ayestra
Ostendra
The Silver Sea
The Choker
Ystwyth
BESERA
South Selga River
Eskis
Fayet
Fayet Desert
OR-HALEE
Or-Halee Cid
Vala
Selt
THE GREAT GREEN OCEAN

ONE

Steel rang through King Vernard's encampment as his bastard daughter, Halina, dueled with the captain of her guard. They lunged, parried, and dodged in an open space among the tents as a group of militairs watched.

"Come now, Captain, where are your bollocks, man?" one of the onlookers jeered.

Halina laughed. "I keep them in a little bag around my neck, Charin, right next to yours."

As the soldiers responded with shouts and laughter Captain Thaksin seized the moment and lunged into the opening beneath His Ladyship's guard. She blocked, though not fast enough, and her captain's sword smacked her left knuckles.

The captain stepped back as the onlookers cheered and jeered. "Settle down, dunderheads," he said.

Halina inclined her head in acceptance of the point as she shook her gloved hand. "Khotyr, take me, that *stings*."

Thaksin laughed. "Margrave, please. You don't have fingers to be pained."

That was a partial truth. Halina was missing a third of her pinkie and half of her ring finger on her left hand. They were just two of many battle scars she bore after spending over half her twenty-seven years in service to her kingdom.

The captain circled his liege, his longsword held low as he basked in the cheers of the small crowd.

"I have fingers enough for this." She saluted him rudely then lunged and scored on his chest. "And to kill you." She flipped her dark auburn hair over her shoulders. It had come loose of its braids again.

Thaksin tsk-tsked and raised his sword. "A cheater's point, Your Ladyship?"

"Death obeys no rules." Her next cut came from above and swept down diagonally, fast and powerful as she tried to break his guard.

The sharp clash of the longswords was quickly muted by heavy fog. The cold, rolling brume enshrouded the encampment, making hulking ghosts of tents and nebulous wraiths of soldiers in a camp that flattened over fifty wind-swept, scrubby acres between the base of Kharayan Tor and the shore of the Silver Sea.

The militairs called and clapped. The militess and her captain parried, blocked, and lunged for a few more minutes before Thaksin suddenly stepped back, lowered his sword, and knelt. The soldiers observing the duel quickly followed the captain's lead.

Halina lowered her own sword, turned, and wasn't surprised to see her brother — Ursinum's crown prince — enter the arena. "Semele's blood."

Prince Ilker's expression was grim as he stopped at her elbow. "Don't invoke the old gods," he said in her ear, his dark blue eyes cold and his tone filled with disapproval.

She kept her voice low, too, as she replied, "Those are your beliefs, not mine." Sweat trickled down her back and salted her upper lip. Mist settled upon her hair and darkened her long, gray leather tabard. "I still prefer the old gods; they've kept me alive and mostly intact through many battles."

Ilker raised his voice and jabbed a finger at the watching militairs. "You men find other things to do." As they hastened away from their margrave and her brother, the crown prince said, "You're a lady, Halina. Try acting like one."

"I'm a soldier. Which I've noticed bothers you when I'm taking men to bed but not when I'm leading them into battle."

"Margrave—"

"Blood and bones, Ilk. You're not my keeper. I'll act like a *lady* when you stop being so sanctimonious." She turned and raised her longsword to re-engage Thaksin, but the captain had disappeared with the other militairs. "Bollocks! I was about to win that match."

Ilker crossed his arms. "Another time you can trounce your captain. The king needs you now."

"Oh, gods, what does he want?" Halina shoved her sword into its scabbard with more force than necessary. She shivered; she was sweatier than a whore on Khotyr's Day and the unseasonable fog was chilling her as quickly as dueling had warmed her. Plus, her mood had gone from fun to foul. Ilker was being a bed tick, and King Vernard never sent him to her with glad tidings.

Her brother's disapproval deepened into a scowl. "The king has chosen you to parley with the Shadow Mage." He proffered a sealed letter. "Here are the final terms for the man — gold, land, and a place in His Majesty's court in exchange for allegiance in this war against Besera. The king's horse is being saddled as we speak. He'll accompany you to the mage's ward-line. I'm to remain in camp."

"It's about time all those nattering goats he calls advisors made a smart decision." She looked from the letter in her brother's hand to the tightness around his mouth. Ilker was worried about her. The mage and his wards were deadly.

The king's first attempt to court the Shadow Mage had been met with scorn. With the second venture the messenger had returned whole of body but unsound of mind. It was assumed that the man's mission had failed. The third attempt, also delivered in person, had produced no reply other than an emissary who appeared to have been turned inside out before death took him at the edge of Kharayan's woods.

Halina accepted the parchment. "I'll hasten to pack my bag and join His Majesty."

She turned away, but Ilker stopped her with a touch on her elbow. "You know I'm against this, Halina."

"Yes. And you know volunteering was my choice."

"A poor one."

"Your opinion. Someone has to speak with the mage. He's my tenant; it should be me." She squeezed his fingers and gave him a crooked smile. "You also know I'm too stubborn to die, 'Ilk. So stop worrying."

When King Vernard had, begrudgingly, granted control of Khara to his elder daughter, he'd also given her dominion over the Shadow Mage, whose dark-gray Ranith Citadel was well within Khara's borders.

That had been six years ago, after the War of the Winds. Like everyone else in Quoregna's four kingdoms, Halina had hoped for many decades without the bloody slaughter of war. But, as if wicked weather drove wicked feelings, trade negotiations between Ursinum and neighboring Besera — with whom they'd been long allied — had turned cold and bitter in lockstep with the abnormally frigid autumn. Vernard had threatened an embargo on salt exports. Besera's King Zelal had responded by massing his army for invasion; if they couldn't buy Ursinum's salt they'd take it. The Silver Sea separated the two kingdoms. And Khara, a long, narrow holding sandwiched between the sea and the nearly impenetrable Valmerian Mountains, was Ursinum's first line of defense.

Ilker said, "This is why you need a husband," as he kissed her temple.

"As much as I need a sword in the gut," Halina replied as he left her, his tall figure quickly becoming a shadowy wraith in the fog.

Her gaze slid to the gothic tower that dominated the tor above Vernard's camp. "Turn this war and the weather, Shadow Mage," she said beneath her breath.

The things Halina knew of the man could be ticked off on her left hand: his name was Gethen Rhysh, he was the elder brother of Besera's king, and he was Quoregna's most powerful necromancer. She'd never seen or spoken with him, nor had any of her men. "I imagine you're bent, bald, and bitter," she muttered as she donned her heavy, gray winter cloak. "Slowly rotting and going mad in that tower, cursed by the evil of your own dark spells." She laughed and thought, *Or maybe you're charming and handsome, with straight teeth and an amiable disposition.* Her humor died. *Let me cross your wards so we can parley, Master Gethen of Ranith. Khara and Ursinum need your help, whether we like it or not.*

Thaksin appeared at the arena's edge, and Halina's attention went to him. "Saddle up and tell our company to make ready to return to Kharaton Castle."

"We're leaving?"

"You're leaving." She held up the letter. "I'm going to meet a mage."

TWO

"**S**omething's not right, my friend. Winter's come too soon."
Gethen slid his fingers through the thick, black coat of
the wolf walking beside him.

He and the wolf wended their way through Kharayan's thick
forest. The black oaks and silver pines were covered with spiky
white hoarfrost, the ground was hard and icy. Autumn had lost its
color before it had fully bloomed. Gone were the fiery golds,
jewel reds, and dusty purples. Instead, the woods and ruins were
dark and forbidding, smothered by an unnatural, gray brume that
seeped from the ground and the air.

"Much too soon. I want to know why."

Warmth and the steady pulse of the wolf's strong heart flowed
into Gethen, and deep within his own body, magic stirred. But it
didn't caress his muscles and mind with the ease and eagerness of
a street whore, as it had not so long ago. His power had become
as reluctant as a virgin and as meek as a baby.

He was a mage balanced upon the cusp of transformation as
his sorcery changed from being powered by the shadows to being
fueled by the sun. A shadow mage becoming a sun mage, he was
the only one of his kind in the four kingdoms of Quoregna.

The black wolf kept its keen amber gaze on him and sat as he knelt beside it. "I'll only take as much as I need," Gethen said, and the wolf closed its eyes. "And I'll stay with you until you're strong again."

He ran his fingers through the animal's coarse guard hairs, leaving a faint trail of green sparks. Beneath his strong, pale hand, the wolf's silver spirit shimmered and, with a small tug, the power that resided within the animal flowed into the man.

This, at least, is still a simple task, he thought as he controlled the draw. Dark, cool magic rose from deep within his body and flooded his nerves. He summoned the forest's shadows, spun them into a thick skein, and wove that into dusky, iridescent armor and a shroud with many magical folds from within which his spirit could spy.

Cloaked and armed thusly, Gethen released the wolf's spirit. The animal settled to the forest's carpet of brittle, frosted leaves and slept. Leaving his own body and part of his consciousness to guard over the wolf, he released his soul to travel through the realm of death in search of answers.

The Void was a colorless reflection of the living world, and the hues of his skin and nacreous armor were striking against the gloom. His soul stepped onto a meandering cobblestone path beneath a slate sky. Worn, dank, and coated with black moss, it wound through a murky, silent forest of spindly, leafless trees.

A few souls loitered near the Voidline, as solid in form as the living but as gray as the surroundings. "Be off before I hurl you deeper into the Void," he said, and with a wave of his hand they scattered like leaves. They were unwelcome so close to the border. Souls lingering in the Void long enough to find Gethen's crossing on their own, were ones who had no business returning to the realm of the living, and it was his responsibility to keep them imprisoned.

His body shivered where it crouched beside the wolf. He focused outward, seeking a thread of dark, disruptive magic. But there was nothing. And that was disturbing, indeed. Death's realm usually bristled with danger. Something was hiding the source of the unnatural winter, and he had an unpleasant suspicion of the cause.

Gethen tightened his shadow shroud and pushed his magic, willing it to find a way past whatever was blocking his view of the Void. Back in the forest, his body shook harder. Pain and cramps flared across his shoulders and back.

Finally, he snagged a faint thread of cold, bitter sorcery, and the path he followed became shiny and slick with black ice. This was old magic, like his, and it was brittle and spiky, filled with malice and death. Such ancient sorcery was rare and rarely benevolent. It was the kind of corruptive power the kings and queens of yore had turned to mages like him to contain.

Following the ribbon of cold magic, he came to a wide, shallow expanse of chalky, white fluid that swallowed his reflection. In its center stood a small, black, octagonal mausoleum. The liquid seeped from beneath its closed doors and flowed down the steps. He crouched and touched it, rubbing his fingers together. The fluid had the silkiness of bleached bones and was so cold it burned. He stood and wiped his fingers on his cloak.

The Rime Witch.

She was an ancient and vindictive sorceress imprisoned in the Void a thousand years ago by one of his long-forgotten predecessors. The wards holding her were unbreakable, which meant she'd been released.

"Who freed you?" he murmured, his voice muted in the Void.

The mausoleum's doors banged open. Gethen was lashed by an icy whip. The faint ribbon of magic he'd been following had become a thick scourge. He stumbled back, shook his head from the sting of it, and summoned more shadows. He transformed them into black, roiling clouds and sent them to blind and confuse his unseen attacker. But a howling, frigid wind tore them into wisps, spun them into sleet, and blasted them back at him. His armor held. Head down he pushed forward.

The wind suddenly reversed, dragging his shadows and the sleet toward the building, sucking at Gethen's spirit. He stumbled, dug in his heels, and resisted the violent pull. Unsheathing his longsword, he plunged it into the ground, an anchor against the shrieking vortex that had engulfed the mausoleum.

Shadows, sleet, and fog coalesced into a gray and glittering whirlwind. Faces churned within it, voices screeched and howled. Visions of war filled his mind: Bodies writhed, blood flowed, kingdoms fell beneath the crush of a shadowy army. Besera's King Zelal — his own brother — bled and begged for mercy. King Vernard's head was displayed on a blood-slicked pike.

Gethen beat back the uninvited images. His arms ached and his tremors grew. His corporeal body convulsed, taxed by the dark magic swelling within it as the attacker attempted to seize his power. His freezing skin burned and his lungs grew heavy and congested.

Don't fight. Walk away. The Rime Witch would twist and manipulate him, if given the chance. And though his sorcery was weakening, it could still give her enough strength to cross the Voidline and spread her malevolence over Quoregna. His responsibility was to contain evil in the Void, not to battle it.

Gethen wrapped his shredded shadow cloak around his spirit and turned from the vortex. He was wasting his flagging power with this fight. Better to return to the Voidline and strengthen his wards to prevent the witch's escape. He could return her to her tomb and reinforce those wards once he'd crossed the cusp and gained the sun's magic.

Like blood and melting flesh, wisps of black shadow dripped from him as he crossed the white water. The violent sorcery followed, lashing at his hem and heels. But Gethen traveled a twisting course, its many turns to the Voidline meant to lead shadows and souls astray, and the witch's scourge weakened.

But as he crossed into the corporeal world, he was struck numb and dumb by a fiery spark that shot from his feet through the top of his head. His body collapsed into the leaves and detritus of the forest.

Voices called him. He couldn't respond. His lungs ached. His muscles knotted. If he couldn't rejoin body and soul, he'd be trapped in this half-life until his physical body wasted and died.

"Open your eyes, Master."

Magod. He knew his groundskeeper's voice. The man and his elderly mother Noni, Gethen's housekeeper, had the distinctive clipped speech of the Ayestran people.

Noni said, "C'mon, Master. Up. You can't sleep here."

He opened his eyes to both realms. A blinding flash of golden light enveloped him. His spirit was aflame, his magic surged, and his soul slammed back into his body so hard he grunted, rolled over, and coughed up phlegm and chalky, white fluid.

Noni held his head and crooned like the mother he barely remembered. Gethen pushed up to his hands and knees and cursed. This transition to sun sorcery was going to kill him. Pain pounded his skull, trying to beat his eyeballs out from the inside. She tutted, but he shoved her hands away. "Enough," he rasped. "I'm not a child."

"Pissed your trouzes like one," Magod said.

Gethen glared at his servant. "Remind me to gut you when I've recovered my strength."

"Yes, Master," Magod replied and helped him stand.

"Did anything else cross the Voidline?"

"Master?"

"A shadow? An entity? Did you see or feel anything unusual in the forest?"

Noni shook her head, and Magod replied, "Nothing."

"Good." Gethen exhaled and looked around. "That's good."

The black wolf sat amid the trees, a dark form against the mist. As Gethen straightened, it turned and disappeared into the fog. The swirl of mist around murky shapes accompanied it; the rest of the Kharayan wolf pack had been watching over Gethen and their brother.

Noni threw her master's gray woolen cloak around his shoulders. "Come. Chilled to the bone. I'll boil the water and Magod'll fill your tub."

Gethen accepted the water skin that the brown-haired groundsman held out. He rinsed his mouth and spat. Tremors rattled him as his servants led him along a familiar path toward the looming gothic spires of Ranith Citadel.

Twenty-two years had passed since Shemel, the previous Shadow Mage, had removed nine-year-old Gethen from his rooms in Besera's capitol and brought him to the citadel. Prior to that day, Gethen had been receiving lessons on politics, warfare, and civil matters — all subjects he, as Besera's future king, would've needed daily. But when he was chosen for apprenticeship, there was no arguing with Shemel. The sorcerer was too feared.

Gethen, Noni, and Magod followed a winding path, emerging from Kharayan Tor's murky woods to tread the centuries-worn switchbacks up to Ranith's fortified stone barbican.

Even summoning the power to lift the arched, iron portcullis made Gethen's head pound, but his gesture warped the air around them and raised it. Leaning heavily on Magod, he passed the crumbling stone huts and buildings of the fortification's abandoned village.

Ranith Citadel stood with one face to the forest and the other to the sea. Perched upon the tor's broken precipice, the citadel's thick masonry — scoured by wind, rain, and time — gave a sense of great weight and solidity. Yet the building's tall, narrow lancet windows, with their delicate gothic tracery and curvilinear patterns, contradicted that solidity, creating an almost lace-like softening of the battlements and façade.

Like the man, the Shadow Mage's abode offered contradiction to the world.

THREE

Ranks of militairs and foot soldiers fanned out in a semi-circle as the small party, led by King Vernard, reached a line of dark, spindly trees atop Kharayan Tor. Halina rode behind her father with Thaksin at her side. The king's camp spread out below them and northward.

Thaksin's saddle creaked as he leaned toward her. "You don't have to do this," he said. "Let me negotiate with the mage. I don't fear him."

Halina's gaze scraped over his rugged, scarred face. *But you think I do?* Her attention turned to the king. "No. I'll do this. You'll return to Kharaton and oversee the castle's fortifications."

Vernard beckoned. Halina urged Abelard forward until the horse reached her father's side. Ursinum's king had stopped at the line of cut, black cobblestones that marked the border of Shadow Mage Gethen's cursed woods.

"Yes, Your Majesty?"

The king was a battle-hardened man whose girth and mood suited his black bear emblem. Shaggy haired, blue-eyed, and fair-skinned, he'd given his auburn locks to all of his children, though Halina's Beseran mother was responsible for her unusual height and long limbs. That Beseran blood had also marred Halina's face, chest, shoulders, and back with a constellation of freckles that Ursinum society — particularly the ladies of the royal court — considered undesirable.

Vernard studied her with dispassionate eyes. "You're certain you can match wits with this mage of yours, girl?"

She squelched the urge to stab him. She'd stopped being a girl in her seventeenth year the first time she was gutted in battle at Gurvan-Sum.

"I won't return until I've secured the Shadow Mage's allegiance. And if Master Gethen won't join our fight, I'll ensure that he won't aid Besera, either." She matched her father's stony expression. "Even a dark sorcerer is subject to the ravages of my knife twisting in his gut."

King Vernard's head tilted back as he took in the imposing gray stone tower that rose out of the dark forest — Ranith Citadel, home to Shadow Mage Gethen. "Very well."

The mage was King Zelal's older brother, a fact that made his home on Ursinum's side of the border uncomfortably close and inconvenient. Unless he was willing to betray his brother and birth country, which Halina doubted, she anticipated her sword would soon wear mage blood.

If she survived crossing his magical wards.

Vernard's advisors were against sending her to parley with the sorcerer. "The militess is too old, too plain, and too quarrelsome," they'd said.

"Maybe so, but she's also a capable negotiator," the king had countered as he studied his elder unmarried daughter. "I've heard the Shadow Mage fancies a battle of acumen and respects strength. Those qualities the girl has aplenty."

King Vernard considered his daughter. "Ilker gave you the sealed document?" When she nodded, he turned his horse to face his sprawling camp and the Silver Sea beyond. "Try to keep your head, girl." He kicked his horse into a jog down the trail, calling after: "Though, if you don't, your mage will be doing me a favor!" His laughter drifted back as his company left her at the forest's edge with her horse, her falcon, and Thaksin.

Halina cursed the old pillock under her breath. For over a decade, he'd been using her as a bargaining chip in military alliances, trade agreements, and political treaties that stretched over Quoregna's four kingdoms.

But Ursinum's king was under pressure to honor his accords. His problem, of course, was Halina's refusal to marry any of the sycophants and tyrants His Majesty's partners proposed. If the Shadow Mage killed her, however, Vernard would be relieved of his contracts.

She swung out of her saddle, and took the bird, Enor, from her captain's arm. "Return Abelard to Kharaton. He'll be no good to me once I step onto that path."

"Halina, I fear for your—"

"Take the horse and return to the castle. Those are your orders." She shouldered her haversack and twitched her cloak over the longsword on her hip. "And take your sentimentality, too. We stand upon the brink of war, and I have an alliance to secure."

He took Abelard's reins even as he slipped from his own saddle and caught Halina's arm. "What of our alliance?"

She settled the falcon on her shoulder and covered her captain's fingers with her gloved hand. "You are the captain of my guard and quite enjoyable in my bed. But we have a dalliance, Thak, not an alliance. Don't make assumptions." She pried his hand off her arm.

The tow-headed man cursed beneath his breath then straightened and said, "Yes, Margrave." He remounted his horse and eyed Ranith's six-story tower with a hard gaze. "Have you any further orders for me?"

"No. I'm counting on you to ready Kharaton to withstand the first assault."

Cold wind whipped Halina's hair across her face. It carried

ribbons of fog and the sounds of Vernard's encampment to the tor — shouts and laughter, metal clanging against metal, the whinnies and snorts of horses.

Her captain's disappointment turned to determination on his face. "I'll keep Khara safe until you return, Your Ladyship."

"I know you will, Thak." She stroked her falcon's salt-and-pepper feathers as she added, "I'll send Enor with messages."

"I'll remain here until you've crossed the line."

"No. Don't waste any time. Return to Kharaton before the king refuses to release you and our militairs."

Thaksin nodded. "Be safe, Halina." He turned his gelding and Abelard, and urged the horses into a lope back down the hill.

She didn't watch him leave. Thaksin wasn't the first soldier she'd tupped to reward for loyalty. Instead, she studied the path into the woods then glanced at Enor; the raptor remained calm.

Terns and crows wheeled overhead, calling raucous challenges to each other in an iron-gray sky. But Kharayan was silent, forbidding, and still as if wind and wildlife didn't dare disturb its mysteries.

Somewhere ahead hovered the mage's wards — spells powerful enough to kill and madden Vernard's previous messengers. Halina searched the gloom ahead of her. "Coward." But fear was an old ally that she counted on to keep her alert.

She exhaled and stepped over the line of black stones. The air wavered and something tugged at her body, like a strong tide pulling at a moored boat. All light failed, and she stopped, blinked, and swallowed, suddenly blind. Her hand went to her sword as a needle chill pricked her exposed skin, penetrated her bones, and made her gasp and shiver.

But on Halina's shoulder, Enor gave a quiet *ki-ki-kee* note, stretched her wings, and then settled. The falcon wasn't afraid. Halina exhaled. "It's the dark spells, woman, and you're not dead yet." She pushed forward through the ward. The incantation yielded and contracted behind her as the forest's gloomy light returned and the chill eased. Nausea rolled through her, strong enough to make her limbs shake and bring bile to her throat. She swallowed and grimaced at the acid burn. Still she'd survived an encounter with the mage's dark magic. "There. You can stop worrying, Ilker."

Halina squared her shoulders and set out on the path to Ranith Citadel with long strides. The sooner she arrived, the sooner she could get warm and press the mage into Ursinum's service.

Sound, absent when she'd stood outside Kharayan, now proved that the Shadow Mage's forest wasn't devoid of life. Crows cawed warnings of her arrival. Black squirrels chittered and scrambled around the tree trunks and through the underbrush. And high in the canopy, a redheaded woodpecker knocked for insects, its sound echoing through the forest.

Fog hung thick and murky amid frosted tree trunks, turning the woods into a world of black, gray, and white. Spindly branches — stripped of brittle leaves by the biting wind — arched across the worn path to grapple like angry old men. Sunlight would've set their frosted bark alight like star-dusted skin, but no sun shone upon Khara, let alone within the forest of the Shadow Mage.

Halina stroked Enor's chest as she entered the tunnel of trees and mist. She searched the darkness as she moved deeper into the woods, following the sounds of creatures that were maddening in their ability to remain just beyond her sight. They watched her, perhaps hunted her. Trees creaked with the biting wind and the fog swirled up and around their trunks.

Movement drew her eye; something large and white parted the gloom. She squinted into the forest depths. Her right hand gripped her sword. The creature was pacing toward her. Fog eddied around it. Branches snapped beneath its feet. Halina stopped. It was a beast of some kind, large and steady in its pace, and unafraid of her.

A massive white stag — an animal that easily stood taller than the king's own warhorse — stepped onto the trail before her. Its antlers spanned the full width of the path, and the animal stared down its nose at her as if considering whether to let her proceed or trample her into the forest floor.

It was possibly a spirit. There were stories that the Shadow Mage gained his power by draining the souls of men, leaving behind shadows that wandered Kharayan in search of bodies in which to dwell. Again Enor shifted and gave her quiet cry. And, as if in response, the stag raised its head and whistled softly then turned and, tail flashing, trotted up the path toward Ranith.

"Not a spirit." Halina released her sword grip. "Letting my superstitions run wild." She shook her head. Then she set off focused only on keeping to the path in the dense fog.

The way to Ranith was long and winding, and grew steeper as she emerged from the timberline and started up the rocky path that led to the ancient village's black iron portcullis. Away from the shelter of the forest, the wind picked up, cold and sharp. Sleet stung her face. It rested upon her leather armor then melted and left a dark stain. Halina shifted Enor to her arm, raised her cloak's gray hood, and pulled the woolen garment close, sheltering the bird against her body. It was unseasonably cold, and down in Kharaton there was hoarfrost upon the new cabbages and orange chard. The farmers were worried that the autumn harvest would fail.

Fog billowed around the tor, swallowing the world below and muting sound. It mixed with the sleet and bejeweled Enor's feathers. Halina lost all sense of time and distance, aware only of her pluming breath and the rhythmic crunch of frosted gravel beneath her boots.

And then, like a castle floating in clouds, Ranith Citadel loomed overhead. She'd reached the village's lowered exterior gate. She cursed and wondered why the portcullis was closed when the whole wood was already warded. Then again, she'd breached the Shadow Mage's spell. Perhaps others could, too.

"Ho!" she shouted and was answered only by the muted echo of her call. "This is Margrave Khara. I order you to open the portcullis! I've come from King Vernard with a message for the Shadow Mage!" No reply came and there was no movement in the village for as far as she could see, which wasn't far through the damnable fog and sleet.

"Khotyr, take me." She surveyed Ranith's gray outer wall. Stacked stone with crumbling mortar in places, the crenelated battlements and angled taluses stood four stories at their lowest points. Without rope, scaling the frosted wall was impossible.

Halina curled her lip, sighed, and dropped her haversack within the recessed barbican. She folded her legs and sat, her back against frigid, gray stone. She settled Enor onto her pulled up knees and wrapped her cloak around both of them. "Let's hope someone comes along soon, bird, or this will be a long, cold wait." She glanced up at the narrow murder hole in the stone entrance directly overhead. "And let's hope he's friendly."

FOUR

I n Gethen's vaulted bathing room, Magod emptied a bucket
of heated water into a wooden tub. Standing before a bank
of gothic windows, and with no witnesses other than his
servant and a few gulls riding the icy wind, Gethen shed his filthy
boots, tunic, and trouzes, stood in the round tub, and cursed as
Magod emptied the last full bucket over his shoulders.

He wetted a rag and said, "Leave me."

The groundsman retreated through his master's apartment to
the citadel's curving halls.

Gethen scrubbed the cold from his skin but couldn't warm his
mood. "Skiron's bones. The witch is loose in the Void, and I've
grown more vulnerable to attack than I thought." The gradual
weakening of his powers over the last year had picked up speed
like a boulder crashing downhill. "Damnably dangerous situation."

As the Sun Mage he'd draw strength from any source of light
— sun, moon, fire, lightning — *and* still control his shadow
magery. It was tremendous power. But making the transition
meant enduring a period of failed magic as his shadow sorcery was
subjugated. Gethen shook his head. "Magod won't be adequate
protection." The witch's attack made it clear that he needed a

much stronger champion. The groundsman, though young and strong, preferred beekeeping over battle and wasn't a trained swordsman.

The water in the tub quickly turned tepid and foul. Gethen grimaced. He'd never encountered magic as cold and jaundiced as what he'd fought in the Void. Few entities could wield such dangerous and powerful sorcery. Was her threat against him or against Quoregna? And what could he do about it before his magic failed?

The wind coming off the Silver Sea whistled through cracks in the citadel's ancient windows and carried the muted sounds of horses and men. Gethen paused to listen. "Vernard. He'll get nothing from me." He ran the rag across his chest then stepped from the tub. "I've no power to give, even if I was willing to battle Zelal, which I'm not."

He dressed in a brown tunic, dark trouzes, and a dark blue surcoat belted at his waist. Rubbing the dampness from his black hair, he strode through his bedchamber and into his study.

A knock sounded at his door.

"What?" he snarled.

Noni's scratchy voice delivered a grating reply: "Message from King Zelal."

"Another?" Gethen wrenched open the door.

She shuffled into the room with a tray of food balanced on her boney shoulder and a bottle of mead in hand. She set the tray on the table before the room's fireplace, and then proffered a small, tight scroll. Gethen took it and cracked his brother's yellow wax seal. He read the message and cursed again. "Zelal's requests for my aid have become threats." He met Noni's worried, brown gaze and added, "Now I'm a traitor to my family if I don't return. His soldiers' first task will be to find and kill me once they cross the Silver Sea."

She frowned, and her wrinkled face folded into more wrinkles. "He's become so unreasonable?"

Gethen waggled the paper between them. "So it appears." He threw the parchment on the table with the others he'd received from Vernard and Zelal and tore a hunk of bread from the loaf she'd brought.

He didn't understand what his brother was doing. This idiocy made no sense, and Zelal was usually level-headed.

"Get me a pot of ink, a quill, and a scroll." He poured a glass of honey-wine and added, "And bring a dram of the aged metheglin. My head still aches from crossing the Voidline."

"Not the hippocras?"

"No. It's too weak."

Noni frowned, offered a scant curtsy, and left the room.

Gethen considered the last messages from Zelal and Vernard as he chewed the coarse bread:

Bring Ursinum to Besera and return to serve your homeland and family, or be judged a traitor and face a death mark.

And:

Besera masses for war. Side with Ursinum, quit my lands, or forfeit your life.

Gethen grimaced and massaged his aching skull. He couldn't aid either of the fools, even if he wanted to. And he had much greater problems than the bickering of kings.

"The Rime Witch is banging on the border of the living and the dead, Zelal and Vernard are marshaling their troops, and my power's lost its teeth."

Noni returned with the dram of medicinal mead and Gethen's writing supplies. She added a log to the fire and lit candles throughout the room, then gathered the Shadow Mage's soiled clothes and towels from the bathing room, and closed the wooden shutters on the high windows, blocking out the jaundiced light of the cold day. "Storm's coming," she said.

"Snow. Tell Magod to winter the bees today."

"So early?"

"Yes."

The bees were what had first alerted him to the weather's strangeness. Magod had started harvesting honey after he'd noticed them clustering inside their hives, a sure sign that winter was coming. "Flowers aren't blooming much, either," he'd said. "They should have another six or seven weeks to make honey. Not this year." He'd scratched the back of his shaggy head and peered up at Gethen, knowing his master wouldn't be happy. "Will have to leave more honey in the hives, too, if winter's coming so soon. Don't want starved bees." And that had meant less honey to make the meads, unguents, and medicinals that Gethen sold.

The Shadow Mage scowled into his dram cup then downed the metheglin. He glared at the older woman for a long moment. Then he blew out hard and fumbled for the honey-wine, his eyes watering and his throat and insides catching fire as the mead went down. His voice was harsh as he croaked, "What did you do, woman? Mix the metheglin with capsicumel?"

Noni retrieved the cup. "Yes. You need warming, but I'm too old and Magod says you're too ugly. Thought you'd benefit from the fire of your own peppers."

Capsicumel was mead mixed with fiery peppers that Gethen obtained from southern Or-Halee's traders. He earned a fine living from selling the drink, his steep prices willingly paid as he imbued it with spells that increased its efficacy and the duration of its fire.

Heat spread through his belly, up his spine, and radiated through his limbs. But his head remained clear as his aches melted away and his body became languid. It was almost as fine as a woman's touch and certainly one of his better brews. He popped a black olive into his mouth then growled, "Next time warn me."

Noni dismissed his words with a wave. "Dead sorcerer's no good to anyone. Especially beggarly kings and servants."

"Beggarly? That remark would get you killed in that camp." Gethen jerked his thumb in the direction of Vernard's tents.

"The army's still down there?"

He spat out the pit and chose another olive from his plate. "King Vernard seems to believe my cooperation, or my death, is a foregone conclusion." He picked up the quill she'd brought and dipped it into the inkstand. "And he's unlikely to leave before sacrificing at least one more messenger. Kings aren't easily dissuaded from stupidity."

Gethen put quill to parchment and began a response to his brother's newest message:

> *To the honorable Zelal, rightful king of Besera, Regent of Rhyshis, Duke of Gryvid, from his brother, Gethen Rhysh, Duke of Rhyshis in absentia, and Shadow Mage of Ranith Citadel,*
>
> *Greetings and wishes for Your Majesty's continued health and prosperity.*
>
> *Brother, I cannot be of service to you ....*

FIVE

Voices. Halina sat up.

What little light there was had dimmed to near-darkness and snow had begun falling — heavy, fat flakes swirling down and piling up against the citadel's outer walls.

A man asked, "What're you doing out in the cold, Mummin? Been looking all over the citadel for you." His voice was deep and gravelly but young.

"Picking blackapples by the pond," a woman replied. Her voice was scratchy with age, and she sounded defensive as she added, "Since when do you need to know where I'm going?"

"Was just wondering. That's all." Boots scraped on cobblestones. "You usually tell me."

"Well, I'll save you more fussing and go back to the tower now. Lock myself in my room so you're not worried."

"Don't be a grump, Mummin."

The woman harrumphed and the sound of her footfalls quickly diminished. The man's muttered curses and the crunch of dirt on stone grew louder as he approached the portcullis. Light and shadows waltzed with a lantern's sway.

Enor complained and ruffled her feathers as Halina lifted the falcon to her shoulder.

The man stopped and called, "Who's there?"

Stiff and sore from sitting on her arse in the cold, Halina stood and faced him, schooling her expression to betray nothing as he held the lantern aloft and approached the lattice gate.

"I'm Militess Halina Persinna, Margrave of Khara. I bear a message from His Majesty, King Vernard, and the royal court at Tatlis for Shadow Mage Gethen."

The man's brown eyes widened and he proffered a deep bow. "Margrave Khara? Welcome, Your Ladyship. Will let you in so you can get warm."

He stumped up the barbican's interior stairs to the guard house above. With deafening screeching and clanking, the gate was released and cranked upward until Halina slipped beneath. She stood in the dark recess of the citadel's passage and studied the young man as he descended the stairs. A servant judging by his plain cloak, he was tall and barrel-chested but slightly stooped, as if he was made uncomfortable by his own presence. "What's your name?" she asked.

"Magod."

"You serve Shadow Mage Gethen?"

"All my twenty-two years, Your Ladyship." He motioned for her to follow as he set off up the main path through the village and toward the looming dark tower that was the Shadow Mage's citadel.

"How was I able to cross into Kharayan despite the mage's wards?"

"Don't know. That's a question for my master. I don't know much of his sorcery, and never cross the wards myself without his aid."

Halina doubted that the man knew nothing of the dark sorcerer's methods, but his loyalty wasn't worth questioning. It wouldn't do to antagonize the Shadow Mage by doubting his man, not if Halina wished to bring his power to bear against Besera *and* keep her life.

Until she'd seen the messengers who'd fallen victim to Gethen's dark magic, she'd been of the mind that he dealt more in convincing trickery and some very good medicinal meads than in actual necromancy and summoning. Now, however, she eyed the grotesques carved into the citadel's walls and corbels — wild-eyed demons, writhing bodies, howling spirits, claws and teeth and tongues — and braced for an unpleasant confrontation, at best.

They crossed through a set of open iron gates to enter the citadel's frosted bailey. The squeal of hinges and clank of a heavy lock echoed off the stone walls as Magod pulled the gates closed behind them. The keep and tower rose above Halina, a dark stone needle that stabbed the snowy sky, its narrow, gothic windows hiding who knew what horrors.

"Watch your step, Your Ladyship," Magod said and gestured toward a hole in the floor to the left of the massive front doors. "Hatch to the oubliette's rotten. Don't want you falling in."

Halina looked away from the cracked wooden boards covering the opening. "Damnable place," she said beneath her breath and fought the urge to take several large steps away from it.

"Cursed, to be sure," Magod replied.

He didn't know the half of it. When she was six years old, Halina had been pushed into Tatlis Castle's oubliette by her second cousin, Waldram. She'd spent what had felt like an eternity sobbing and screaming for help, up to her neck in fetid water and standing on bones. She bore the scars from that experience under her skin, as well as on it.

As he led her through the arched entry and into the great hall, a small, white-haired woman, who shared the man's protuberant brown eyes, appeared upon the broad, dark stairs. The woman reminded Halina of a stoat, a small and seemingly harmless creature that was dangerous if provoked.

Magod said, "Here's an important guest, Mummin. Margrave

Khara with another message from King Vernard." The man turned back to Halina. "Wait here, Militess? Will tell my master you're here." Magod indicated the woman and added, "Noni's my mother and Master Gethen's housekeeper."

Noni curtsied. "Take your cloak, Your Ladyship? And provide some warm mead? Master's evening repast hasn't been served. You'll join his table?"

"Mead would be most appreciated," Halina said as she offered Enor to Magod then removed her cloak. "And it would be an honor to join your master's evening meal." She frowned. Whatever quality had made her compare Noni to a stoat was gone, and she now saw only an elderly woman with a kind smile and a solicitous manner.

The man settled the falcon onto his shoulder and ran his hand gently over the bird's back. "Will take good care of this fine little bird, Your Ladyship." Golden candlelight flickered in his wake as he retreated up the winding, stone stairs. Noni disappeared, presumably to the kitchen, leaving Halina to study the great hall.

Dominated by a wide stone hearth, the room, like the entry, boasted soaring wooden ribs atop massive marble columns that upheld its arched ceiling. Rows of clerestory and triforium windows allowed in plentiful light along its gently curving walls. An elaborate wool rug padded the white marble floor and stretched the length and breadth of the room. Its design delighted her eyes with deep jewel-toned flowers, birds, and scrollwork. Tapestries decorated the walls — forest scenes and banquets depicted in more jeweled hues, sumptuous against the room's white walls. A third of the size of Kharaton Castle's great hall, it was an infinitely more comfortable room. Halina's lips twitched. Had she expected cobwebs, cauldrons, and paintings of death, dismemberment, and torture?

"I'm *humbled* by your presence in my home, Lady Khara."

She turned at the baritone rumble of the voice. Sarcasm oozed from the Shadow Mage's mouth, emphasized by his scant bow.

There was power behind that voice and a sword's sharp steel. Uncompromising and angry beneath a refined robe, the sorcerer was anything but humbled, and instinct alerted her to danger. The man was a wolf waiting for her to run.

Noni stepped up. Halina took an empty crystal glass from the tray that the woman offered first to her then to the mage. She smiled, knowing the expression wouldn't reach her eyes. She was no rabbit to flee from his jaws. "Shadow Mage Gethen, thank you for your hospitality. Your servants represent you admirably."

"Yes. They do." He pointed toward two chairs and a couch arrayed around the fireplace. "Sit, Your Ladyship."

A command, not an offer. She remained standing and returned his cold, gray gaze. She held out her glass and Noni filled it from a glass-and-silver decanter. The sweet heady scent of the honey wine was a delight and her first sip didn't disappoint. "Imperial Tokay?"

"It's quite good this year." Gethen scowled at her over his glass even as he savored his first sip. "Noni will prepare a room for you, Militess. I don't recommend a return trip through Kharayan's woods this late. The wolves will be on the hunt, the snow promises to fall unabated, and I've no interest in leaving Ranith's warmth to escort wayward ladies."

"How kind, Master Sorcerer. Since you're inconvenienced by my presence, let's parley quickly; there's much to do before Besera invades."

Something in the mage's face changed — darkness crossed it but was gone in a blink, and Halina, though accustomed to the subtleties of Vernard's court, wasn't sure that she hadn't seen a mere shadow cast by the flickering fire.

"We've nothing to discuss, Margrave. Tomorrow you will leave Kharayan." Gethen turned to address Noni.

Halina replied, "We have your cooperation to discuss, Shadow Mage."

While he ignored her and instructed his housekeeper on preparing a room, Halina sized him up.

Gethen of Ranith presented a formidable figure. He was broad across the shoulders, narrow at the waist, and long-legged. He wore his hair in the style of his homeland's men, cropped close on the sides but left longer on top, and he sported the shadow of a beard. The silver dusting his thick, black hair defied a youthful face but affirmed his haunted, hard expression; she'd heard that the mages aged quickly, their lives consumed by their own dark magic.

He moved with economy and power, and Halina, court-born and having served in the king's army for two decades, recognized him as a man trained for warfare and command. But it was Gethen's dark gray eyes that both fascinated and warned her. He assessed her as a wolf does a stag — potential meal, potential danger. It was much the same way she studied him. And his disregard of her demand proved that he was unimpressed by royal command and military might.

This man was far more dangerous than Vernard realized.

When he'd replied to King Vernard's first command, the Shadow Mage's note had been curt and lacked all courtesies. It had not ingratiated him to the king. However, it had amused Halina greatly, and served as a warning about the man behind the message: Shadow Mage Gethen was no one's lapdog. She was inclined to admire him because of it, and that made him all the more dangerous.

You're here on duty. This man may be your tenant, but he also may be your country's enemy.

Militess Halina no longer fell for a man's face or demeanor. She'd be impressed when the mage demonstrated loyalty to his king and prowess in battle. That was the true test of a man or woman.

Noni disappeared up the wide stairs and the sorcerer turned back to Halina. His eyes had gone from warning to threat. Wrath deepened his voice and darkened his expression, changing his face from handsome to hostile. He bared his teeth and snarled, "How is it that King Vernard continues to misunderstand my clear rejection of his demands, Margrave?"

Halina schooled her expression and kept a tight hold on her ire.

Never run from wolves; they live for the chase.

Her voice was steady and cool as she replied, "How is it that you refuse your king's commands, Shadow Mage?"

"I'm beholden to no man."

A little bit of her control slipped. "You are beholden to me and to our king. You have lived in Khara for two decades."

The mage grew still. "So you decline my fourth refusal?"

It was a dangerous shift in his demeanor, and Halina's hand strayed to the misericord, a thin dagger, on her belt. "I'm here to negotiate your cooperation."

"I despise repeating myself. Worse, when reason returns me to the same madness again and again."

"I see no *reason* at all in your refusal."

Gethen smirked. "Then enjoy the madness." He made a gesture with his open palm and intoned a few strange words beneath his breath.

Halina's grip tightened on her dagger, but the room became a blur of green light and icy wind. And before she could pull the weapon or protest, she was sitting on her arse in the middle of the snowy bailey.

"He used his sorcery. On *me*. That insolent fen-sucker!" She stood and stomped up the steps to the citadel's wide main doors. She didn't bother knocking; she'd spare no more courtesy on the stinking mage. Halina heaved back the door. She strode through the doorway. And walked right back into the frigid bailey.

"What?" She stared around. "How?"

She tried the door to the kitchen and returned, again, to the bailey. The stable entrance and the postern door yielded the same result. Every entrance to the round, towering citadel and its curved outbuildings brought her back to the snow-bound, circular bailey. Again and again Halina tried the front doors, always to return to the place from which she'd come. Finally, cold and frustrated at her easy defeat, she drew her sword and hacked at the iron-banded doors. Even the front gates refused to exit the bailey when she lifted their frozen lock.

He'd trapped her. Somehow the Shadow Mage had trapped her in the bailey where she'd freeze to death. Halina grew still. Snow fell like a curtain around her and her sweat froze upon her face. Her muscles trembled and fear stuck in her throat. She'd survived battles with men and demons, been gutted, burned, and scarred. She'd endured the cruelty of royals who believed that their pure Ursinum blood was finer than hers with its Beseran taint. Now she would die alone, fighting no one, a failure dismissed and discarded by her own intractable tenant.

"No." Halina's hands, cramping and burning with the cold, tightened into fists. "I won't give up," she whispered. "I will *not* die."

Then, as if summoned by those words, the arched front doors creaked open and the white-haired housekeeper appeared upon the stoop, a lantern in her hand. "Your room has been prepared, Lady Khara."

Halina swallowed.

The lantern cast flickering green light, and she closed her eyes to its glare.

Noni said, "This way, Your Ladyship."

Halina blinked and stared around her. She was standing in Ranith's great hall beside the crackling fire. Her body was warm and no snow covered her clothes. The housekeeper stood before her with a flickering candle to help light the way up to the guest room.

The Shadow Mage was gone.

"Your Ladyship, are you unwell?"

Halina found her voice. "No. I'm ... hungry." As she followed the old woman up the wide, curving staircase, she felt a stare upon her back. She glanced down as they reached the second floor landing. The mage was watching her from the foot of the stairs. The man moved as quietly as the shadows he was named for.

Halina shivered. His was a mad kind of sorcery, and it was wise to fear it if she wanted to remain alive and successfully secure his loyalty.

They climbed to the citadel's third floor, and Halina appreciated the warmth and comfort of the residence all the more for her waking nightmare. It did, indeed, feel more like a courtier's residence than a military fortress or a place where the dead were summoned to reveal their secrets and murderous, deceptive spells were cast. And certainly it was much warmer than the snowy bailey.

Noni showed her into an elegant room. A fire burned bright and warm in the grate opposite a wide, black oak, canopied bed that was curtained and covered with sumptuous, gold-and-white bedding. A writing desk stood beneath a shuttered window, a sapphire blue couch encouraged lounging, and a small table with two padded chairs positioned before the fire allowed meals to be taken in privacy. A dressing table, more beautiful tapestries, and another large, colorful rug completed the room.

"Help you with your bath, Your Ladyship?"

Halina stripped off her leather gloves. "That's unnecessary. I'm a militess first, a lady of King Vernard's court second. I can see to my own toilet." She wanted to be alone with her jumbled thoughts.

Noni's hopeful expression settled into bland disinterest. She curtsied and left.

She only wanted an opportunity to help a lady. What's the harm in that? Halina thought. "Poor woman's stuck waiting on that pignut day and night."

She made use of a white pitcher and basin to splash her face and wash grime from her shaking hands. She was still angry and ... scared.

The mage had promised madness.

"Damnation."

She stared at the fire in the grate as she dried her skin. She hated that she didn't know if what she'd experienced was illusion or reality, or if she'd ever really been in the bailey.

What if he'd left me trapped?

It was terrifying to think he'd twisted her mind so easily that she would've died because she'd *believed* she was freezing to death. She shivered, then changed into her only chemise. She didn't even know how long the dark spell had lasted; minutes had felt like hours. As with a dream, it had been vivid and irrational, and had left her more frightened than she'd been in years.

That fear clung to her as Halina eyed her chain mail and breast plate. She would've been content to wear them to dinner with the Shadow Mage. But the negotiations were moving to a new field that required a different set of skills and the silk-and-lace armor of a court lady.

"I won't let him see how much he unnerved me." Halina squared her shoulders and stepped into one of the two gowns she'd brought then fumbled with the ties on the deep blue velvet bodice and light blue sleeves. She was far more comfortable slitting a man's throat than whispering honeyed words in his ear, and she was greatly tempted to knife the mage after his nightmare incantation. He was possibly the most dangerous man she'd ever met. She should hasten to kill him. But that dark and savage power, frightening as it was, also made him indescribably compelling.

"He could've at least done me the courtesy of being hideous," she muttered.

Leaving in the morning was the wise thing to do. But that

would be running away from danger and duty, which was something Halina had never done.

She shook her head. *No. I'll find a way to bend him to my will.* She tucked her flat misericord into a sheath on her left forearm beneath her sleeve. *Or I'll kill him.*

SIX

"I won't give up. I will not die."

Some emotion that felt too much like shame lodged in Gethen's throat, thick and dry, as he sat in Ranith's small solar and stared out the windows at fat, falling snowflakes. The room held a desk, several well-padded chairs before the fireplace, and a worn, leather sofa.

He'd tormented a woman who'd faced down armies. "Shemel would be proud," Gethen said, his voice thick with self-derision.

He turned a tarnished Beseran coin between his fingers. One face sported a golden bee upon a liminth flower, a sign of good fortune for his family. The other side had a golden circle struck into its center — the sun symbol that represented his birth country's military. The old coin had been a gift from Noni when he was a boy; a precious token she'd pressed into his palm on the day he'd arrived at Ranith, a nine-year-old child scared witless by the necromancer who'd claimed him as his apprentice.

What kind of man humiliates his guest, uninvited or not? He shook his head and lied to himself. "It was necessary to make her leave." It was a weak excuse, and it hadn't worked. Her terror hadn't lasted, but her distrust would. He cursed and downed another small glass of sack-mead. Strong, full-bodied, and ensorcelled, the drink brought him clarity and buried his guilt.

The margrave, here, in Ranith.

Things had gone from bad to worse. How in the name of all that was dark and ungodly had she gotten past his wards? He hadn't even sensed her presence until she'd rattled his front gate.

"It's impossible." Gethen glared at the fire flickering in the solar's grate as if awaiting an explanation that would never come. He always knew when something crossed his wards. Animals, insects, demons, beasts, and people. *Always.* He'd sensed the king's first two emissaries and had known they'd not survive the wards. Yet this woman had evaded detection.

Had his power weakened so much so quickly? He stood and dropped the coin onto the wooden mantle. "Vernard and Zelal be damned for not accepting my refusal."

His illusion had kept the militess in thrall as he'd studied her and contemplated her presence in his great hall. True, he needed a champion, but not one who'd come to conscript or kill him.

Any of the previous shadow mages would've left her trapped in the waking dream until she'd died. The mind was more powerful than most people knew. But her whispered words had gutted his resolve.

Gethen poured one last cup of sack-mead and lifted it in an ironic salute to his much-despised former master. "You'd laugh your arse off at my weakness, Shemel." He sipped his drink. "Then you'd slit my throat, steal my power, and take my place on the cusp. I'm glad I murdered you, you rat-faced churl."

He capped the mead bottle and left the room, sipping the rest of his drink as he passed through the library and ascended the citadel's curving, stone staircase. With Her Ladyship in Ranith, he'd have to dress for supper and dine with her in the great hall. His habit was to break his fast in his room every morning, take his afternoon meal in the stillroom, his study, or wherever he was working that day, and sup alone in the solar.

Reaching his chamber, he changed into a gray tunic trimmed with silver thread, a belted, forest green surcoat, and black trouzes. Gethen eschewed the robes and staff that most mages seemed to consider a uniform of sorts. He wanted a sword, not a stick, when things got evil.

Royalty were disruptive at best, dangerous at worst, and an utter pain in the arse at all times. And this woman's reputation preceded her. Her title of Militess was earned not bought, a rarity among men and almost unprecedented among the women of Ursinum's court. King Vernard's elder bastard daughter was well known for her ferocity in battle and her chivalry among her tenants.

Gethen admired a woman who didn't hide behind her husband's or father's trouzes, but this woman *wore* the trouzes and had bigger bollocks than most men. He'd have to consider every move and word with care or he'd find his flesh and bones separated permanently.

She'd assessed him, his servants, and his home with a practiced eye, weighing his potential as an enemy or an ally. He hoped that, unlike her father, she would accept his wish to be neither.

He was content to let the kings squabble. Their bickering had nothing to do with his duties or him, and they helped no one. But the margrave didn't see things that way.

He'd have to convince her he was useless to anyone's cause before she murdered him. He ran his fingers through his thick hair and left his room.

If she sends me permanently into the Void, I'll make every effort to take her soul with me.

Gethen arrived in the great hall to find Militess Halina studying one of the room's more gruesome paintings — *Absolom Feeds the Wolves*. She turned, inclined her head at his bow, and sat to his left — his weak side — at the long, wooden table.

The blue silk gown she wore accentuated her trim figure and

the color of her eyes. Its fitted sleeves revealed the slim shape of a sheathed dagger upon her left forearm.

Of course she's armed, he thought.

The militess was like the doe a hunter assumed would flee but which, instead, battered and stomped him until he was nothing but bloody flesh and broken bones.

The first course served was a thin broth made from strained vegetables and parboiled grain. She blew steam from her soup and gestured around the room at the portraits hanging upon the walls. "Are these your predecessors?"

"Yes."

She finished her soup. "Where has your man taken my falcon?"

"Magod has her in his room. He's quite capable with animals, domestic and wild. If you need her just ask."

"He's skilled in falconry?"

"Yes."

He said no more. She didn't ask. And supper continued through six more silent courses until, finally, the meal concluded with shiny, black ebonberries picked from a large patch that grew behind Ranith's abandoned basilica.

"These berries surpass any I've had in Khara or Tatlis."

Gethen chose one of the shiny, oblong fruits from his plate. "We're blessed with berries that flourish upon consecrated ground."

"Oh?"

"They grow in the fertile soil of Ranith's burial grounds, among the oldest graves."

Only the slightest movement of her lips revealed her surprise, and then she replied, "How unusual," before popping another into her mouth. Her gaze held his as she savored the fruit.

After the meal, they adjourned to the solar to talk and enjoy one of the sweeter meads. Gethen would've preferred to retire to his room and brood over his transitioning magic, the mystery and threat of the witch's release, and the margrave's ease with his wards. But that wasn't part of the diversion they now played. Each had a role — he the dark and evil mage, she the insistent and loyal militess.

As soon as they settled into the chairs before the fireplace, the margrave said, "Explain your refusal of His Majesty's request for your services."

"Why are the kingdoms at odds?"

She cocked an eyebrow. "You don't know?"

Gethen's gesture took in the entire citadel. "I live an isolated life, and neither Zelal nor Vernard have included anything but demands and threats in their messages to me. I'm not a trained dog to come running at the snap of any man's fingers. Or any woman's."

She inclined her head at his remark then replied, "Salt."

"Salt? Why?"

"Just as the weather turned cold and it became clear that we were facing an unusually early winter, Besera demanded a twenty-five percent price cut in salt imports. The collapse of the Siladur Mine during the late-summer rains has reduced our exports by a quarter. Yet the salt union had planned to honor this year's prices with Besera; prices that should be rising."

Gethen frowned. "And Ursinum's response was what?"

"Threat of embargo."

He shook his head. "You can't restrict salt."

"Of course we can. Besera has other sources—"

"At a far greater expense."

"Zelal should've considered that. Trying to squeeze more money from the union is never a good idea."

That was true. "And this disagreement began when the weather turned evil?"

"Yes."

Gethen grunted and took a sip of his mead.

Halina watched him. "You still haven't explained your lack of cooperation."

He met her gaze and replied, "I cannot help, Militess, because I'm becoming a sun mage, only the second in Quoregna's recorded history. As such I'll harness the power of the sun, but I must endure the loss of my shadow magery first." He looked at the mead in his cup. *Why in damnation did I tell her that?*

She leaned forward. "I didn't know such a thing was possible." There was suspicion in her narrowed blue eyes

"It is. Soon I'll be powerless."

"For how long?"

He shrugged. "I have no idea." Gethen smiled bitterly into his cup. "Remarkably poor timing that's beyond my control."

"And have your skills also failed for your brother?" There was flint in her tone and her eyes.

"Yes, Margrave." This was dangerous territory. Her animosity had gained teeth and claws thanks to his parlor trick. "I don't have the strength to battle for Ursinum *or* Besera. Nor would I if my power was wholly restored. As I've already asserted to King Vernard *and* King Zelal, I'm disinterested in this conflict. I suggested to both that they solve it with less stupidity."

"If I were to attack you now, could you defend yourself?"

"Against one foe who has no sorcery? Yes. That's an easy spell. Against thousands of soldiers and other sorcerers? Unlikely."

She nodded. "Magic or not, you're an invaluable source of information about Besera's king, his troops, and methods of attack. Your aid is required by your adopted king."

Gethen snorted and cocked an eyebrow at her. "What? Ursinum has no spies in King Zelal's court?"

"Of course we do. But in court isn't the same as among the king's advisors and generals."

Gethen eyed her. She took a risk in revealing this information to him. He could be a spy for Besera. Then again, as with all things courtly and strategic, lies and half-truths came as easily as smiles and usually wore them. "I've been estranged from my homeland and my brother for more than twenty years. I have nothing to offer."

"I doubt that. You were trained to rule."

"Just as the princes and princesses of Ursinum were. I bring nothing new to this, Militess."

"You're renowned for your control of dark magic. Even with your failing power, I'm sure you can bring a great deal to this." She held out a letter, sealed with black wax and the bear of Ursinum. "King Vernard sends you greetings and makes you offers."

Gethen stood. "I've already answered your king, Lady Khara." He drank the last of his mead and put the glass down on the mantle harder than intended. The cut crystal landed upon the Beseran coin he'd left there and rang through the room. "Goodnight, Your Ladyship." He offered a stiff bow and left the room without accepting the letter.

What was so compelling about the margrave that he'd willingly shared the truth of his waning power with her? She didn't need to know that. Revealing his vulnerability was a foolish risk.

"Idiot," he grumbled beneath his breath as he strode through the great hall.

In the kitchen Noni was preparing bread for the next day. A thin layer of flour coated the long wooden table that dominated the center of the stone room, and the dull thud of dough being punched and kneaded kept rhythm with her low, tuneless humming.

Every evening she mixed the ingredients for fresh sourbread, punched down the dough, and left it to rise until the next morning when she then placed several loaves onto the hearth before the sun came up. The delicious smell of freshly baked bread wafted up the rear stairwell to Gethen's bedchamber and awakened him.

"Her Ladyship retired to her room?" Noni asked.

"I wouldn't know." Gethen stopped beside the kitchen's blackened brick hearth and warmed his hands over the fire. "I left her in the solar with King Vernard's unopened letter."

Noni paused. "Was that wise?"

Gethen scowled. "Possibly not, but I won't be backed into a corner by anyone." He took a few whitenuts from a bowl upon a smaller table beside the hearth and popped them into his mouth one-by-one while watching the orange-and-blue fire dance upon the grate. Then he wandered to Noni's side and reached for the pine nuts she was adding to the bread, but she slapped his hand away.

Gethen sneered. "Let the Militess take the king's offer back to him tomorrow and tell him that I'm useless to his cause. As long as I have strength to breathe, I'll have strength to keep my wards up and those yaldsons at bay."

Noni brushed her hands on her apron, adding to the room's hovering cloud of white flour. She cocked an eyebrow at her master and her lips twisted with disapproval and worry. "*She* crossed them. And what of your brother? Will he stay away?"

Gethen watched the wrinkled, discolored skin on the back of her hand stretch and fold as she worked the dough. "Zelal and Vernard will have to destroy the tor if they wish to cross my wards."

Her smile was rueful. "You have sorcery and power over the shadows now, but what'll happen to your wards as that magic fails?"

Gethen had no answer for her. Outside, the wind wailed like desperate souls. A faint tapping drew his attention to the kitchen's window. Sleet. It struck the glass and slid down to create little piles of ice and white frost against the ledge. He frowned. This weather was bad for the harvest, and that meant the loss of bees, honey, mead, and, worst of all, the loss of income.

Noni's gaze followed his. "Unnatural."

"Yes, it is," he replied. "But I can't address the weather or its cause while the king and his emissary are treading on my shadow."

"What'll you do?" Magod asked as he came up from the larder, his arms laden with a basket of root vegetables, several wine bottles, and a large sack of coarse, ground redgrain.

"Send the margrave back to her king tomorrow," Gethen replied. "The sooner our liege leaves Ranith, the sooner I can focus what power I have left to fix this mess and strengthen my wards." He jabbed his finger at the sleet-coated window.

Ceramic bowls clattered as Noni cleared a spot on her long worktable for her son. Magod deposited his burdens there, straightened, and gawked at the window. "The weather's worse?"

"Did you cover the hives?" Gethen asked.

"All wrapped. Hope that turns to snow; bees'll be warmer and dryer with snow."

"It will. Let's get the animals into the stable before they freeze. None have winter coats yet. I can't afford to lose the cow, goats, or even those clod-brained chickens."

Noni grabbed her heavy shawl from the peg beside the door that led out to the bailey, but Gethen called her up. "Finish the bread." And he followed Magod out the door.

The bite and sting of sleet, and his lack of a cloak, made him regret his decision. "I'll chase the chickens into their coop," he said as Magod herded the wooly sheep toward the stable.

Not for the first time Gethen cursed the red-and-white speckled hens. How could the creatures be so thick-skulled? Every winter he found himself chasing the little beasts about his bailey in a snowstorm. If they hadn't needed the eggs to sustain themselves through the long winter months at Ranith — and this year's winter looked to be far longer than any he could recall — he would've traded the chickens at market for more potatoes, cabbages, and some of that good, black rye that came from Etherias every year.

The other animals had enough wisdom to be under the eaves or already within the stables, so Magod soon joined Gethen in chasing chickens. Had the weather not been so miserable, and his hands so painfully cold, the Shadow Mage would've laughed at the ridiculousness of two grown men running about the bailey after squawking hens in the snow.

When they'd rounded up and bedded down all the birds and beasts, Magod and Gethen headed toward the warm, yellow light spilling from the kitchen's window. But before going into the citadel Gethen paused on the stone steps to consider the flat, slate-colored sky and the shadowy forest.

Kharayan was beginning to resemble the Void.

Magod turned in the doorway. "Bring you a cloak, Master?"

Gethen waved his servant into the kitchen. "I need to be alone with the storm and my magic. Put a decanter of warm mead in my room." Magod nodded and left him to a storm that threatened to turn the world from gray to white.

Gethen stepped away from the shelter of the tower and focused on the night and the cold, turning a slow circle in the bailey. Weather work challenged him more than it had Shemel and most of the former shadow mages. He tilted his head back and, ignoring the burning sting of the sleet as the howling wind slammed it sideways into him, he parted his lips and inhaled the storm.

Gethen tasted emotions in it: abandonment was salty and resentment was bitter. The Rime Witch was controlling the storm, and she was powerful, vindictive, and dangerous. Somehow she was reaching into the corporeal world to manipulate the weather. He wiped sleet from his face. "But how?"

He longed to return to his rooms, sink into his strength, and pass into the Void, again. He wanted to redouble the power of his Voidline wards, then confront the witch, draw down her power, and turn it back upon her. But he wasn't strong enough. He hadn't yet recovered from their last meeting.

Something tugged on Gethen's focus. He opened his eyes, and his gaze strayed up the tower, its dark grey stone now plastered white with sleet and snow. Flickering yellow candlelight spilled from the guest room he'd assigned to Militess Halina. The woman stood at the window, a backlit shadow. He couldn't see her eyes, but he knew she was watching him.

She'd let her hair down and the room's candlelight set it aglow like a banked fire. The tug on Gethen's focus became a tug on his body. Desire stirred in him, uninvited and unexpected. He watched her until Margrave Khara stepped back and closed the shutters.

Her disappearance left him feeling colder than before he'd noticed her in the window. His breath plumed in the frigid air; it was like he'd slipped from beneath warm covers into an icy room.

Gethen refocused on the storm. He was accustomed to the cold. Being the Shadow Mage and traveling among the shades meant cold that had seeped deep into his bones and lingered. But this was different. An intent to kill and destroy fueled this abnormal winter. He turned away, rubbed his hands together, and re-entered the kitchen, relishing the room's heat.

Noni gave him a wool cloak and a hot mug of mead. "Well?" she asked, "Learn anything new while freezing your bollocks off?"

"I learned that we have chickens without brains and a cold, menacing entity who's getting uncomfortably close."

"Anything to be done about it?"

"The chickens? No. The entity? Hopefully. But not tonight or tomorrow." He gulped the mead and handed her the cup. "Thank you for thawing my bollocks." He smiled when she slapped her towel across his arm.

"Take your wolfish grin from my kitchen." She always said he looked predatory when he smiled.

I should smile more at the margrave. Or snarl. He yawned. "I'm going, old woman. In the morning, weather permitting and gods willing, I'll toss Militess Halina out of Kharayan."

Noni turned back to her bread as Gethen took the rear stairs to his fourth-floor apartment. Winding up the dark, uneven steps absorbed in his own thoughts, he took no notice of the shadows that always haunted the narrow stairwell.

In his study he went to the small table beside the fire and filled another glass with warm mead. He settled in one of the stuffed chairs facing the fireplace and contemplated the storms — snowy, political, and, possibly, carnal — that had arrived upon his doorstep.

Ursinum and Besera being at odds made no sense. The two kingdoms had been allies for so long that much of their shared border had no guards and their yearly trade meeting was more celebration than negotiation.

Vernard and his daughter laying siege was senseless, too. In his two decades at Ranith, the only interaction between Gethen and his liege had come in the form of a yearly tax collector whom Magod paid when he visited Kharaton's market every spring and fall.

The wind whistled through thin gaps between the ancient citadel's walls and its windows, a ghostly ululation. The weather had turned ugly and so had relations between the kingdoms. The storm had worsened and Vernard's army had arrived at Gethen's doorstep. The witch was affecting more than just the weather. She was manipulating the people of Quoregna, too.

His gaze strayed to the carved wooden mantle above his fireplace. There perched the unwanted letter from Vernard still sealed and awaiting his eyes. Magod must have brought it when he'd delivered the mead.

"Blood and bones." Gethen snatched down the letter, settled back into his chair, and ran his fingers across the wax seal, contemplating the royal bear and how best to be rid of the woman who'd delivered it. He tossed the missive onto the table beside him and went back to pondering the many storms in his life.

Hours later the citadel had grown quiet, its stone walls keeping out the worst of the storm's chill. The night was dark and Gethen should've been long asleep, but rest wouldn't come to him. He was no closer to escaping any of his troubles for all the hours of consideration. The mead was gone, the fire and candles burned low, but the letter and the militess remained.

The vision of the woman at her window haunted him. She was beautiful and powerful.

With another curse, he retrieved the sealed offering and snapped the wax bear in half. He scowled as he scanned the letter — its words written with bold black strokes. Much of what King Vernard had to say was uninspiring and unoriginal: Gethen owed him allegiance, Gethen's power and knowledge were invaluable, and either he joined Ursinum's cause and helped defend their borders or he would be judged a traitor and earn a death mark so highly rewarded that even toothless grandmums would hunt his hide. The offerings were as he'd expected: Gold, gratitude — at which he sneered — and a position in Vernard's court as the royal mage. None of this held any temptation, even if he were able to access the full power of his magic.

There was, however, one item that was both surprising and enticing:

Finally, His Majesty, King Vernard, offers to you, Shadow Mage Gethen, marriage to His Majesty's elder daughter, Militess Halina, Margrave of Khara. Such a union will guarantee you domain over all her holdings, and paramountcy over her, her soldiers, and her tenants.

That Vernard would barter his daughter and her lands for Gethen's loyalty wasn't astonishing; royalty always considered their own flesh and blood a commodity worthy of trading. What made Gethen's eyebrows arch was that it wasn't Arevik, the king's younger daughter, but the militess, a woman desired by kings and not far removed from Ursinum's throne.

Instinct told Gethen that the margrave didn't know her father had offered to trade her like a sow for a handful of dubious enchantments. It wasn't an equitable match.

"She'll kick over tables then stick a knife in her bastard father when she reads this." Gethen smiled, wide and wicked. He could use this to his advantage. The knowledge eased his agitation and, strangely, satisfied his desire, and finally — well past midnight — he yawned, banked the fire, and crawled beneath the thick blankets on his bed.

Doubtless the coming hours with the margrave under his roof would prove to be more interesting than he'd anticipated. He smiled to think of the woman's fury when she learned of her father's treachery. Her wrath might even eclipse the power of the storm raging beyond Ranith's walls.

SEVEN

"He's lying about his sorcery." Halina lay awake, watching lines of gray, predawn light seeping through cracks in the citadel's ancient walls. Her gold-and-white bedding was warm and thick, but the banked fire in the fireplace meant the floor would be frigid under foot. *Trying to distract me from my agenda. Why? Is he already serving his brother?*

With a growl, she kicked off her covers and reached for her tunic and trouzes. She quickly dressed, including her leather tabard and sword belt, though she left off her sword and its frog. She was adding her misericord to the belt when a knock on the door announced the housekeeper's arrival.

"Come," she said as she slid her feet into her worn, black leather boots.

Noni entered with a tray. "Thought you'd like breakfast in your room, Your Ladyship; that's my master's habit."

"Very well," Halina replied as the woman placed the tray upon the wooden table before the fireplace.

The housekeeper bustled around the room securing the curtains back from the windows and opening the shutters, adding a log to the fire, and retrieving the washbasin from its stand in the corner.

Halina glared at the window as she sat. She'd hoped to see blue sky. Instead, ice filmed the glass.

Breakfast included fresh bread, still warm and fragrant, a hearty white cheese, and another bottle of mead, plus more tart ebonberries and hard-boiled eggs. The housekeeper came and went as Halina ate, and finally said, "Master went into the woods to put out fodder and grain for the animals. He bids you to enjoy his library until his return."

Finished eating, Halina brushed crumbs onto her plate and stood. "Thank you. I'm sure your master has an extensive collection of books on the dark arcana."

"Poetry and tales from Besera, too." Noni retrieved the dirty dishes and beckoned Halina to follow.

They descended to the first floor, crossed through the great room, and took a dim, curving corridor that led to the long, narrow library. Halina liked the room's multiple, arched windows. A door led out to a small courtyard ringed by a low wall and snow-shrouded, redthorn bushes. Polished wood shelves, laden with books, lined the walls from floor to ceiling, and several square tables with chairs occupied the center of the space.

Noni unbanked the fire and coaxed it from its sleep then left Halina alone. Soon a cheery glow and warmth spread through the area.

As with the other rooms in the Shadow Mage's citadel, the library floor was covered with thick, soft, colorful rugs, and where the walls had no shelves, portraits and tapestries hung. Several large inviting chairs occupied the area before the fireplace, and the dark blue sofa along one wall showed dips and fraying where centuries of mages had lain upon its length.

Halina selected a book of tales from Eastern Besera. It included the story of Soraine, who evaded a monstrous captor only to discover that the monster was a mouse, and that she'd been held captive by her own misbeliefs.

There was much to be learned from the folklore of a country, although Vernard's military advisers turned up their noses at the idea. Of course, most of them were idiots.

She didn't settle into one of the comfortable chairs before the fireplace, however. Instead, Halina went to the closest window and gazed out at the white world. Kharayan's trees bowed, burdened by ice that hung thick upon their limbs. Wind whooshed around the citadel and through the trees. Cracking and crashing followed in its wake as tree branches broke, surrendering to the weight of the ice and the sway of the wind.

Halina glowered at the white wonderland. A very early and angry ice storm had come to Khara and trapped her in Ranith with the Shadow Mage for a day, at least. Well, she hadn't planned to go anywhere until she had the sorcerer's ink on her agreement or his blood on her blade, so the snow and ice changed nothing, though it put her in a black mood.

If he's losing his powers, why tell me? She wondered what he thought to gain from revealing vulnerability. *Sympathy?* She pursed her lips. He didn't seem the kind of man to seek pity. More likely he was putting her off, distracting her. He didn't know her very well if he thought that would work. She considered the leather-bound book. She was the monster not the mouse. "Good luck, Shadow Mage," she said beneath her breath.

Sound and movement drew her attention to the far end of the courtyard. Gethen and Magod were coming through the postern door. The Shadow Mage was supporting his man who limped and grimaced. A trail of red marked their passage. Dropping the book upon the couch, Halina forced her way through the snow-blocked door into the bailey and, her feet crunching upon the icy snow, she moved to the other side of Magod.

"Take him into the kitchen. Noni can tend the wound."

Gethen said. At Halina's nod, he released the man and disappeared back through the postern.

"Most kind, Your Ladyship," Magod said through clenched teeth as they made their way across the treacherous bailey.

When they reach the kitchen's stoop, Noni emerged and helped her son into the tower. "What've you done to yourself this time?" she asked as they settled him onto a bench beside the long kitchen table. One look at Magod's right leg answered that question. Blood soaked his trouzes from mid-thigh to boot top.

Halina pulled her dagger. "Bring me hot water and clean cloths, needle and thread for stitching, and the stiffest, clearest drink you've got."

Noni didn't argue with the woman who owned the very land upon which she stood. The housekeeper poured boiling water into a bowl from the kettle, fetched a bottle of whitewood alcohol from the stores, and placed them upon the table beside Halina. Then she disappeared in search of the other supplies.

"Your Ladyship's kind," Magod said, "but Mummin can fix me up. Don't dirty your hands."

"I'm sure she can, but I can do it faster. I've been up to my elbows in blood and guts more times than I care to recall." Halina put the knife to his trouze leg and slit it from ankle to wound. A wide, bloody gash revealed striated muscle and pinkish bone. Without looking up she asked, "Ax?"

"Yes, Margrave."

Halina pointed to the alcohol. "You better take a few good pulls from that. This is going to hurt." She waited while Magod downed half the bottle, then she poured a good portion of its remainder into the wound and over her hands and knife while the man groaned and gripped the bench. Noni returned with the towels, needle, and thread as Halina spread the wound and checked for debris.

"The good news is that you're not bleeding enough to die from this. The bad news is that I can't stitch straight."

When she was satisfied that the wound was clean, she took a threaded needle from Noni. "How is my falcon?" she asked to distract him.

"Eh?" Magod replied through clenched teeth. "Fine, Your Ladyship. Keeping her in my room."

"Are you hunting her?" She closed the gash with quick, efficient stitches.

"I am. There's a good, dry place in the citadel. Plenty of rats." His shaking fists evinced his agony.

Halina glanced up from bandaging his leg. "She'll grow fat and lazy in Ranith."

Something drew her attention toward the kitchen doorway. A new sound had been added to the citadel: panting, whining, and the click and scratch of many claws upon marble. She looked at Noni. "Does your master own dogs?" She'd seen no sign of pets in the keep.

"Those're wolves, Your Ladyship."

"Wolves? *Inside* the citadel?"

"Yes, Margrave." Noni helped Magod to stand, maneuver around the table, and through the room. They headed up a narrow staircase at the back of the kitchen. Magod swayed and cursed drunkenly with each slow step.

The Shadow Mage arrived in the arched kitchen entryway. His gaze went from the empty bench, to the bottle and bowl upon the table, to Halina and the bloody rag in her hand. "You stitched his wound?"

"Of course. I know how to treat battle wounds, Master Sorcerer." She wiped her misericord's blade clean and tossed the rag on the table as Gethen ducked his chin in acknowledgement. She ignored his scant thanks and asked, "You've brought wolves into the citadel?"

"They're housed in my stillroom." He cleared the table, found a wet rag in the wash tub, and wiped blood from the bench. "I'm more reliant upon the animals in Kharayan's woods than they are upon me, but when the weather turns vicious I do what I can to shelter them."

She leaned in the arch that led to the great hall and watched him. "But to bring them within your own home seems a dire risk, especially with a wounded man beneath your roof."

He turn his disconcerting gray gaze upon her. Blood dripped from the cleaning rag to the floor. After a heavy second passed he replied, "There's no danger to those who are my friends and allies." He offered her a wide, wolfish smile that didn't reach his eyes and added, "But you needn't worry about that, Your Ladyship. Your father intends for us to be *close* allies, doesn't he?"

Wary of his emphasis on *close* she muttered, "Indeed, he does."

He studied her with unblinking intensity. "Your king's offering was mildly interesting, Militess." He stooped and wiped blood from the floor.

He wants something. She quickly thought through the offerings. Gold didn't seem like a temptation to him, nor land. *Power?* Vernard had offered him a prominent position in the court. "You're willing to parley now?"

He smirked and tossed the rag in the wash tub, then cleaned and dried his hands. "I'm willing to hear your arguments all day, but you'll have to present them while I work." He strode past her into the great hall, leaving the scent of pinewood and herbs in his wake. "I'll be in my second-floor stillroom, Margrave."

Halina inhaled. He smelled good, masculine, clean. Clean was a bonus. *Damnation.* She watched him ascend the wide stairs. *I'm not here to play chase.* She looked at her hands. Magod's blood was under her fingernails and her palms were stained with it. "Thinks he can lead me around by the nose." She sniffed again then snorted, amused by her own appetites. "Better be careful or he'll be right." She washed her hands at the same tub he'd used then followed him.

Reaching the second floor, she was surprised to find Gethen waiting outside a darkened room, his arms folded. He watched her from beneath his black brows as she approached. She glanced through the doorway. The dim candlelight flickering in from the hall illuminated the glint of glass, the bulk of a large table, and dark lumps scattered across the floor. Wolves. He'd told her they were housed in his stillroom.

"Wait here." He entered the room. He blew across his fingers and gestured toward the fireplace. A fire burst to life on the grate tinged green by magic before turning its normal yellow, red, and orange. He walked around the room, threading past the gray, brown, silver, and black animals as he lit the brazier beside his desk and the wall candles with the same magical method. Then he turned. "Come in and take a seat beside the fireplace."

Two of the largest wolves raised their heads and watched with keen amber eyes as she passed. One silently bared sharp teeth, but a gesture from Gethen calmed it. Halina threaded past them, careful not to tread on paws or tails, and took the covered gray chair with what she hoped appeared to be confidence. She liked wolves — at a good distance and not in packs.

There were two windows in the room. A desk beneath one held a neat pile of parchment, three quills in a glass holder, an inkstand, and a blotter. Cabinets and shelves of varying heights lined the walls of the room. They contained books, boxes, jars, and instruments of origins and uses unknown to her. Herbs and branches hung from the rafters, baskets held all manner of plants, objects, and substances. She recognized a copper still at one end of the table and assumed the covered wooden pins occupying a sturdy rack at the far end of the room held fermenting meads.

The mage unrolled a cloth upon his table then considered a collection of squat glass containers before selecting one. He went to a corner cabinet and opened it to reveal an assortment of jars and small wooden boxes stacked by size. He selected two jars. From a small, recessed drawer he removed several tiny stone boxes and another low-sided dish. All of this he took to the table.

"Kharayan's paths are blocked. The snow became an ice storm

overnight and the weight of it has been toppling trees and snapping branches all morning."

Noni appeared from the hall with a coffee service. She poured two cups of the hot brew then crossed the room to a closed door.

"Wait." Gethen began to mix a combination of unguent, powders, and herbs that he took from the jars and boxes. He continued to work as he glanced at Halina. "It seems that Ranith must shelter you for several more days, Militess."

Lovely. More threatening spells, ill-timed temptation, and now slinking wolves. She smiled. "Better than freezing my tits off in a tent."

He paused mid-task to eye her from beneath his brow as Noni snickered. "True," he said and returned to mixing.

She'd surprised him. *Good,* she thought.

The coffee was pleasantly sharp. She sipped it and lowered her cup. "Perhaps we should look upon this blizzard as a gift, Master Sorcerer. While His Majesty can do little to prevent Besera's aggression, King Zelal will be unable to attack, as well. The snow has bought Ursinum time to rally troops and find allies, and provided you and me with an unfettered period during which to negotiate."

"A gift," the Shadow Mage said. Noni waited patiently. Her master finished mixing and uttered a few strange words over the unguent. A faint blue-green vapor formed beneath his palm and drifted down to mingle with the ointment. He watched the container for a moment, then wiped his hands upon a rag and passed her the dish. "Apply this now and with every change of his bandages. The wound will heal within two days, and you can remove the stitches on the third." She curtsied, opened the door, and disappeared into an adjoining room.

Halina said, "That's impressive sorcery, if you can heal your man's wounds in so few days. I'd expect him to be crippled for weeks." Gethen capped containers, closed boxes, and ignored her until she added, "Your ability with medicinals makes you invaluable at a time of war." She gave him a shrewd smile. "Of course war makes your medicinals invaluable, too. Besera's aggression could fill your coffers many times over. So I doubt His Majesty's offer of gold compels you."

His gaze was equally perceptive as he slowly stepped back from his desk. He returned the jars and boxes to the cabinet. Yet he remained silent as he came and sat in the chair opposite her.

"Land isn't much temptation to a man comfortably housed in a citadel that's served him and his predecessors for centuries. Particularly with no children squabbling for an inheritance. So that leaves power. A position in His Majesty's court comes with a great deal of influence. Is that what tempts you, Master Gethen?"

His silence stretched on as he sipped his coffee and watched the fire dance upon the grate. Halina persisted. "Your knowledge *is* invaluable, supported by magic or not. And your duty is to share it with Ursinum."

His voice was icy when he replied. "I may not live in Besera, but my brother remains dear to me. I won't betray him. Nor will I serve him in this idiotic war." The burning wood on the grate settled and sent up a small whoosh of orange embers. "Enjoy Ranith's hospitality but stop prattling about my loyalty and duty. Those belong to all of Quoregna's living things, not just to arrogant fools who think nothing of killing to further their *might*." He stood and put the last two logs on the fire.

The contempt filling his voice felt like a slap. He believed she went to battle only to elevate her position. *He*, the Shadow Mage, a *necromancer*, had criticized *her* for killing? She took a moment to control her anger before replying with a steady voice. "I don't kill for power."

He turned quickly. "Don't you?" His expression was cold and calculating as he slowly circled her chair to return to his. "So you haven't led thousands of soldiers to their deaths to prove to the king that you're too powerful to become a man's pretty plaything?"

Halina swallowed as a little seed of regret sprouted in her mind, fed by the bitter waters of truth. "No." She hated the feeling of someone's disdain washing over her; it always threatened to resurrect the ghosts of her childhood. She glared at him. "Interesting criticism from a man who prefers to stick his head up his arse rather than help his fellow countrymen. I've not heard you offering to parley with your brother to avert this war and save those lives you chastise *me* for ending."

A little bit of the cool in Gethen's expression thawed. He ducked his head slightly then raised his closed fist before his chest, saluting her with an invisible sword. "Fair point, Your Ladyship." He considered the coffee remaining in his cup, downed it with a grimace, and stood. "If you wish to continue this game, you'll have to accompany me to the extraction room. Ranith needs candles." He turned and strode from the room, leaving her surrounded by sleeping wolves.

She cursed him colorfully beneath her breath.

"Never run from wolves, Halina," Ilker had taught her when she was very young. "Stand your ground to survive. Run, and they'll chase you down and tear you apart." He'd meant both the animals and the royals, and it was advice that had served her well.

She wended her way around the predators, ignoring the growls following her footsteps and finally breathing again when she reached the hall. She'd kill that mage. That seemed an appropriate response to abandoning her to the wolves. She gripped her thin misericord. She'd stick him with it then finish him with her longsword. "He may be able to heal wounds, but he can't return his head to his shoulders."

Footfalls on the stairs alerted her to his whereabouts and she strode after him, considering adding the removal of his bollocks to her agenda, too.

Halina stalked the mage from the keep, across the snowy bailey, and into an outbuilding. He was arranging wood and kindling inside a fire pit in the middle of the room when she yanked open the door. A nearby worktable held a spool of white wick cord, small metal weights, a long drying rack, and three wick holders.

He flashed her another of his wolfish grins as he set a wide, iron cauldron into the pit. "I hope you don't mind if I dip my wick before you kill me, Margrave."

If he was trying to shock her, he'd woefully misjudged. She spent her days surrounded by soldiers; ribaldry was her second language. She cocked her head and smiled seductively. "By all means, Master Sorcerer, dip away." She strode across the room to his work area, adding a little extra sway to her step. He still gripped the cauldron as she stopped beside the table. Her tone gained weight, however, as she added, "But beware, I'll set the bed afire. The best way I've found to kill a louse is to burn it first then crush it beneath my heel."

He held her gaze as he slowly straightened, raised his fingers to his lips, and blew across them. "I'll remember that." He lowered his hand and the wood beneath the cauldron caught fire with a *whoosh*.

Halina hadn't expected the heady tension that filled the space between them and beckoned her closer to the man. *Don't let him distract you.*

Gethen broke the moment by pulling a rickety wooden stool from beneath the table. "If you're here to stay, have a seat."

She inclined her head. She looked around the space, hoping the stool remained intact as it creaked beneath her. It was a large room, lit by hanging lanterns. Wooden bee hive frames and boxes were stacked side-by-side and floor-to-ceiling against the long back wall. Others awaited scrubbing and repairs. Barrels and filtering and extraction equipment were neatly stockpiled. This was where Gethen filtered and stored honey and kept any beeswax that was leftover after extraction.

"I didn't come here to play games and chase you, Master Gethen," she said.

The ring of glass against metal reverberated through the room. "I'm aware of that, Militess. But your presence mustn't keep me from my responsibilities." He placed a tall jar inside the pot. "Last night I gave much thought to Ursinum's predicament, as well as my own situation." He tipped water into the pot from a bucket then moved to the table and started chopping yellow beeswax into small chunks. "And I believe there's a mutually beneficial solution."

"I'm listening."

Gethen tossed wax into the jar. "Before your arrival I crossed the Voidline to learn what I could about this blizzard. It isn't a natural occurrence, and what I met within the Void has convinced me that the threat to Ursinum isn't Besera."

"No?"

He brushed off his hands over the jar. "No. It's what I encountered when I walked with the shadows and the dead."

"And what's that?"

"The Rime Witch." He warmed his hands over the fire. "A miserable, bitter, and spiteful entity who's been long imprisoned in the Void. This storm and the tension between Ursinum and Besera are her doing."

The stool creaked. "You enter the Void? I thought your duty was to keep the line sealed."

He nodded. "I guard the Voidline and prevent anything from coming into this world uninvited. That means driving back entities that wander too close to the border. And interning those that are the greatest danger to the living, like this witch. On this side of the Void the only things that should be incorporeal are shadows; all that's spirit or soul must dwell within a body or beyond the Voidline."

"So is this Rime Witch a spirit?"

"For now." He began measuring and cutting lengths of cord for the candle wicks. "But she's manipulating the living from beyond the Voidline; something she shouldn't be able to do. She's broken free of her bonds. Or been released." He tied small, metal weights to both ends of three wicks then hung all on a circular, wooden handle. The setup allowed him to dip six candles simultaneously — two per long wick to be cut apart once they were dry.

"Released by whom?"

He shook his head. "There are mages, like myself, who can pass between the corporeal and incorporeal with the use of our power—"

"You mean that power that's failing you?" Her caustic tone could corrode metal.

He gave her a tight-lipped smile. He seemed to have lost his humor and conceit. "I understand your doubt, Margrave. But all you've seen me work are simple tricks and illusions. Crossing the Voidline takes tremendous power, and remaining safe while straddling two realms requires even more. As my sorcery has waned I've become dependent upon strength drawn from the spirits of the animals that dwell within Kharayan's woods."

"You take the lives around you to power your magic?" Halina's hand went to her dagger. "So the murderous practices that occur behind Ranith's stone walls aren't old wives' tales." She'd too easily forgotten he was dangerous.

The wax was melting. Gethen tossed more pieces into the jar and began preparing more wicks. "Shadow mages have a well-earned reputation for killing." He pinned her with that spellbinding gaze. "Yet here you sit, unharmed, Militess Halina." His voice turned from sand to silk. "I prefer not to destroy what I touch."

She arched her right eyebrow at him, but her hand didn't relax upon the weapon. "How fortunate for me."

His lips twitched, and he turned back to the wax. "The Rime Witch is a growing threat at a time when my power's waning. I'm sure you can see the problem that presents to all of us."

"I can." *If what you say is true.* Halina leaned forward. The stool creaked beneath her arse. "Tell me more of this transition in your sorcery. Will you be more powerful as the Sun Mage?" She released the misericord's grip. She had little understanding of magic, but she knew military might. If his sorcery really was changing, and he'd be stronger as a result, it behooved her to redouble her efforts to secure his fealty. Ursinum couldn't lose such a powerful ally to Besera.

The warm musk of melted wax filled the room. Gethen began the process of dipping the wicks, hanging them to dry, and moving to the next holder, so that each layer had time to set between passes. When he was finished, he'd have eighteen candles and could easily repeat the process until the wax was gone.

"Yes. Once the transition is complete I'll wield the magic of the sun *and* the shadows," he answered as he worked. "Unfortunately, if the Rime Witch continues to strengthen, we won't have the luxury of time for my sun sorcery to grow and be mastered."

"Hmm." She didn't quite know what to think of his claims. What wasn't he telling her? "If your sorcery is failing, how can you hope to stop this witch?"

He put up the candles to dry while he added more wood to the fire and water to the pot. "I need a protector as my magic wanes. Once I've shifted from shadow to sun sorcery, I'll quickly regain my strength. But there are things that must be done now to contain the threat." He straightened and met her gaze. "I need a champion to guard my physical body while my spirit strengthens the Voidline wards and drives the Rime Witch back. I'd thought to use Magod, but he hasn't the heart or the skill for such a battle."

"A champion." There it was, the rub. "You mean me?"

He nodded and dropped more unmelted beeswax into the jar.

"You're placing a great deal of trust in me," she said. "How do you know I won't kill you myself?"

"Because you need me." He jabbed his finger toward the building's small, square windows. "That storm is unnatural, as is the hostility between Ursinum and Besera. I'm your only way out of this mess, Militess Halina, unless you want the blood of twenty thousand more soldiers on your hands."

Ouch. She watched the blowing snow. "Prove you're not with Besera. Prove that your sorcery is waning, that this witch is real, and that you didn't create this storm to hamper Ursinum." People said Halina had her father's murderous gaze. "Do that and I'll help you." She turned that gaze on the mage. "Your word isn't unquestionable, Shadow Mage, and from what I've experienced of your sorcery, your word sounds like lies."

He began to respond, but she cut him off. "*If* I choose to guard you, it will constitute an agreement to the terms of His Majesty's request. After returning from the Void, you'll lower your wards around Kharayan and join Ursinum's troops on the shores of the Silver Sea. You'll wield magic and sword in service to His Majesty, King Vernard of Ursinum."

Gethen's manner had cooled as hers had heated. "Help me contain the Rime Witch and there'll be no war or storm," he said.

"Those are my terms. Do you accept them?"

He crossed his arms. "No."

A spark of rage flashed through Halina. She yanked it under control, but the stool clattered against a table leg as she stood. "I suggest you reconsider your answer."

She strode into the bailey where the storm raged unabated. Snow blew sideways and plastered the trees and tower. It snatched at the braids she'd too loosely secured, and whipped her hair into her mouth as she cursed. She entered the kitchen and slammed the door hard enough to bring down a cascade of snow and icicles on the stoop.

"I'm not finished, Mage."

She stomped up Ranith's wide, winding staircase, leaving snowy boot prints in her wake.

Either he'd accept her terms, or she'd run a knife across his throat. *Then* she'd be through with him.

EIGHT

Gethen rubbed his chin and watched the militess kick snow across the bailey. The demon wind lashed her red hair. He shook his head and laughed quietly. He admired her just a little more than he wanted to kill her. The woman had a steel spine and would bend quite far before she broke. The trick would be easing off before she snapped and stuck a knife in him.

More and more he believed having her as a protector and ally would be key to his survival and triumph when he faced the Rime Witch. There was a reason why Margrave Khara had arrived on his doorstep when he most needed a champion. "But a woman like that isn't easily swayed," he said. "And she's meaner than anything hiding under the furniture and behind the doors."

His amusement evaporated. He needed the margrave's strength if he was to imprison the witch. But, damnation, she was strong-willed and sharp-minded. And uncompromising.

And desirable.

He cleared his throat.

The militess understood power, and he hadn't missed the shift in her judgment when he'd told her more about his transitioning sorcery. That was another hook he had in her mouth.

He could gain her trust and cooperation with the promise of his greater sorcery. If he was careful he could do it without losing his freedom to her king. But if she sensed manipulation, she'd slaughter him like a fattened goose and feed him to his own wolves.

Snow and sleet peppered the extraction building's windows. The fire crackled and popped beneath the cauldron. He returned to candle making. He could let the woman cool off. He had more than enough work to keep him out of range of her sword for the remainder of the day.

And he had the king's letter. He didn't need to antagonize her.

When Gethen finally had three sets of eighteen candles, he raised his hand and flicked his fingers toward each lantern, summoning their flames to him. An orb of green mage fire formed as each drifting flame joined together. It hovered before him then dimmed as he closed his hand around it. Mage fire didn't burn unless he directed it to; in Gethen's palm it was cool and buzzed with potential. A smile curved his lips. The militess was much like mage fire, albeit much hotter.

"What would it take to coax her to burn for me?" He laughed. He already knew she was willing to set his bed on fire with him in it.

Darkness closed in. Shadows danced and writhed across the floors, walls and ceiling, created by the still-flickering firelight beneath the melting pot. They whispered his name and beckoned their mage to join them in the cold. They were power shackled, awaiting his command, an unstoppable, immortal army created by the shadow mages who'd preceded Gethen and anchored to the tor beneath his feet.

Vernard and Zelal were right to want his allegiance, and they weren't the first kings to court, or threaten, a shadow mage. With a shadow army at his command, a king could crush his enemies and rule Quoregna.

But that army couldn't leave the tor no matter how much the mages had wished it. The anchor chaining the shades to Kharayan existed for the protection of all four kingdoms.

"But what if the Sun Mage can release them?" Gethen said to no one. "The witch would want that power, too." That was a disturbing thought.

He cursed the shadows, mages, and the Rime Witch beneath his breath. He didn't want to lead that army.

Necromancy had corrupted the former shadow mages. After death they'd become cold, wandering wraiths, eternally chained to Kharayan Tor for the safety of Quoregna. That was a fate Gethen planned to avoid.

The fire sputtered in the pit. His breath fogged. But he still held the green mage fire. He opened his palm and its glow and heat surged. He cursed as it burned his hand even as he welcomed the rare warmth. It cast light through the extraction room, pushing the shadows back. He hurled the fireball at the pit. The fire burst to life beneath the cauldron and all the lanterns flared.

"I won't be used by kings or spirits." He strode into the storm. The mage fire followed him, leaving the lanterns and fire pit dark again. Gethen returned to the citadel and the flickering ball set the wall candles aflame as he approached and pulled their fire back into itself as he passed out of their pools of light. Thus did he make his way up to the stillroom on the second floor of Ranith Citadel.

The hearth and candles flared as he entered the room. He took his brewing apron from its wall peg and looked around at the sleeping wolves. There were fourteen, including several young pups.

"Hergid, find Noni." A large, brown wolf eyed him from its resting place beside the work table. When Gethen added, "Please," the animal stood, stretched, and lumbered from the room. He called after, "Make some noise as you approach. Her heart can't bear the surprise of a silent wolf."

The stillroom held vats of honey, oils, spirits, and sweet nectars of all kinds. Bundles of dried black, green, and red peppers filled wooden boxes. Sprays of herbs — blue gillim, sweet brambles, and monk's blood, among many — hung from the walls and rafters, and a variety of jars contained roots, grains, and spices.

He prepared medicinal meads and unguents, and infused them with the power of dark incantations to destroy contagion and banish ague. He traded them to hedge witches and healers from all over Khara and beyond. They claimed the salves and medicines as their own creations, while paying the Shadow Mage for his products in food, coin, or sex.

In working this simple magic, Gethen found peace and purpose.

He retrieved a shallow dish from a cabinet, collected eyespice oil, maluk, liminth seeds, hayper, and a half-dozen other spices, along with a handful of dried ebonberries, and settled at his table. There he began the task of grinding the spices with a mortar and pestle while around him wolves dozed.

Hergid returned. Noni appeared in the stillroom doorway a few moments later, bearing a tray. She looked around, a frown creasing her wrinkles until her eyes almost disappeared beneath them. "Lunch for Her Ladyship."

"Take it to her room."

She peered at him. "Make any effort not to insult your guest this morning?"

"Very little." He held his breath as he uncapped a bottle of undiluted somniferum ether. One whiff and he'd be dizzy, two and he'd be on the floor.

"Go hungry 'til I've seen to Her Ladyship's meal then." She turned and disappeared with the food. The stairs creaked and the crockery and silver clattered as she climbed to Ranith's third floor guest chamber.

Gethen added four drops of the ether to his tincture, capped the larger bottle, and exhaled a curse. "I called you here for a reason, old woman."

Hergid curled up beneath the worktable and upon Gethen's feet. The Shadow Mage's leg twitched, the one where he'd been bitten as a young apprentice.

He'd been left in the woods to find a deer, drain its soul, and use its strength to harness a travel spell that would permit him to return to the citadel.

"Use your magic as it's intended or die in the forest," Shemel had growled.

But Gethen hadn't wanted to kill a deer, so he'd tried summoning enough power from the flora around him. But plants and trees are stingy with their power, clinging to it as their roots hold fast to the earth and burying it deep.

Instead of growing powerful, Gethen had been weakened by the effort. The sun had set and the light in the forest had failed. Soon he was lost and surrounded by Kharayan's snarling wolf pack. Foolishly, he'd run. The pack had given chase, howling and baying. Suddenly, with a great leap, Hergid's sire, Trahearn, had pulled him down, his teeth tearing jagged holes in Gethen's calf.

He'd expected to die then, but the wolves had ceased their attack. Peering into the darkness, Gethen had found that he lay only inches from the tor's cliff. The wolf had stopped him from plummeting to his death on the rocky shore of the Silver Sea. The pack hadn't been hunting him.

Gethen leaned down, and scratched Hergid behind his ear, then returned to his mortar and pestle. The tincture was for Magod.

As the afternoon dimmed in Gethen's stillroom he banked the fire beneath his mead kettle, strained the concentration into a pin, and covered the open end with a doubled bolter-cloth to cool. As he wiped his hands on his apron the wolves looked up, their sleepy eyes becoming keen as he surrendered his hold on their spirits. Like Ranith's master, they stood and stretched.

Gethen pushed open the room's only window, melting the ice around its frame with a touch of his hand and a whispered incantation. He leaned out. The snowfall had eased but drifts were piled as high as the bottom ledges of the first floor's windows.

Yipping and squealing drew his attention back to the wolves; the beasts needed to get outside.

"Come. You can hunt while I finish cutting firewood." The wolves gathered around Gethen's legs, rubbing and snuffling against him, licking and nuzzling his hands and each other, excited by the prospect of running beneath the wide sky and dark trees.

He encountered Noni on the way downstairs. She stiffened and stared at the ceiling as the wolf pack thundered past her. She seemed more discomfited than usual by them.

"I'll let them out until nightfall," Gethen said, and his house-keeper's face and figure relaxed like a flag that had lost its breeze. He chuckled as he passed her, and hearing it, she snapped her apron at him. Gethen paused and turned back. "How is Magod's leg? I trust the unguent is doing its job?"

"Indeed. Looks much better, and stitches should come out by tomorrow evening. Pain's much improved and no fever or sign of infection. Thank you, Master."

"Good. I left a draught on my worktable. Give it to him tonight with his supper." Gethen continued down the stairs and across the great hall to open the front door for the milling wolves.

The moment the pack smelled snow and felt cold air upon their faces they started howling. The eerie sound echoed and undulated around the bailey and within the great hall.

"Go on, ingrates," the Shadow Mage said.

Raising white plumes of snow, the wolves charged across the courtyard, through the citadel's open main gates, and disappeared among the ruins of the village below.

Gethen trudged the length of the bailey, rounded the corner, and came up short as Militess Halina turned away from the small postern door that opened into the forest opposite the library. He bowed. "Your Ladyship." *What's she doing out here?*

Her fiery hair had been re-braided — two thick plaits on the sides that were drawn back to secure the hair off her face. It was the style of Ursinum's soldiers, and it highlighted the angles of her cheekbones, the almond shape of her blue eyes, and the generous sprinkling of copper freckles across her cheeks and nose.

Gethen hadn't missed her stare and the furrowing of her brow as she'd spied him emerging from around the corner of the stone building, but he ignored it, and her expression had turned dispassionate.

"Shadow Mage." Halina jerked a thumb toward the dwindling pile of firewood. "I can wield an ax, if you'll provide one." She nodded toward the sea. "With heavy clouds looming on the horizon and your man injured I'm sure the citadel will need more wood than what's here."

Gethen continued to the outbuilding where Magod stored tools. "I can manage this task alone."

"Worried someone might get hurt, again?"

"Yes. Me."

Her smile was slow and her voice deep as she said, "I don't need an ax to reduce your wood to kindling, Master Gethen."

His lips twitched. Once again the woman proved to have more smolder than he expected. He forced the outbuilding's door open past drifts of snow and ice, and retrieved two heavy axes and a wooden sledge.

"Magod and I began chopping a good-sized oak that fell in the storm," he said upon returning. "A sapling came back on him, caught his ax, and did the damage to his leg. It was, however, the last large sapling that we needed to free, which leaves a lot of wood waiting to be chopped."

The militess followed the sledge past the postern door. A narrow trail wound through the forest, but it was slow going as they frequently stopped to remove fallen branches from the path.

Kharayan's forest was a white cathedral, its peace broken by the sledge's creaking leathers and the crunch of snow beneath their boots. Trees snapped and groaned as snow slid from their limbs, brushed aside by an unsteady breeze. Bushes crackled as birds, rabbits, and other small beasts emerged from their hiding places to forage for food in the respite between storms.

They hadn't gone far, though it had taken much longer than Gethen had anticipated, when they reached the fallen black oak tree.

He hefted the axes and handed one to Halina. "If you'll hold the blade steady, Your Ladyship, I'll warm it. Then we can work from opposite ends towards the middle."

She grasped the handle and turn the blade toward him, and as the green glow of mage fire lit his hands and glinted off the blade, her brows rose. However, she made no remark when he'd finished. She simply draped her heavy wool cloak over the lowest branch of a nearby pine tree and set to work.

Gethen watched her as he warmed his blade. Halina lined up each stroke with care, raised her ax, and brought it down without hesitation. He couldn't help but imagine the woman doing the same thing to a man's skull with a sword.

The rhythmic knock and ring of falling axes and the crunch of splitting wood soon drowned out all other sounds. As they finished chopping large branches into manageable sizes, Gethen carried them to the growing pile upon the sledge. He paused after depositing two large cuts and his gaze strayed to the militess.

She was tireless and focused completely on her task. The rhythmic sound of her breathing caught his attention and held him in thrall. She drew a slow, deep breath and exhaled to power each swing of her ax. It was the way a soldier breathed in the heat of battle or a lover did in the throes of passion.

Gethen's own breathing matched hers and he turned away when he realized it. *Damnation, man. Don't get bewitched.* He gripped his ax handle tighter, focusing on the bite of a blister where his ring finger met his palm. The sting was a welcome distraction.

After they'd worked a while, pausing occasionally to reheat the ax blades, Gethen called a halt to the work. "That's enough wood."

The margrave glanced at the pile on the sledge then cocked an eyebrow at him. A fine sheen of perspiration dampened her skin. Wisps of her hair had escaped their braids to cling to her forehead and neck. "You can't take much more?" She licked her upper lip and Gethen's mouth went dry. He rubbed his palms on his trouzes as she retrieved her final cut of wood.

"Quitting before I've got too much to handle," he replied and added his ax to the sledge. "Most of Ranith is closed for the winter. My quarters on the fourth floor are as high as we go. The fifth and sixth floors are ruins open to the elements and tainted by some long-dead shadow mage who tried to harness powers that he had no business touching."

Her eyes narrowed and a small smile played at the corner of her mouth. "Are you superstitious?"

"No. Experienced. I came to Ranith as a boy, and I've explored every inch of the citadel and woods. The catacombs beneath this tor entomb generations of shadow mages. Their spirits once haunted these woods and the citadel, but I grew tired of their corruption. So I contained them with the use of some very strong wards." He leaned toward her and added, "But I wouldn't go wandering alone, Margrave. A steel blade can't stop everything." Gethen took up the sledge's leather traces and pulled it down the path toward his fortress. Halina donned her cloak and followed.

He considered the dark gray tower that rose out of the woods and perched upon Kharayan's sheer black cliff. Cursed and haunted Ranith may have been, but it was home.

When they finally reached the citadel — with much pushing, cursing, and pulling of the sledge over icy ruts — Noni was waiting with cups of warm bracket. "Something to fortify you and Your Ladyship." They thanked her and enjoyed the drink, sitting on the sledge, close but not too close.

Halina wrapped her hands around the warm pottery and blew upon the steaming liquid, her eyes downcast. She had impossibly long, thick eyelashes. Cold air and exertion had brought a rosy flush to her fair, freckled cheeks. Gethen liked the look of her and cursed inward at the magic all women commanded.

"Go inside, Militess." He left his mead cup on the sledge and began stacking the newly cut wood at the end of the woodpile. "I can split enough firewood alone to keep us warm and fed today and tomorrow."

She lowered her drink and looked back to where fog shrouded the Silver Sea. "Very well." She stood and returned to the citadel through the kitchen door.

Gethen watched her, surprised by her complacency. It seemed that she was still giving him time to reconsider his refusal. He glanced around the bailey and his gaze stopped on the postern. "Why were you out here?"

He finished stacking the cut logs, put the axes and sledge in the outbuilding, and returned to the bailey with a maul. He set up an old, cured log for his chopping block then finished his mead.

"Vernard knows me better than I thought." The king had deduced that Gethen wouldn't be intrigued by a kittenish girl or an experienced trollop, both too willingly used and tossed aside.

He put down his cup, selected a large, seasoned log, and wrapped a length of cord loosely around it. "Bastard sent me my equal."

He brought the maul's heavy, wedged blade down upon a

narrow groove in the wood. With a satisfying *crack*, the log split. He moved around it, continuing to split it until the entire log was sectioned. Then he untied the cord, tossed the wood into a pile beside the kitchen door, and started on another large log.

"That tricky prick."

The king had chosen a woman who was powerful and unyielding, with the combined beauty of Gethen's native people and those of his adopted home. A woman he'd hunger for.

Crack. Another log split.

The challenge Halina presented — taking the woman without losing to her king — was almost unwinnable. Almost. And it was that glimmering possibility that intrigued Gethen too much.

"I underestimated you, Vernard." He glanced up at the guest room window. She wasn't watching him. He smiled as he set up another log. "And you underestimated me." He hefted the maul overhead and let it fall. Four more pieces of wood were quickly added to the citadel's fuel.

"You don't reach into a humming beehive and grab a handful of honey." He turned the next log this way and that, looking for a crack in the grain. "Bees have to be coaxed, soothed and seduced into cooperating. They require great patience." Gethen placed the log for splitting. "Especially the queens."

NINE

Halina paced her room. "He's insolent." For refusing to obey his king's and liege's command. "He's insulting." For demanding that she serve him. "He's intriguing." That was the worst of all.

It didn't help her agitation that a little hitch had tightened her chest when the mage had come around the corner of the citadel and found her standing in the snow gazing through the iron lattice postern. She'd gone outside to get a closer look at the enormous white stag that had appeared as she'd stood scowling at the bailey through her bedroom window. But with Gethen's sudden arrival, she'd forgotten the deer and, instead, found herself admiring the man's broad shoulders and feral gaze. She'd yanked herself up hard when she'd realized she was staring.

He must know magic hums off him. She'd struggled not to show how his proximity warmed and distracted her.

Halina unbuckled her sword belt and left it on the bed. Why had that stag appeared to her? If it was a warning from the gods, it was coming much too late. She tossed her tunic and trouzes beside the sword and glanced out the window at a world that had turned white again. "Trapped in Ranith for another day."

Her fingers lingered on the hem of her sweat-dampened shift. Experience said she should kill the mage. But he hadn't really given her a reason to. Soldier she may be, ruthless upon the field of battle she always was, but wanton with life Halina never acted, despite Gethen's assertion. She'd spent enough time dancing with death to have a great love for life, even the life of an insolent, insulting, intriguing dark mage.

The power he wielded gave her pause again, especially knowing it was soon to increase. She wanted that for Ursinum. Killing him would make him a wasted opportunity.

She looked down at her bare legs. He'd watched her as she'd chopped wood; his gray eyes had followed her movements and studied her body. She'd enjoyed that attention. She'd licked the sweat from her lip to see his reaction and found he was as affected by her as she was by him.

"I can use that."

The knock and ring of steel splitting wood carried faintly in from the bailey. Halina swallowed, went to the window, and pulled the shutters closed. Yes, she could use his attraction to her, but only if she wasn't ensnared by the same stupid spell. She cursed. "Damned inconvenient. All of this."

She shivered and pulled her shift over her head. She draped it upon a wooden chair to dry then turned to the washbasin that Noni had filled with warm water. Removing the sweat from her skin would put her in the right mood again. Just in time to sup with the damnable mage and be pushed back out of it. She snorted. How easily he slid under her skin. Certainly he'd been court-raised; he demonstrated a level of confidence that she'd rarely encountered outside of her father's circle of advisors and sycophants.

Once she was clean Halina dressed in a dry chemise and considered the other gown she'd brought. Made of pleated silver and gold silk, it was one of her favorites. But she'd need help with its laces. She blew out a breath and tugged the bell pull to summon Noni. Sooner than she'd expected, the elderly woman knocked on her door.

"I was a fool not to accept your assistance yesterday evening," Halina said as she invited the woman into her room. "Tonight I'm taking up that offer." She indicated the silver-and-gold silk surcoat.

Noni's face dimpled with delight as she produced a nearly toothless smile and took the garment from Halina. "An honor to assist you in dressing this evening, Your Ladyship."

Halina raised her arms as the woman wrapped stiff, boned stays around her torso. "How long have you served your master?" she asked and held the stays in place over her breasts as Noni laced them.

The housekeeper retrieved Halina's gown next, squinting as she thought. "Was belly-heavy with Magod when Master Gethen's father bought me from the Chancellor's brothel in Umasera." She held the surcoat open.

Halina slipped her arms through the gown's armholes. "You came from Besera's capitol?" It was surprising. Neither the woman nor her son had the characteristic Beseran mottled skin. Hers was discolored by age rather than heredity. Magod had the flawless complexion of a Northern man still in his second decade.

"I was born in Ayestra," Noni replied, as she slid one sleeve up Halina's arm and tied it in place.

"I see." Halina held up her left arm for the other sleeve as Noni fetched it from the bed.

Ayestra was a small, northeastern island situated between Besera and Nalvika. Before the War of the Winds it had been an independent kingdom; the Nalviks' attempt to subjugate it had been the flashpoint for the war.

"So Master Gethen was only a boy when you went to serve him?"

"Yes. His Majesty, King Maczen, purchased me after Queen Tegwen's death."

"Ah." Halina fingered her skirt's fine silk. "I'd forgotten that he's Tegwen's eldest."

"The king wanted my master to have a loyal, female servant to comfort him. Good thing, too, because only a few weeks later Shemel claimed him for apprenticeship." Noni secured the second sleeve then tightened and tied the surcoat's back laces. She smoothed wrinkles from the pleated skirt, her fingers lingering upon the clear crystals that formed small stars at the apex of each pleat. "Such beautiful workmanship."

It was a lovely gown. Even Halina knew that. One of the finest her seamstress had sewn, the dress made her feel beautiful and womanly. "Were you forced to come to Ranith?"

"Oh, no. I was happy to remain at my master's side."

"You're quite devoted to him."

"Yes, Your Ladyship. He's been very good to Magod and me."

Halina removed the plaits from her hair and shook out its waves and curls. "I'm afraid that sorting through this mess will be the most difficult task you'll face today." She handed her wooden comb to the housekeeper.

Noni waved away Halina's words. "Been decades since I've had the pleasure of preparing a lady's hair. There's little artistry in twisting my wiry, old locks."

Halina closed her eyes and relaxed as Noni removed the snarls from her hair with little tugging and less cursing. "Does your master often bring wolves into Ranith?"

"No. Only with evil weather and young pups in the pack. Adults fare well enough; don't feel the cold. A wonder to see them curled up, nose under tail, even in the fiercest blizzard. But my master keeps the wolves close now because of the pups and because he needs their power."

"Power with which to harness his shadow sorcery?"

"Exactly so, Your Ladyship. It's why he houses them in his stillroom when they visit the citadel."

"Have you observed any lessening of his abilities?"

"Sadly, yes." Noni sighed. "He's taxed after crossing the Void-line now and needs the animals' strength more. He broods that he'll harm them."

That supported the mage's claims. However, like all servants whose housing and meals relied upon the well-being of their master, Halina didn't doubt that Noni would lie to protect him and Ranith. "He creates all the medicinals himself?"

"He does. Master's tinctures, unguents, and meads are well-known among healers from all parts of Quoregna." Pride filled her voice.

Snow had formed elaborate lacework upon the window, and Halina's gaze followed the shimmering lines of nature's handiwork.

Noni added, "I'd follow my master into the Void, if he asked."

When the housekeeper was finished combing she began braiding and twisting Halina's hair into an elaborate style, holding it in place with the silver-and-pearl hairpins that Halina's lady-in-waiting had packed with her belongings.

She turned her head this way and that, admiring Noni's handiwork in the dressing table mirror. "You possess artistry worthy of the ladies in His Majesty's court," Halina said.

Noni smiled so widely that her face resembled one of the little, dried blackapple dolls that Halina's childhood governess had created every fall. "Thanks is mine to give, Your Ladyship," Noni replied as she bowed. "Only keep my master's hair cut and can't do anything with Magod's. Ranith's never seen as fine a lady as yourself." Halina nodded as the housekeeper excused herself to return to the kitchen and her preparations for the evening meal.

Tired of staring at the same four walls, Halina returned to the library and retrieved the book she'd left upon the sofa earlier that day. However, once again as she opened its cover, she noticed movement from the corner of her eye. White shifted against white, traveling counter to the storm's rhythm.

She faced the window.

Her stag had returned.

The animal watched her from beyond the closed postern. Its black unblinking eyes drew her toward it.

"Why are you back?" Halina tossed her book aside. She went to the library's heavy wooden door. But so much snow had accumulated against it that she was unable to push it open. She turned, meaning to go through the great hall to the front entrance and into the bailey. However, as she entered the larger room, the dinner bell chimed, high and sweet.

Halina sighed. She'd have to ask the mage about the animal. The strangeness of its return couldn't be ignored. If it was some figment summoned by the man to vex her, she would know by his reaction when she asked about it. And if it wasn't, well, then she'd bow to his expertise in the area of mysterious entities. Though outwardly harmless, its black gaze and haunting return made the hairs stand on Halina's arms.

At the sound of boot heels upon the marble floor, she turned and was face-to-face once again with Ranith's enigmatic master. This time instead of cold arrogance upon his face, fatigue cast dark circles beneath his eyes and his hands trembled.

"Are you unwell, Master Sorcerer?"

Gethen looked at her sharply. "I'm tired. Storm-scrying is draining, even when I have the full extent of my sorcery. It's not one of my stronger gifts." The corner of his mouth curled as he added, "Thank you for your concern. I doubt you feel it deeply enough to aid me." He looked down his nose at her.

Halina ground her teeth then replied, "No, Shadow Mage Gethen, I have not altered my decision. And I'll thank you to remember that we're not negotiating *my* service to *you*, but your fealty to our king and country." With that she turned on her heel and strode to the great hall, her dark host trailing behind and her skirt singing an angry, rustling chorus.

Doubtless the white stag was some form of persecution that the Shadow Mage had created for his own amusement. Likely that was the source of his fatigue. Well, she found no humor in it and would make certain that he understood the displeasure she took from his jape.

As Gethen sat opposite her Halina asked, "What animals dwell in your woods with the wolves? Do you have deer?"

His eyes narrowed as he regarded her, perhaps alerted by her false tone. "Yes, numerous blackthorns and a small herd of redcoats. You'll also encounter large black grizzlies like the one that adorns your father's signet, wild pigs, many forms of grouse, black squirrels, and coneys aplenty." He paused as Noni served soup made from sweet root vegetables, as well as more of her fragrant bread, toasted and spread with a mixture of sharp white cheese and black olives.

"Have you any white deer?" Halina asked, watching his expression as she spooned soup into her mouth.

"No. Hoar-deer are only found in Nalvika's far north."

"Hmm." Like every meal she'd had at Ranith, the soup and bread were excellent. But also like every meal, meat wasn't served. "No pet stag?"

The sorcerer's spoon clinked against his white bowl as Gethen put it down. "I have no pets, Lady Khara. The animals of Kharayan Tor belong to no one. Why this curiosity about deer in those dark woods?"

Halina enjoyed another spoonful of soup before answering. "I wonder at the origin of the large white stag that I've seen three times since my arrival. The animal stands much taller than any blackthorn or redcoat that I've ever seen and possesses a coat that rivals the snow in its absence of color."

Gethen's brow furrowed. "White stag? There's no such animal in my forest or village." He cocked his head and added, "I'm truly at a loss." Then his lips twisted into his customary half-smirk, half-smile. "Are you certain it wasn't a trick of the light upon the snow? I've seen many strange things in snowstorms, and few of them proved to be corporeal." Halina frowned, not appreciating his implication and liking it even less when he added, "And those that were real but incorporeal proved to be unpleasant at best."

She put her unfinished soup aside and turned to the thick vegetable and grain stew that Noni placed before her. It smelled fragrant and delicious, but her appetite went lax after two bites. She pushed the stew around her plate with her spoon. "I find your answer lacking, Master Sorcerer."

Gethen sampled the stew before answering. "Pity. It's the only answer I have."

Halina drained her cup of mead then leaned forward. "The stag was neither a figment of my imagination nor an incorporeal wisp. It wasn't caused by snow madness or dimwitted paranoia. I know what I saw. And perhaps it's a game, a sorcerer's jest, meant to distract me from the negotiations for which I came to Ranith."

Noni reappeared in the great hall, carrying a bowl of fruit. She glanced surreptitiously from her master to the margrave before placing the fruit upon the table between them. She set out small bowls and a tiny carafe of sweet cream then returned to the kitchen.

As the door closed behind her Gethen also leaned forward. "I don't jest, play games, or avoid negotiating with you, Lady Khara. Whatever you saw in Kharayan's forest isn't mine. That raises my suspicions; either it's a figment created by the storm or it's another *uninvited* guest." He cocked an eyebrow at her and added, "I prefer that it be an illusion of snow and light than a rogue entity sent by the Rime Witch or some other foe to haunt my woods and taunt Your Ladyship."

He took a blackapple from the bowl of fruit and held it out to her, but Halina shook her head. Gethen began to pare the apple's reddish-black skin in a long, curling strip. "As for your negotiations, I've taken them seriously and replied honestly. I won't throw my aid and fealty to Ursinum or Besera; I can't." He neatly sliced the apple's yellowish-pink flesh from the core and its sweet fragrance filled the room.

Halina sat back and folded her arms. "Your demands can't come before Ursinum's needs. The threat to my land isn't an early snowstorm or some angry, magical slattern that you claim to have encountered in the Void. This storm will abate and Besera will cross the Silver Sea, its vast army ready to destroy Khara and, beyond that, Ursinum. I have people to protect, Master Gethen."

He dropped the rest of the apple into his bowl and pushed it aside, then sat back and folded his arms. "The storm, Ursinum's contrived hostilities with Besera, and the Rime Witch are pieces of the same puzzle."

"Contrived? The threat your brother's massed troops presents is all too real, and no more imaginary than is my white stag."

"Nor is my *magical slattern*." Gethen pushed away from the table. He stood and, hands clasped behind his back, strode to the room's tall windows. His voice was quiet as he added, "Nor my growing need for your aid." Beyond his shoulders and the glass there was white where the Silver Sea should have sparkled, silver light on blue-green water. Only the muffled moan and howl of the ceaseless wind gave voice in the room as Halina held her tongue and waited for her host to continue. He finally turned and the fatigue on his face had deepened.

"I don't ask for your help lightly," Gethen said. "I've dwelled in Ranith for twenty-two years with only the aid of my servants and Kharayan's animals. Had I known that I'd become the Sun Mage, perhaps I could've been better prepared for this weakness. Militess, you're strong and have the might of many soldiers behind you when you go into battle. I've nothing but my sorcery and my wits to keep me alive when I face dark entities within the Void." He stared at the floor between them and ran his hand through his hair before adding, "Never before have I known such impotence against such a powerful foe."

Impotence. The Shadow Mage's confession held far more sway over Halina than any of his prior tactics had. It was as if he'd cast an incantation upon the room, so completely did her opinion swing in his favor. Halina, court-raised and battle-hardened, understood all too well the horror of helplessness against an overwhelming enemy. Gethen's frustration and shame filled the room, and she swallowed, having tasted those exact emotions as she'd watched soldiers, friends, and family die in battle after battle.

She slowly stood. "I hear the honesty behind your words." He looked up as she added, "But I can't answer your request without giving more consideration to the needs of my holding, His Majesty, and Ursinum's people." She stepped away from the table and toward him then stopped. "Tonight I'll ponder your situation as well as my country's. And tomorrow I'll give you a decision."

"Thank you, Militess." Gethen moved a few steps closer to her and added, "I'm not unaware of the delicacy of your position as the king's emissary. But I must act quickly to stop the witch from breaching the Voidline and becoming corporeal. For that, I require your help."

Halina turned as he bowed. She passed Noni as she left the great hall for her room on the third floor. Gethen had given her much to contemplate, and as she climbed the shadowy stairs, the cold and the dark of the early winter pressed down upon her.

When she reached her room, Halina placed another log upon the fire and stoked the ashes. The chamber seemed colder, its shadows deeper, and the glare of the snow outside her window somehow deadlier than it had been only an hour before.

Gethen's surrender of his pride weighed heavily upon her, as did her responsibility to the people of Ursinum. Yes, she was Vernard's emissary and owed it to him to extend her greatest efforts into seeing that his needs — the needs of Ursinum's citizens — were met. But the possibility that this Rime Witch was deliberately creating the storm and the war meant a threat that went well beyond Khara and Ursinum. And she owed it to all of Quoregna to prevent another disaster like the War of the Winds.

Halina paced the room, rubbing her hands together and

blowing upon them. She stopped before the fire and held them toward the grate trying to warm her icy fingers. But to no avail.

If the mage was correct, she should do all she could to protect and empower him as he returned to the Void and confronted what was surely their greatest mutual enemy.

A knock at the door announced Noni's arrival. "Thought some warm mead and help with your gown and hair would be wanted, Your Ladyship. Unless you'll be joining my master in the solar this evening?"

Halina accepted the cup of hot honey-wine. "You and this drink are most welcome. But I'll spend the remainder of the night here." She sat and sipped the mead, happy to let it warm her insides while Noni removed the pins from her hair then braided it into a single thick plait that fell past her shoulders.

"Added a log to the fire?" Noni asked as she untied the sleeves from Halina's gown. "I'll put two on tomorrow evening after turning down your bed."

"I can't get warm tonight." Halina raised her cup and added, "This, however, is a great help, as are you."

Noni's smile enveloped her face and brightened the room.

When she was finally down to her white nightgown and comfortably tucked beneath the thick bedding, Noni snuffed the candles and left the room, closing the door behind her. Halina smiled. She enjoyed the woman's gentle presence. It had been a long time since she'd appreciated the help of a competent servant; all of Vernard's were spies and thieves, and she'd long ago learned not to trust any of them, especially the ladies-in-waiting that he'd placed in Halina's castle in Kharaton.

She stared at the softly changing light upon her room's walls and ceiling as, somewhere above the storm, the sun lowered and the stars brightened. There was no view through her room's windows, only sparkling white as snow built up, cold and thick, upon the glass. She knew the day had ended and night had arrived from the light's changing hues as the storm continued to rage outside and the snow upon the windows turned from white to gray to black.

"I thought I closed the shutters," she muttered. The fire's heat would escape with them open. But she was warm, the room was cold, and sleep drew her down into its depths.

The fire burned low when Halina awoke. Despite her heavy covers, she shivered. Her hands and feet were chilled to the bone. Something had awakened her, maybe the cold. She rolled over coming fully awake in the room's frigid darkness.

The curtains and shutters. She peered at them in the dark. They were closed. She didn't recall doing that. Maybe Noni had come back.

"Get up. Stoke the fire," she ordered herself and slipped from the warm covers. Her feet touched the icy wood floor and she cursed, "Khotyr, take me." Her teeth chattered hard enough to hurt and her body shook in the painful cold. She pulled a blanket from the bed and wrapped it around her shoulders.

The rug was slick and frosted beneath her bare feet, and Halina hastened to the grate. The feeble fire's warmth and glow failed to penetrate the room's heavy chill and darkness. She stirred the ashes and put another large log upon the low coals. The anemic flames continued to sputter, and she cursed under her breath as she searched the iron firewood box for good tinder. But everything was ice cold and none of it would coax the fire to a roaring flame.

Her hand cramped around the poker's handle and Halina abandoned it upon the grate. The warmth of her thick bedding would be better against the room's bone-deep chill than the dying fire's meager heat would be.

She turned away from the hearth, and her cold body went colder.

The white stag stood between Halina and her bed. Its eyes were chalky orbs, and its breath plumed.

It was impossible for the beast to be in her room. *This is a dream.* Yet Halina's chest constricted. Her fingers itched to hold her sword. She was exposed and vulnerable. The weapon hung in its scabbard on the back of the chair beside her bed, inconveniently located behind the stag.

She shook her head. *You can't slay dreams with steel.* "You aren't real," she said through chattering teeth, hoping that the words spoken aloud would reveal the beast to be shadow and dream.

Defying her wishes, the massive animal turned his white head and empty eyes toward her.

"Bollocks," Halina cursed as the creature's flesh began to peel away, sloughing off in chunks and strips that splattered the floor and her feet with cold, viscous fluid. Its jaw opened to reveal bleached bone and jagged, bloody teeth. "Great big bollocky bollocks."

It whistled a sharp challenge that echoed in the room, and Halina covered her ears.

The stag reared and transformed further. Its cloven front hooves lengthened, split, and flexed into long, grasping fingers, its rear hooves flattened and grew toes, and its body took on a human form, though its head and antlers remained unchanged. It came down and crouched, gnashing its teeth as blood frothed from its mouth and nostrils.

Impossibly, the room chilled further, and Halina's muscles shuddered with cold and fear as white hoarfrost raced across the floor and up the walls. The sword was beyond her reach and useless against spirits.

Behind her the fire popped as frozen wood expanded on the grate.

The hot poker. Halina dropped her blanket, turned, and seized the iron rod. The creature attacked. She ducked and rolled beneath its grasping fingers. But its claws raked her left shoulder and numbness paralyzed her arm. She came up fast and thrust the red-hot poker into the beast's flank. The thing shrieked and retreated, limping. The wound smoked and frothed where she'd struck. Halina pressed her advantage, lunging forward and stabbing at the beast's throat.

It whistled in rage and grabbed the poker, yanking it away with inhuman strength. Its hands steamed, a nauseating stench filled the room, and Halina swallowed her gorge. She kicked out. Her foot connected with the beast's belly and the thing stumbled back, sending the washstand flying. Pottery shattered upon the floor; water splashed Halina's feet and instantly froze. She slipped on the ice and shouted as the creature lunged toward her, the poker raised for a killing blow.

Halina rolled clear as the iron rod smashed into the floor, splintering wooden planks and catching beneath the tongue-and-groove boards. But she couldn't stand. Her foot had gone as numb as her arm, deadened by its contact with the beast.

The ancient hemlock flooring screeched and snapped as the monster twisted the poker free. Once again its whistle pierced the room as it raised the iron weapon to bludgeon her into oblivion.

But fortune and a quick shadow mage smiled upon Halina as a flash of green light and a shouted incantation stopped the beast's attack. It turned and roared, enveloped from feet to antlers by a cold, whirlwind haze that Gethen conjured as he strode into the room.

The mage wore living armor. Shadows seeped from the room's darkness and encased his body, growing hard and reflective as they tightened and formed to his figure. He carried a longsword and faced his enemy with admirable ease.

The beast found its voice — high and garbled, like it spoke from beyond the grave with dirt still filling its throat. "You're getting slow and stupid, Shadow Mage. Far less challenging than when we last met." It turned to point at Halina, the white brume flickering over its form and cracks spreading across its flesh. "Though I thank you for inviting vulnerability into your home."

At Gethen's side, two black wolves snarled and snapped, advancing with raised hackles and flattened ears.

"I disagree, witch," the Shadow Mage replied. "And I didn't invite your mouthpiece across my threshold." At a flick of the mage's fingers the creature stiffened and arched, its face a rictus of agony. "You may have it back."

Gethen uttered something low and guttural — an ancient language Halina didn't know. The beast writhed and shrieked within a whorling plume of white that plunged the temperature of the room and exploded upward. Frost bloomed across the ceiling. The poker fell from the monster's grasp and clattered at Halina's feet. She grabbed it as the Shadow Mage raised his sword and stepped forward. He slammed the flat side of his blade into the wraith as Halina thrust the poker upward into its belly. The beast shattered into thousands of glittering fragments, some so small they hung in the air like white ash and filled the frigid room with a nauseating stench.

The wolves roamed from Gethen to Halina, their lips curled and ears flat as they rumbled their displeasure. But, much to her shock, they paused to nuzzle her face and hands.

Again, Gethen spoke unfamiliar words and the animals left the room, passing Noni and Magod in the doorway. The servants were armed, he with a longsword and she with a cleaver. Their master considered them and said, "You're late."

Magod smiled sheepishly. "Slower than Mummin on the stairs tonight, Master."

Gethen went to Halina. "Can you walk?"

"No. Its touch made my left arm and foot useless."

He frowned. "May I carry you?"

"I encourage it," she replied through clenched teeth. Now that the threat was gone, she felt the damage that had been done. The cold nothingness in her limbs was sickening and, compounded by the creature's lingering stench, had her swallowing her supper again. Vomiting on the mage would be mortification far worse than being carried like an invalid by him.

Then again this was war and she'd seen many a strong man piss himself and spew his last meal before and after engaging the enemy. There was no shame in it. It was pride that made her want to keep her stomach; she'd never cried, pissed, or puked upon the battlefield. She wasn't about to do so in front of a man she didn't quite trust but, maybe, desired.

His expression neutral, the Shadow Mage wrapped her in the discarded blanket, easily lifted her, and strode into the hall. He carried Halina to his second floor stillroom, navigated an ever-changing landscape of pacing wolves, and entered the smaller room beyond it, an infirmary. He laid her upon another comfortable bed and summoned fire to the grate and candles throughout the room.

The two male guard wolves had accompanied them from the guest room and now stood beside Gethen as he ran his fingers through their shiny black coats. Silvery light lifted from their fur and trailed his fingers. It mingled with the green glow of his mage fire, spread through his body, and set him alight from the inside out.

Halina gaped as he stepped away from the animals. They settled down and slumbered as the Shadow Mage paced the room's perimeter, murmuring incantations and scribing fiery, green symbols that slowly dissipated on the air. When he'd circled the room thrice, he stopped in its center and clapped his hands three times. With each clap, the witch light within him surged outward, shredding his strange armor and filling the room. Then, with a nod at his handiwork, Gethen turned to Halina as the light dispersed.

"The room is warded. Let me see your shoulder and foot."

She'd received countless battle wounds and had the scars to prove it. There was no room for modesty in war, yet she clutched the blanket to her breast and gritted her teeth as the mage cut through the shoulder seam of her shredded, white nightgown. He touched her skin where the witch's beast had clawed her. It took all her strength not to scramble off the bed as the contact sent a hot jolt down her back and into her belly. It was his magic flowing into her; it had to be.

He jerked away from her and cursed beneath his breath.

Halina was relieved her voice was even as she asked, "Is the wound that bad?" She looked up. Gethen was staring at her, his gaze intense and hungry. "Will I lose the arm?" she asked as the heat of his magic spread through her.

He swallowed and his expression turned stony. "No. I can treat this." He moved to the foot of the bed. "Did the creature break the skin on your heel, as well?"

"I don't think so. I kicked it." He'd mastered whatever his sorcery had tried to break loose, but she didn't have the luxury of his self-control. Halina steeled herself to the heat and power of his touch as he lifted the blanket to inspect her heel and toes.

"There are cuts here." He stepped back. His eyes narrowed, and he pressed his thumb to his lips and stared at nothing as he thought. "Was there pain or only numbness?"

"Just numbness."

He nodded then returned to the stillroom.

She eased back into the pillows and yawned. Her body ached everywhere that wasn't numb. The clatter of glass, stone, and metal carried through the open door, but she couldn't fathom what the mage was concocting, and she was too tired to care. This room was much warmer than her chamber had been. Her eyelids grew heavy.

"Militess." Gethen's weight shifted the bed.

Halina jerked up from the pillows. "What?"

His smile was slightly less wolfish than those he'd previously worn. "Don't sleep yet." He held out a pewter cup. "Drink."

She peered at the steaming yellowish liquid. "What is it?"

"Metheglin. It'll ease the pain you're going to experience as the numbness retreats from your limbs. And it'll help destroy the poison in those wounds."

"Poison? How delightful." The concoction smelled like rotting apples, sweet and astringent. She wrinkled her nose then tipped the cup back and drained it. The metheglin burned from her throat to her gut and spread warmth and lethargy throughout her body. "You make it stiff," she rasped.

"I've prepared a salve and poultices to draw out the evil that the beast's claws left behind." He beckoned her to lean forward. She did so and this time didn't flinch as he eased her shift off her shoulder and spread a liberal amount of warm unguent across her skin.

"Mmm, that's much improved," she mumbled. Her eyes closed and her chin rested upon her chest by the time he'd finished securing a poultice around her shoulder.

"Rest." He tugged her shift into place, gently pushed her back into the pillows, then pulled the blankets over her.

Sleep tugged Halina into its embrace as Gethen treated her foot.

TEN

"Halina Persinna." She was taut muscle, strong bones, and soft skin. Unflinching. Unafraid. "Extraordinary," Gethen said.

He paced her ruined and stinking room. It was morning and he'd gotten no sleep. A white haze hung in the chamber, swirling in his wake and dancing around the candle flames. He rubbed his hands over his face and stalked from the fireplace to the bed and back again. Shattering the attacking wraith hadn't been enough; Gethen wanted to maim its master.

"That was beyond cowardly, sending your monstrosity into my guest's room and attacking her where she slept."

He retrieved the fire poker from the floor where it had fallen and threw it at the hearth. It struck the stones with a deafening clatter then ricocheted away, bounced off a wall, and rolled across the floor. It came to rest where the demon had torn apart the flooring.

The creature had been a benign forest wraith before the Rime Witch had twisted it into a horror. That proved that the Shadow Mage's power was dangerously depleted. She shouldn't have been able to touch anything or anyone protected by his wards. He should've been alerted to her activities in Kharayan. But he'd been ignorant until Halina's shout had drawn him from the solar.

There was no doubt that the witch had reached across the Voidline to ensnare the deer. Which meant that she'd followed Gethen's curving path to the border. That was a dangerous change. Before she'd been hurling her rage toward the entire Voidline, resulting in the storm and the animosity between Ursinum and Besera. This was a new tactic, a focused, personal attack.

He ran his hands through his hair. "How did the Rime Witch breach my wards? And why attack the militess instead of me?" Halina had crossed into Kharayan unharmed while her predecessors had failed. And the witch hadn't just targeted her; she'd called her his vulnerability.

Was the witch's goal to deplete his strength?

He clenched his fists. Between the battle with the stag and the warding and healing he'd performed afterward, Gethen's sorcery was at its weakest yet. If he faced another confrontation now, he'd be unable to wield the cold spell that had destroyed the beast.

He spat on the floor where the stag wraith had last stood.

Gethen had sent Magod to verify that the wards remained in place and were effective. The wolves guarded Halina as she slept, and Noni was searching Ranith's stores for suitable clothing for the margrave.

He took in the rumpled bed and Her Ladyship's clothing. The stench that permeated the room had also seeped into the fabric. It was doubtful that the terrible stink could be removed from her gowns.

Gethen retrieved her sword and armor. He closed his eyes and fingered the rough leather and cold metal. Magic moved beneath his fingers, seeping from Halina's armaments into him. "Blood magic." He opened his eyes. "Maybe that's what attracted the witch."

It was the kind of power that had to be earned in battle with the deaths of soldiers, the spilling of their blood and hers. Blood magic couldn't be wielded deliberately by those untrained in sorcery. Nonetheless, it conferred power to the armor and weapons that had shed blood and taken lives, and to the one responsible for the killing, the soldier who wore and wielded them. Blood carried its own dark magic. Judiciously wielded it brought peace, injudiciously used it caused suffering and war.

Militess Halina had fought hard and admirably against the stag wraith. She'd shown no fear and had refused to back down despite her wounds and the viciousness of the monstrosity.

Gethen grunted. "So the white stag wasn't a figment of her imagination. Lady Khara will appreciate me acceding that point." His fingers twitched; her fair skin was scarred, souvenirs from many battles. Her shoulders were dusted with freckles, proof of her mixed heritage. The people of Ursinum had unmarked skin, but the Beserans bore mottling across their shoulders, back, and chest. A rare few, like him, even had striped patterns — brown- or rust-colored pigmentation that encircled their arms and legs, darkened their spines, and traced their ribs. In Beseran culture, Militess Halina's mottled skin would be prized for its beauty.

Gethen's pacing slowed until he was still. Halina was so many contrasts — brutal against her foes but kind with the servants, determined to forge her own future yet haunted by her past, ugly by her own people's standards, but he found beauty in her direct gaze and freckled skin.

"Her loss would be acutely felt and mourned."

He pivoted and left the room, closing the door to the destruction and stench, as well as his tumultuous feelings. He admired the militess, but that's where his interest had to stop. She was a means to an end, a powerful ally he needed. Anything more was trouble.

He returned to his stillroom and left Halina's belongings on a table beside the doorway to the infirmary, then he opened one of the windows, knocking off an accumulation of snow that reached mid-pane. He squinted. Glaring sun bounced off the white snow, blinding him for a moment. Shielding his eyes, Gethen looked out over the snow-softened remains of Ranith's empty village to the frozen forest beyond, and then returned to the bailey. Magod had cleared snow from the roofs of the outbuildings, stable, and henhouse.

"I should check on the livestock." He pulled the window closed and headed down to the bailey.

In the stable the animals were munching on hay and grain and happily bedded down in thick piles of straw. Satisfied by their quiet contentment he turned to go into the kitchen but paused when he heard whistling and the crunch of snow under large feet. Magod came around the corner of the citadel's front wall and through the gate, Halina's falcon upon his shoulder. He carried a woven basket, and a slight limp was the only sign of his healing injury.

"What of the wards?" Gethen called as he moved to meet his groundsman.

"In place and strong enough to drop a herd of oxen," Magod replied.

"And the hives?"

"Covered in snow. Bees should stay dry and warm all clustered up. As long as they have enough food." He presented the basket and added, "Found some mushrooms that've survived the cold."

"Noni will be happy." Gethen inspected them and added, "and so will we at supper tonight."

"Her Ladyship all right?"

"Yes. Resting well." He took the mushrooms from his man. "The bird responds to you?"

Magod nodded. "Been well trained." He rubbed the back of his neck and peered from underneath his eyebrows at his master. "How'd the beast get through strong wards? And the militess before it?"

Gethen stomped his heel into a frozen rut in the ground. "That's the mystery isn't it? And an even greater mystery is how our visitor last night breached the Voidline and the citadel without gaining my notice."

Magod frowned. "What help do you need to fight it, Master?"

"Continue as you are. Care for the hives and the animals, see to the citadel and our guest, and check the wards daily. Let's hope last evening's attack has convinced our militess to aid me, and not increased her distrust of my word."

"Why would she distrust you?"

"She's not convinced that my sorcery fails. She could conclude that I'm responsible for the wraith."

Magod shook his head. "Should set her straight on that."

"Yes, well, that woman requires more careful handling than her bird does."

Magod nodded and stumped off to his storage shed.

In the citadel Gethen found a warm but empty kitchen. He left the basket of mushrooms upon the table and ladled porridge into a bowl from the iron pot on the hearth. He sat and let the porridge warm his gut as he slowly ate.

The bowl of fruit Noni had served the previous evening sat on a nearby worktable. Gethen stood and plucked two sunfruits from it. Their yellow, pebbly skin tickled him as he rolled them between his palms. That was the trick to freeing the tart fruits from their peels; once warmed, their flesh slid away easily. Fail to warm them and there'd be only a sticky mess. Strange how heat was both beneficial and destructive.

"People are overly fond of warmth," he said as he sliced the end off one of the sunfruits. He was never warm, even laboring outside under the midsummer sun his bones remained cold.

It hadn't always been that way.

"Cold is the fate of the Shadow Mage, boy," Shemel had sneered when Gethen had complained as a young apprentice. "You crave heat?" he'd asked. When Gethen had nodded, the prick had snuffed his smoke stick on Gethen's left cheek and cackled as the boy retreated to a corner of the stillroom and swallowed snot and tears. Gethen still bore the scar. It was one among many he'd received at his dead master's hands.

He scratched his stubbled jaw. "You can't ignore this." His voice echoed in the empty kitchen. The sun was coming. And so was something cold and evil.

When he'd touched Halina the previous evening, heat and blinding light had almost overwhelmed him, and iron bands of yearning had encased his chest, ensnaring him in no way he'd ever known before. She'd felt it too, he was sure. She'd nearly jumped off the bed.

"Semele's blood." This powerful desire couldn't possibly have arrived at a worse time. He didn't know whether to embrace it or beat it down, but nothing ever occurred without a reason.

The militess was Vernard's emissary, potentially an assassin, and becoming a deadly trap. Somehow she'd attracted the Rime Witch's interest.

"'I thank you for inviting vulnerability into your home'," Gethen repeated. "Vulnerability." He stared at the banked fire on the hearth and slowly straightened. "Halina. I invited Halina in my home." He clenched his fists. "*Damnation*."

The Rime Witch had isolated him and his champion with the storm. On this side of the Voidline her sorcery wasn't more powerful than his. Yet. So she'd found a way to use the militess against him: The witch had attacked Halina, forcing Gethen to expend his strength in her defense. The margrave was endangered if she remained at Ranith, but he'd be without a champion if she left.

He slammed his fists upon the table. "*Gods!*"

He went to the kitchen door, stepped out, and stood beneath the bright sun, squinting past the blinding white world into the shadows that swallowed his forest. They'd always sheltered him from spying eyes.

He peered at the stone gargoyles and beasts guarding Ranith's heights then pushed through thigh-deep snow until he reached the stacked stone wall bordering the citadel's cliff. Though a lake, the Silver Sea was vast enough to have tides. Waves crashed against the tor's granite cliffs below him. Black-and-white sea crows wheeled high above.

Why did he share an unexpected connection with Halina? There was nothing of that in the records.

A cloud scudded across the sun and plunged the world into shadow and chill. He looked up. The sun was obscured, but it wasn't gone. The cloud continued its journey and Gethen squinted as the sun's brilliance sallied forth once more.

"The shadow needs the sun, or it's lost to darkness." He slowly turned away from the wall and cliff. Once again he peered at the citadel. Snow, warmed by weak sunshine, slid off stone and glass to splatter upon the ground. A face appeared in a window on the second floor. Halina was watching him. She pressed her hand to the glass. His fingers twitched. She turned as if called then disappeared from view.

She'd been lured there to weaken him. Another slab of snow slid from the citadel's wall and crashed upon the kitchen stoop. "Maybe." He pushed back through the trough he'd made and found the stiff broom Noni kept by the door for cleaning the bailey's paths. He contemplated Halina as he cleared the snow. How was it possible? Kharayan's wards remained strong.

When the stoop was clear he returned the broom to its home and entered the citadel. He passed through the kitchen's warmth without feeling it and made his way to the library without casting mage fire to light the gloomy halls.

Gethen needed more information about the Rime Witch. He scanned the shelves and books. He knew what knowledge each one contained, and there was very little written about his foe. *Beasts and demons. Incantations. Necromancy.* He meandered along the shelves. *Potions and tinctures. Predictions. Summoning. Traveling.* He stepped back.

"Necromancy." His fingers hovered before the broken spine of a tattered book. This was a tool at his disposal, but one he rarely employed. Unlike his predecessors, Gethen never used human spirits to power his sorcery. There was a dangerous taint to human souls that too easily seduced shadow mages into practices far more sinister than strolling through the Void, manipulating shadows, and speaking with the dead.

This integrity had made Gethen a "mistake" in Shemel's opinion, and the old necromancer had tried to torture the decency out of him for eight relentless years. In payment, Gethen had murdered the man and taken his power.

He left the book on its shelf. The information he needed remained in the mind of a miscreant. Gethen made a fist and stepped back. "Bollocks."

A shushing sound pulled his attention to the window in time to see a gust of wind swirl snow into powder. It danced upon the windowsill for a moment before blowing away. The wind was returning. The aberrant storm was far from over.

He left the library. With the militess's help he would summon Shemel to get his answers.

On the stairs he encountered Noni. She carried a laden, bronze firewood basket in one hand and a coal scuttle in the other. "Is that wood for the infirmary?" he asked.

"It is."

"I'll take it. I'm on my way to see the margrave."

He reached for the flat, footed basket, but she turned away and said, "My job to attend Her Ladyship. Don't get in the way."

"What's gotten into you, old nag?"

Noni harrumphed and continued up the stairs, the heavy wood pulling her shoulder down.

After a moment, he followed, shaking his head. The woman had turned serving the margrave into fawning over her.

Halina was upright in bed and wore a moth-eaten, dark green gown that reeked of dried herbs. But it was better than the sharp, sour musk of death that had ruined her own clothing.

"Knew that color would be fetching on you, Your Ladyship." Noni placed the wood and scuttle before the hearth beside Halina's bed. "Tonight, I'll fix those moth holes and alter that dress and the others to fit you better."

The militess fingered a hole in her left sleeve. "I don't know where you found one dress, let alone three, and I certainly won't complain about their fit or condition. I'm happy not to smell like death." Her gaze slid past Gethen. She smoothed her bedding then tucked a loose lock of hair behind her right ear.

He stared at her. Then, realizing that he was staring, Gethen pulled a chair away from the wall and moved it to her bedside. Its wooden legs clattered across the floor. "Are you in pain?" He gripped the chair's ladder back without sitting.

She glanced at him then quickly looked away. "No. Thanks to you."

"Good. When you're feeling well enough, I'd like to enlist your help in discovering more about the Rime Witch."

Her gaze finally settled on him and her expression hardened. "You have my cooperation in this, Master Gethen."

He clasped his hands behind his back, nodded, then returned to the stillroom. He'd formulate a dose of metheglin to fortify her and return her strength. As he moved about the room, the murmur of voices carried from the infirmary.

"There's two more chemises, Your Ladyship. Not as fine as yours were, but clean and fresh. Will do my best to remove that awful stink from your clothing."

"I'm sure these will suit my daily needs. But I wear armor when I ride and fight. If the smell won't come out of the leather, then I'll just have to reek."

"Still searching for suitable trouzes. I've only found ones to fit the men. But maybe among the 'prentices's storage."

Gethen poured metheglin into a dram cup and summoned Bength, one of the male wolves that he'd assigned to guard the militess. "Just a small touch of your spirit," he said as he stroked the wolf's muzzle and ears. The animal sat and cocked its head, ears perked and golden eyes keen. Gethen smiled then gently pulled the wolf's spirit into himself.

Wolf energy was feral and unpredictable, and it had taken Gethen many years of practice to master its enticing ferocity.

When he'd accumulated enough power from Bength, he withdrew his will and released the wolf. "Rest. You've served my liege and me well today." The wolf slinked to his companion's side while Gethen added pulverized nermica, nightshrooms, and liminth root to the metheglin, then held his hand above the mixture and spoke a healing incantation. A dark green mist formed around his fingers and flowed into the cup, like heavy smoke. The liquid churned as Gethen said more incantations. Vapors rose to fill his nostrils with a harsh, bitter odor. When the concoction finally quieted, he ceased the incantation and stoppered the metheglin bottle. He fetched clean rags from one of his cabinets and a jar of healing unguent then went to the infirmary and offered the dram to the militess.

She took it, sniffed its contents, and grimaced. "Gods, that's foul." She cocked an eyebrow at him. "Is this what made me insensible last night?"

"Metheglin, yes, but this is a different variant." He folded his arms. "Don't you trust me?"

A small smile curved Halina's lips. Then she downed the tincture like a soldier drinking soma before a battle. She coughed, shuddered, and held out the empty cup. "Not at all," she croaked.

Gethen arched a brow at her. She had spirit, and that made her powerful and attractive. He held up the jar of unguent and the rag. "That's unfortunate, as now I need to come closer, Your Ladyship."

Halina eyed the shallow dish in his hand. "Wonderful."

"The wounds on your shoulder require stitches." He held up the small dish. "Fortunately for you this will numb your skin." Gethen sat, laid a leather medical roll on the bed, and spread it out.

She said, "I'm disappointed to learn that you're not nearly as monstrous as you wanted me to believe when I arrived at Ranith."

Noni stood in the corner, watching them, and Gethen ordered, "Bring me a basin of hot water and another clean rag." The housekeeper curtsied and left the room. He gestured toward Halina's gown. "May I?"

She stiffened as if she was holding her breath, then she leaned forward from the pillows and pulled her braid aside. "Of course." With deft fingers, she unlaced the front of the garment and lowered the fabric off her shoulder to reveal the bandaging and poultice that he'd fashioned earlier.

Gethen moved to get a better view of the wound.

"How do you do this?" she asked.

"Do what?"

"Heal wounds and cure illness so well. That's always puzzled me about you, even before we met."

"Because I'm a necromancer?" She nodded and he continued as he steeled his nerves against the first touch. "Dark sorcery doesn't have to be destructive. There are things, invisible to the eye, which thrive on wounds and cause ague. Shadow magic can be directed against such plagues and used for healing." Both he and Halina reacted as his fingers brushed her skin; a surge of heat flashed through his hand and she gasped. "My apologies, Militess." He gently removed the bandaging taking care to touch her skin as little as possible.

Her voice sounded breathy as she asked, "Does that always happen when you touch people?"

His mouth was suddenly dry and he swallowed. "No. It's never happened before." Gethen peeled back the poultice. The wound wept and bled. Its edges were red, swollen, and crusted with blood and some foul black substance. She shivered and he asked, "Do I make you uneasy?"

"A little."

He chuckled. "Just a little?"

Her voice was tight. "I suppose you're the sort of man who makes people a lot uneasy."

"I suppose I am." He cleaned the long gouges. "Tell me if I'm hurting you."

"It's fine. I'm accustomed to pain."

Gethen paused at that. *No one should be accustomed to suffering.* "The beast's poison lingers."

Reflexively, Halina turned her head and, suddenly, their faces were mere inches apart. Their gazes met and her lips parted. Gethen held his breath. She did the same. Gods he wanted to taste her mouth. Without thought beyond that overwhelming yearning, Gethen feathered his fingers from her ear to her jaw. He cupped her chin and stroked his thumb across her parted lips. Her breath was warm, her skin so soft.

Then Noni's shuffling footsteps broke the spell. He straightened, and Halina faced forward, her expression stony and her voice emotionless as she asked, "Will I lose the use of the arm?"

Gethen swallowed that dryness again. "No, Margrave. The unguent will destroy the rest of the poison. But you'll be my patient for at least another day."

She looked askance at him. "I'll strive for obedience, though I'm not known for that quality."

"We've that in common." He took the damp rag Noni held out and scrubbed the wound. He swallowed a curse at the stench that came from the poison as he removed it and cut away bits of dead and dying flesh.

But Halina had no such compunctions as she held her blanket to her nose and mouth. "Skiron's bones, that's putrid. Did that beast crawl into the jakes, die, rot, and then return to life?"

Gethen laughed. "An apt description, and possibly close to the truth." He finished removing diseased flesh. "Noni, fetch the medicinal wash from the cabinet; the one in the green bottle." She did and its application removed the last traces of the poison, then Gethen began stitching. "I can't guarantee a pretty scar."

Halina snorted. "Oh, no. A scar."

"Most of the women I've known would care."

Halina toyed with her blanket's weave. "I've no delusions about my appearance, Master Gethen. I'm not valued by King Vernard for my age, my opinions, or my beauty."

Your king is an idiot. "Wisdom comes with years. Opinion gains value with intellect. But nothing good ever comes to a woman whose only quality is the comeliness of her face."

Halina laughed heartily enough to make both wolves look up from where they'd been sleeping on the floor. The militess shook her head and said, "You're a disappointment, Shadow Mage. First you allowed me past your wards, then you provided excellent hospitality, and now you've proven to be a romantic."

Gethen leaned forward and knotted the stitches then cut the thread.

"What next?" she asked.

"I thought we'd embroider alter cloths, Your Ladyship." He slathered the wound with unguent. Halina laughed again, and he added, "It's my understanding that you're a fair and genteel lady who enjoys her stitches." He handed the needle to Noni, ignoring the little knowing smile the woman wore, and began winding a fresh bandage over and around the cap of Halina's shoulder.

Finished with that, Gethen turned to minister the wounds on the margrave's foot. They were superficial and well on their way to healing, so he cleaned them quickly and applied salve and new bandages.

Noni came and went, dumping the dirty water in the jakes then returning for begrimed rags, Halina's stinking clothes over her arm. "Anymore help needed, Master?"

"No. You may leave."

The old woman curtsied and closed the infirmary door.

The militess had grown quiet as Gethen worked and, as he finished wrapping a bandage around her foot, he hazarded a glance at her face.

She was watching him. "You're not what I'd expected when I volunteered to parley with you."

Gethen twitched the blankets back over her leg. "Few people know what to expect from me."

Her head tilted and her eyes narrowed. "You obviously weren't happy to see me that first night. So why *did* you permit me to cross into Kharayan?"

He rolled up the medical kit and tied it securely. "I didn't."

Her eyes widened. "Have your wards failed?"

Gethen straightened. "No, the forest's wards are as strong as ever. Magod checked them last night after the arrival of my newest uninvited visitor."

"So what does that mean?"

"That the Rime Witch is gaining strength as I lose mine. And she's reaching across the Voidline to attack us."

"What needs to be done?"

"You're to rest and heal. I'm to discover our mutual foe's purpose."

She nodded. He turned for the door but stopped when she said, "I'm your liege. I could kill you for the way you touched me, you know."

Gethen faced her. "Will you?"

She gave him a crooked smile. "We'll see."

ELEVEN

To the most venerable Vernard, rightful king of Ursinum, from his daughter, Halina Persinna, Militess of the Order of the Red Blade, and Margrave of Khara,

Greetings and wishes for Your Majesty's continued health.

Knowing that Your Majesty most anxiously awaits news of my negotiations with Shadow Mage Gethen, I write to give council on their progress. Your Majesty's offer has been received and countered. The mage requests my cooperation in ...

Halina stopped writing and frowned. What could she tell Vernard about the mage's request? This was dangerous territory; if she didn't phrase it carefully, the king could conclude that she'd allied with the Shadow Mage and turned against Ursinum.

Something clattered in the hall outside the stillroom, and Noni's scratchy voice carried a curse all the way into the infirmary.

It had been five days since Halina had come to Ranith and, with the wraith's destruction of the guest's bedchamber, the infirmary had become her room.

"Let me help," Magod said. He was good to his mother and his master.

Halina smiled and glanced at her falcon. She'd had the bird brought to her room that morning. "Master Gethen. Now there's an enigma, Enor." Noni had doted on Halina, but Ranith's mage had come no closer to her than the stillroom door for the last three days. Which was unfortunate as she missed that surge of heat and lust he unleashed with his fingers.

She touched her lips. When he'd brushed his thumb over her mouth she'd nearly pulled him onto the bed. If the housekeeper hadn't interrupted them, she would've. But he'd gone dark and quiet since then, wrapped himself in the shadows and said nothing, even when he watched her from the infirmary door late at night while she pretended to sleep. It was irritating, this distancing.

Her smile became a scowl. "Maybe it was all a ploy to gain my trust." But she shook her head. She'd seen his expression; he couldn't hide the surprise and desire that had captivated him, too.

The old housekeeper cursed again, and Magod said, "What's ruffling you?"

Halina couldn't see them from her place at the writing desk before the infirmary window, but she knew they must be standing near the stillroom's doorway.

"Worried about the master. He's shouldering too much burden for one man. He's not keen on betrayal, and someone's going to be hurt."

"Mummin, stop fretting. Master can handle a couple of kings."

"It's his own brother."

"Who hasn't seen him for twenty-two years." Feet scuffed and Magod muttered, "Give me those."

"Here. My fingers hurt today." Noni sighed. "When blood calls, blood answers, Magod. King Zelal's messages were clear: Master's to bring Ursinum to Besera. Watch, we'll go back. Don't want to, but we'll go. And take the militess; Ursinum royalty to sweeten a sour reunion."

Halina stiffened, and her hand's pressure on her writing quill broke the tip.

It was Magod's turn to curse. "We're not going back. Ranith's our home. The Shadow Mage has always lived here. Stop running wild in your mind."

Their feet scuffed the floor as they continued down the hall, and the remainder of their words were muffled.

Halina stared at the parchment. A black spot spread where her quill had spilled its ink.

King Zelal was pressuring Gethen far more than he'd revealed. "'Bring Ursinum to Besera'," she whispered. "Is that why he's evading our negotiations? His loyalty's already been bought and my freedom sold?" She bared her teeth at the ink bleeding across the parchment. "Then you chose the wrong hostage."

Her misericord was on the desk. She glared at it. "If I'm taken prisoner—" Maybe she already was Gethen's prisoner. It would explain how she'd crossed his wards. Well, she didn't intend to fail her king or tenants. She balanced the stiletto upon her palm then slid it into her wrist sheath and took up a new quill and fresh parchment.

To the most venerable Vernard, rightful king of Ursinum, from his daughter, Halina Persinna, Militess of the Order of the Red Blade, and Margrave of Khara.

Greetings and wishes for His Majesty's continued health and favor.

Knowing that Your Majesty most anxiously awaits news of my negotiations with Shadow Mage Gethen, I write to give council on my progress. Your Majesty's offerings and commands have been presented to the mage but have been complicated by demands of fealty placed upon your subject by Ursinum's adversary and the mage's brother by blood, His Majesty, King Zelal. I am not dissuaded by this obstacle and continue to advocate with the Shadow Mage for Your Majesty's needs. I will not return to Your Majesty's side until I have secured an agreement favorable to Ursinum or met the mage in battle and defeated him. If I am not heard from again, know that I have died fighting for Your Majesty's cause and the protection of the land most cherished by my ancestors.

Your daughter and servant most faithfully in peace and war, Halina, Militess and Margrave.

She crumpled the rejected letter into a ball and threw it upon the fire in the grate. Then she rolled the finished parchment tightly and slid it into a small leather tube strapped to Enor's back. The bird ruffled her feathers.

Halina glanced out the window. There'd been a lessening of the storm for the first time since the day they'd chopped wood, and there were even a few glimpses of blue sky and sunshine, though snow still drifted down.

"Eat first, then fly home," she said as she stroked the falcon's wings and chest. She lifted Enor from her perch on a chair back and headed for the citadel's unused east wing and the massive space there that had once been a basilica.

The Shadow Mage's groundsman had shown her the empty, echoing chamber the previous afternoon. "Been hunting your Enor here, Your Ladyship. Plenty of prey for her to catch, and she's been doing me a favor," Magod had said as he'd brought her into the dim space. "Can't convince the rats to stay here. Keep finding them in the rest of the citadel, too." He'd considered Enor and added, "Nice little bird. Should find me a falcon."

Now Halina went down the stairs, through the great hall, and along a dark, narrow, low-walled corridor that sloped downward and beneath the bailey. It ended at a pair of copper-faced double doors that led into the basilica.

She pushed through the creaking doors, and Enor called a soft *ki-ki-kee* as the echo of fluttering wings carried down to them from the rafters. Halina removed the falcon's hood and untied her jesses. The bird took flight and made a fast circle around the room, stretching her wings.

Halina leaned back against the large door and pushed it closed. Its loud, metallic *thud* disturbed the doves and pigeons that had taken up residence within the rafters. Droppings, feathers, and bones fell from above as several birds made the mistake of launching from their perches. Enor flashed upward and struck, knocking one of the pigeons from the air. Halina scuffed a clean space on the filthy floor and sat. She wrapped her cloak around her, while the black-and-white falcon took her meal to a windowsill.

Halina bumped her fingers over her dagger's grip and contemplated the dim, dusty space. It differed from the gothic style that comprised the remainder of Ranith Citadel. The basilica's ceiling was lower, its arches lacked the pointed apex that was typical in the citadel's other rooms, and the building's columns were heavier. "I could kill a man in here and no one would hear his screams," she said.

The windows in the room's curved apse were more elaborate than any others in the citadel, with jewel-toned stained glass depicting the old gods, she assumed, though it was difficult to make out the figures in the low light. Some of the windows were broken, allowing animals, dirt, and snow to enter the basilica. Vines, brown and brittle from the sudden cold, crept along the walls. Arched colonnades marched like soldiers from the double doors to the apse, each so enormous that it would take two people standing opposite to encircle them with open arms. And, in the sanctuary, a massive, circular window dominated the wall above where an altar once must have stood.

"Why does Ranith have this space?" Halina saw no evidence of worship in the history of the shadow mages, and the building already contained a great hall. So why have another large gathering area?

She stood, brushed her hands upon the wine-colored gown

that Noni had provided for her, and strolled down the long nave of the building. The largest window was set high on the wall above the apse, and she squinted at it as she approached. She stepped carefully. The years of debris from pigeons, doves, songbirds, and owls had accumulated upon the floor, a heap of droppings, feathers, nests, and tiny bones. It was strange that Gethen permitted this large space to fall into ruin while he maintained the remainder of the citadel so admirably.

When she reached the apse she peered at the windows, but the light was still too dim to see clearly. She was about to turn away when sunlight struck the building, illuminating the walls and floor with a kaleidoscope of jeweled colors, and revealing that which was sacred and profane.

Halina recoiled. "Damnation."

These weren't depictions of gods, but of the current Shadow Mage's dark and dangerous predecessors. Vividly depicted in beautiful stained glass were nightmare visions of torture, murder, and madness. Red-bodied demons ate human sacrifices while victims drowned in rivers of blood. Black-robed mages offered hearts and severed limbs to savage beasts. Naked babies were skewered upon ramparts while men, mages, and demons assaulted their wailing mothers.

Only the large central window differed in theme and offered rest for the horrified viewer. The glass of this window remained clean and intact and depicted the sun at its zenith above a snow-covered world. And, mid-ground, a black-hooded mage knelt over a fallen dark-haired girl whose feet were encased in ice and whose face twisted with agony. A blue river ran from the mage's outstretched fingers. Where the water flowed, flowers bloomed and animals came to drink.

"For bringing you into this room, I'll have Magod clean the jakes with his tongue."

Halina pivoted.

Gethen had entered silently and stood halfway between her

and the exit. "Horrific, aren't they?" he said as he continued toward her, his gray gaze as cold and angry as his voice.

Halina fought the urge to touch him as he stopped just a little too close. *Traitor*. She didn't know if she meant that insult for him or for her own body. "Not the most pleasant stained-glass I've ever seen, though the craftsmanship is undeniably fine."

Gethen spied the falcon feasting on the sill. His eyes narrowed as he studied Enor, but he said nothing about the message tube on the bird's back. Halina hadn't thought he would. The bird's purpose was unsurprising; of course she'd send messages to her king.

He spread his arms wide and said, "Strange isn't it? It seems like a house of worship. But who would worship such atrocities?" The bitterness in his deep voice echoed from the ceiling back to them.

"I'm mystified, Master Gethen." Halina meandered along the curve of the apse and studied each grotesque depiction. "What's the history of this space?"

"Villainy and cruelty. If I could I would pull down this part of Ranith and throw every stone, brick, and shard of glass over the cliff into the sea. The shadow mages' reputation for brutality was well earned." He glared around the large space. "Unfortunately demolishing this part of the building would bring down the rest of the citadel. It's the foundation upon which the tower and keep are built."

Halina studied him. Once again, shadowy circles ringed his eyes, but they'd grown darker. Combined with a new hollowing of his cheeks, he had the look of a man haunted and ill. Yet he moved with the same power and grace that she recognized from the first day they'd met, the poise of a king and the control of a soldier.

Enor launched from her perch and circled the cavernous room, diving and banking, clearly enjoying the freedom of flight. Halina cursed inwardly as Gethen tracked the falcon's course. The message wasn't his business, but she didn't want to play guessing games with the mage.

"I regret that you disapprove of my presence here, but Enor must fly and feed." She raised her arm and the falcon flew to her glove. "She requires meat, but that's in short supply at Ranith. And your groundsman is content to see her removing some of the vermin infesting this part of the citadel." The bird seemed well pleased with herself and her meal. Halina turned her attention to the basilica itself and added, "It's clear that you're unconcerned with the mess."

The hardness in the Shadow Mage's manner didn't ease. "Indeed, there's no need to worry about more blood and guts littering these floors. That's not what troubles me. In places such as this, where death waltzed with suffering, evil leaves traces of intention. And it's attracted to the spark of life that burns so brightly within you, Militess." He pointed toward the door, his expression saying that he would brook no argument. "Monsters have shown no interest in my groundsman, but we both know the same can't be said for you."

She met his gaze and was surprised to see that his anger had turned to dread. What a strange world this was. The mage required her protection, yet feared for her safety. He toed the line between loyalty and betrayal, held the border between the living and the dead, and crept from shadow to sun. *Is he or isn't he a traitor?* Halina nodded, hooded Enor, and followed the man. "What am I to do for my falcon?"

Gethen opened the doors and stepped aside for her. Once outside the basilica, he closed them and placed his hands just above their handles. He said an incantation. With a heavy, grinding sound and a *thud* the doors shuddered and an unseen lock slid home.

"Let her take your message to His Majesty while the break in the storm holds." His gaze was intense and unreadable. It was impossible that he should know what she'd written to Vernard, yet Halina couldn't shrug off the feeling that he did.

She was too aware of Gethen. They were near in height, though he topped her by a hand. He smelled of honey, liminth flowers, maluk, wax, and something astringent — the scents of his trade. And he exuded power, unheard, unseen, but somehow thrumming through her like the vibrations of a hidden beehive.

He led her upward through the passage to the great hall and beyond it into the bailey.

Halina stopped and stroked Enor's back. "Fly to Vernard," she said. "Let the king know I'm well." She removed the bird's hood and jesses and sent her into the sky.

She glanced at Gethen from the corner of her eye. He remained grim as if the mass of his thoughts weighed on him. *Have I just condemned an innocent man?* An overheard conversation wasn't proof of treason, but the falcon would return to the king's camp and Vernard would issue a death mark upon reading the letter. "I'll stay away from the basilica," she said quietly.

He nodded and clasped his hands behind his back. "Another favor, Militess? One which I believe you'll better understand now that you've seen what assaults us from across the Voidline."

Halina turned from watching the diminishing speck that was Enor rising.

"I require your sword tonight as I summon my predecessor's spirit and question him about the Rime Witch. The finest source of information about dark sorcery and the creatures of the Void is the collective knowledge of the former shadow mages. But to summon Shemel from the catacombs and hold him without meeting my own death requires your sword. I haven't the strength left to bring him forth and protect my own skin at the same time. The blood magic embedded within your sword and armor will protect us. But it's a power only you can wield."

Halina shook her head. "I have no magic." She toyed with the tangled ends of Enor's jesses. "I have skills as a trained soldier, but obviously I can't keep demons and magical creatures at bay." Gethen stepped closer, and her traitorous heart thumped faster.

"Everyone has some magic. You've killed men, and in doing so you've wielded blood magic." His voice deepened and his gray eyes darkened. He fingered a lock of her hair and said, "I feel it in you." Slowly he lowered his arm and stepped back. "That's why our enemy studied you so thoroughly before attacking."

Halina swallowed. Her mouth had gone dry. "Why would the witch care about me? I'm no threat to her."

Gethen's shoulders relaxed. A soft smile and a little, ironic laugh banished the seriousness that had drawn down his features. "Believe that if you must." He turned from her and added, "I don't," as he crossed the bailey and disappeared into the extraction room.

He's got you right where he wants you, hostage or not.

Wisps of Halina's hair lifted with the breeze and tickled her face. Snow dusted her cloak and gown. She peered upward. Leering stone demons perched on Ranith's heights, icicles hanging from their noses and toes. "What are you looking at?" she snarled beneath her breath.

Every time she thought she'd gotten a firm hold on her situation with the Shadow Mage, something pulled it from her grasp. Maybe she was still in the illusion he'd spun around her the night she'd arrived at Ranith. Halina bit her tongue until pain made her wince. Nothing changed and she sighed. This was her new reality. She bared her teeth at the gargoyles then turned away from the outbuilding and went into the keep.

It didn't help that the mage twisted her around whenever he came close. She got addle-brained and agreed to something stupid. "Blood and bones, woman. He's as likely an enemy as an ally, and only a man. Stop acting like a bitch in heat." Who knew what she'd face that night. But knowing more about her adversaries — both the mage and the entity — would increase her chances of remaining alive and bringing Gethen into Ursinum's fold. She hoped.

Gethen wrinkled his nose when Halina appeared at the citadel's massive, carved front doors several hours after their evening meal. "Your stench will kill Shemel again."

She'd worn her tabard and vambraces, mail shirt, and plate armor. Noni had tried to remove the stench of death and decay from the leather but had only succeeded in making it tolerable. She had, however, altered several pairs of trouzes to fit Halina, for which the militess was grateful.

"If I'm offending your delicate mage sensibilities with my stink, perhaps we should move outside." She stepped around him and opened the smaller inset-door. Halina inhaled the fresh air and shivered. It was damnably cold. She pulled her borrowed green wool scarf up to cover her mouth, nose, and ears, then raised the hood of her matching cloak, grateful for the warmth of her armor.

Gethen, similarly dressed, followed her into the bailey where Magod waited with two warhorses. The full moon's silver light made the snow sparkle like powdered diamonds.

The horses were fine animals and more substantial than she'd expected to find in a non-military hold. Then again, Gethen had been destined to rule until chosen for Ranith. Perhaps he and Zelal still thought kingship was in his future. In Ursinum. By force.

Over my dead body will I let anyone take Ursinum from my family. She glanced at Gethen as he easily mounted his own horse, Remig. If this adventure was actually a steel trap, the mage and his Beseran brother would find that she was willing to chew off her own foot, and theirs, to escape it.

With a leg up from Magod, she settled into the saddle as he said, "This fine fellow's named Idris, Your Ladyship."

"Thank you for loaning your back and legs to this adventure, Idris," she said. Heavy blankets enrobed the dark chestnut coats of both horses. Their thick flaxen manes offered plentiful protection to their necks and faces, but their breath still billowed in the cold.

Gethen led the way through the front lattice gates. "We'll return before sunrise," he told Magod. "Keep the gate locked." At his murmured incantation and a flick of his fingers, an orb of green glowing mage light sprang into being, illuminating the path before them.

The iron gates squealed in protest as Magod pulled them closed. "Try not to die, Master."

Gethen raised a hand. "I make no promises."

"That's reassuring," Halina said beneath her breath.

The Shadow Mage chuckled.

As they turned the horses off the main path and onto one that was no more than an irregular ditch through the thigh-deep snow, the eerie howling of wolves split the air. The horses' ears flicked toward the sound, but neither reacted otherwise. It was an impressive display of control that continued even as the wolf pack appeared through the trees, ghostly company for their trek. The animals' eyes glowed in the eerie light that floated around their party.

A week ago Halina wouldn't have considered a wolf pack good company on a snowy nighttime ride. Her life had taken some interesting turns since she'd entered Kharayan.

"How long is our journey?" The wool of her scarf muffled her words. She didn't think he'd heard her until Gethen turned slightly in his saddle and replied, "Almost two hours to get there in this heavy snow. The wolves are along to keep the horses safe."

She nodded and he turned back. "And I'm along to keep you

safe," she muttered under her breath, "but who will protect me from you?"

"I'm not your enemy, Militess."

Halina gaped at his back. How had he heard her mumbled words? Her teeth clicked as she snapped her mouth shut. Yet another reminder to not underestimate the Shadow Mage.

She considered the man. He sat his saddle with ease, straight and relaxed, the reins loose in his left hand, his right hand free to draw the longsword that he now wore on his hip.

An owl hooted from somewhere deep in the woods. Some of the wolves paused, their ears perked and eyes alert. Then they moved onward; there was no threat.

Halina frowned. She needed a plan to gain the advantage if he and King Zelal attacked. What did she have that Gethen wanted or needed? He claimed it was her ability in battle, but she still doubted his supposed weakness. Certainly there were signs of strain in his manner and on his face, but those could be explained away by the pressure from kings and her presence in his home.

He looked left into the darkness, and she studied his profile. A strong jaw, a slightly crooked nose that, perhaps, had been broken in the past, and always those intense gray eyes. He'd looked at her with desire, touched her mouth, and come close more than once. The lust and heat she felt when they touched was mutual. She swallowed.

Maybe seduction is his weakness. Loneliness. A man has needs. Halina knew how to use those needs for and against men. She had a reputation in Vernard's army; one carefully cultivated to make her soldiers want to please her. It was one more thorn in Ilker's self-righteous side.

It wouldn't be a chore to seduce you, Shadow Mage. Not at all. Her breathing deepened and warmth crept from her chest to her thighs. Bedding Master Gethen on behalf of Ursinum wouldn't be the worst sacrifice she'd ever made. And what better way to capture an enemy or ally than bind him with her body in her bed? *I'd enjoy that battle.*

Gethen still scanned the woods. Halina looked where he did but saw no further than the first line of trees. All was fog and darkness, a deep, eerie quiet broken by the jingle and creak of their tack and saddles, the shush of snow sliding from branches, and the occasional scrabble of some small animal through the underbrush. Thick snow muffled the horses' hooves, and the wolves moved on silent feet.

They passed through a small gap in the trees and moonlight spilled to the ground, tinting the snow amber rather than silver. Halina glanced up. A dark crescent shadow covered half the moon.

"We ride under a blood moon?" Her voice was swallowed by the night.

"Yes."

"That's bad luck."

"Are you superstitious, Militess?" There was mockery in his tone. He hadn't forgotten her question from when they'd chopped wood together.

"Superstition has kept me alive through many battles."

He chuckled then faced forward.

Blood moon. Blood magic.

She considered the mage's back again. What had made her the Rime Witch's target? Gethen claimed it had something to do with blood magic. But he was mistaken to believe that she had even a speck of sorcery within her fingers, let alone enough to capture the attention of a witch or hold Gethen's magical enemies at bay. Yet here she was, in service to the man who owed her his allegiance. Somehow he'd managed to twist her to his will. She pursed her lips. If he hadn't been so enraged by the stag's attack and so concerned with her well being, she might have suspected that *he'd* summoned the creature to convince her of the danger coming from the Void.

Still, there was the strange connection they unexpectedly shared. What *was* it?

Relief and release, perhaps. She'd experienced that before and after battles. She wasn't inexperienced with the intimacy of a shared bed, and the mage was an attractive and powerful man, made even more appealing by his aid to her when she was under attack. Halina was no weak damsel, but she knew when to call for aid and how to thank a soldier who went above and beyond fealty to assist his liege.

You're lying to yourself. Her desire for the mage wasn't the need for post-battle release. It wasn't gratitude. It was unlike anything she'd felt before, and it was making her stupid. "Semele's blood," she whispered and was glad when Gethen didn't respond.

Halina was cursing the cramping of her frozen arse in the saddle when Gethen finally reined in his horse, dismounted, and drew his sword. The path had ended at a snowy glade. Trees formed a ring around a small, single-story, octagonal building in the middle of the clearing. He raised his hand, uttered an incantation, and directed his mage fire into the circle. Gothic arches topped carved marble columns that supported the building's domed roof. Its sides were enclosed and bore elaborate designs of demons and skeletons, weapons, snakes, and all manner of evil creatures.

"Is it a mausoleum?" Halina asked. She didn't like the white building; it had the air of something malevolent and crouching, a thing waiting for a victim to come too close.

"Yes. It's the entry to the catacombs beneath Kharayan where the bones of all the shadow mages are entombed." Gethen peered at the cold, clear sky then looked at her. "We'll enter the clearing on foot. I'll cast a protective circle around you. The horses and the wolves will be safe outside the clearing. My warded circle will be the first level of protection. When Shemel emerges from the catacombs I must bend him to my will. Should I fail, he'll attack. That's when I'll need your sword."

"You'll have it." She dismounted and tied her horse to a tree beside his. Magic was a mystery, but using a sword was something Halina understood.

The wolves moved into the forest, shying from the clearing. They yipped and howled, either agitated by the location or by a full moon that hung overhead, too large, too close, and the hue of old blood.

Halina studied the solid, marble mausoleum. No snow dusted it or the area from an outer circle of black cobblestones set into the ground to the edge of the building's base. "Is it warded?" she asked and jerked her chin toward it.

Gethen was tight-lipped and grim as he eyed the stone structure. "It's cursed and, yes, warded by me to keep evil trapped within it."

"You imprisoned the spirits of the previous shadow mages? Why?"

"To find some peace. You have no idea how unpleasant my predecessors are."

"I have some notion. Khara's reputation as a blighted holding owes much to their deviant practices."

"True."

The mausoleum's elaborate, filigreed carvings did nothing to alleviate the sense of heaviness that permeated the clearing.

Halina said, "Had I known this existed within my holdings, Master Gethen, I would've asked you to inter a few individuals whose absence from my life would bring me a great deal of peace."

He turned and bowed. "If we survive the coming months, Lady Khara, I'll offer you my services as Warden of Irritating and Overbearing Souls."

"I shall hold you to that."

"Good. It'll motivate you to swing your sword tonight." He led her closer to the stone structure.

"And if I miss?"

"Shemel will escape his prison, take my power, and join forces with the Rime Witch." He jerked his thumb toward the mausoleum. "Shadow mages are opportunists. So I encourage you to put forth your best effort to protect me."

"I perform to the utmost of my abilities in all things, Sorcerer."

He held her gaze and murmured, "I'd like to see that." Then he recalled the mage light to his hand and slid his fingers down the blade of his sword. A sickly hue in the blood moon's light, the green fire glinted off the blade and set the ground aglow as Gethen walked a circle around Halina, dragging the blade in the snow as he went and uttering a stream of incantations. The snow glowed greenish with the fire, and her skin tingled. When he'd walked the circle three times, the last in reverse to lock it, he stepped outside its boundary and cast a similar one around himself.

Gethen sheathed the sword and looked up at the sky. "The blood moon is apexing. It's time to open the mausoleum. Remain where you are unless I step from this circle. I'll only do that under duress, and it's then that I'll require your strength. Keep your sword drawn. The battle blood it's worn and that's stained your hands, will keep the shadows at bay."

"But how can I defend against spirits? Will I even be able to see Shemel?"

"You'll see him; he's a wraith, simultaneously incorporeal and corporeal as he straddles the Voidline. And the blood magic that's bound to your sword can wound him. But he's not unarmed. Terror is his greatest weapon. He'll seek your darkest memories and worst fears, hone them, and strike your mind hard and fast. If you must come to my side, brace for the onslaught. In death, as in life, shadow mages seek to pull everything into the cold misery of the shade."

Halina cocked her head. "Do *you*, Shadow Mage?"

He looked sidelong at her. "I seek to escape it, Militess." Gethen bowed his head and began a low, chanting incantation.

The clearing was bathed in old blood as the moon's red shadow spilled across the snow and the white mausoleum. Gethen raised his head and gestured toward the building's iron door. Rumbling sounded, echoing across the clearing and beneath their feet, and he said something that was lost to the sound.

The hair stood on Halina's arms and her bones rattled. She drew her sword, its weight in her hands reassuring as not one, but three hooded figures appeared in the doorway. A chill crept across her scalp, crawled down her neck, slid over her shoulders and into her chest.

Whereas Gethen wore the clothes of a soldier and healer, the wraiths wore black robes and hoods. Jewels winked on their desiccated fingers and at their leathery throats, dull in the bloody moonlight. Like the stag wraith, they were both substantial and insubstantial, and their flesh and black shrouds shifted upon their clacking bones like masses of ants scuttling over the remains of undead things.

Dread filled Halina. Her grip upon the sword tightened and her mouth went dry. This was battle fear; she knew it well. It had always kept her sharp and alive, one more weapon in her arsenal.

The wraiths emerged from the mausoleum, thudded down the steps, and crossed the ground to halt at the edge of the black cobblestones. The musk of death and decay, worse than the stag's stink, wafted across the clearing.

Gethen's voice became hoarse, and his incantation stopped.

Halina's discomfort increased. Fear, thick and sickening, wormed into her gut. It was as if she stood upon the battlefield for the first time at Sum, facing Arik-bohk's long, serrated swords and hearing the screams of dying men and horses.

A sepulcher voice threaded out from one of the hooded wraiths. "Why have you summoned me, Shadow Mage?"

Gethen kept his sword raised and his left hand poised to ward at the first sign of trouble. "I require the collective wisdom of the shadow mages."

"You seek our guidance?" A different wraith spoke, this one shorter than the first, its voice reedy like wind squeezing through cracks in ancient stone walls.

Gethen sneered. "I wasn't speaking to you or Volker, Olegário."

The third wraith had drifted toward Halina. It pointed a boney, mummified finger at her. "Who is this woman? Her sword and armor stink of blood magic and cold corruption." Its voice was low and grated like claws across her soul.

The first wraith to speak turned to Halina, as well. Disgust filled his voice. "Your champion is a *woman?*"

Gethen ignored the question and the wraith's disparaging tone. "I stand upon the cusp, Shemel."

The wraiths surged forward at that but halted, once again, at the black stones and Gethen's raise hand.

"You grow weak." The third wraith jabbed its bony finger at him, bits of mummified flesh dangling from it. "And the corruption upon the woman came from beyond the Voidline."

"Yes, Volker." Gethen watched the wraiths' every move. "The Rime Witch has escaped her bonds. She enslaved a wraith from within the Void to spy on me and destroy the militess."

Shemel laughed and lowered his hood. "Cusp mage. Weakling. Soft-hearted lick-spigot." His eye-less face was sunken and wrapped with folds of mummified, brown flesh. Wisps of red hair clung to his chin and skull. He'd been tall and powerful in life. The dead mage waved a skeletal hand dismissively and added, "You've even failed to procure a competent champion."

"Not once have I regretted your murder." Hatred deepened

Gethen's voice. "And old insults are a waste of my time. I want answers. Who releas—"

"It does not matter who released her," Olegário interrupted.

Gethen stepped forward. His toe touched the warded circle. "I disagree."

Halina raised her sword and watched Gethen closely.

"Those bonds were ancient," Volker said. "And you failed to renew them, Shadow Mage."

"Don't turn this upon me, chitterling." Gethen's left hand scribed a spell and the wraiths hissed.

Shemel stepped upon the black stones and leaned over the line. "Your complacency freed her."

"Wrong. Those bonds were strong," Gethen said.

"You'll fail. The woman will die. This pathetic world will fall to cold and shadows." Shemel flicked his wrist dismissively again, shedding dust and bits of brown, papery flesh. An emerald ring plopped into the snow on Gethen's side of the black stone circle.

Halina glared. They were doing exactly as Gethen had warned, preying upon his fears. "And then you, too, will be enslaved," she said. "If he fails, it will be *your* failure first, Master Mage."

Gethen's gaze jerked to her. But her words had worked, and he straightened and stepped back to the center of his tight circle. "The militess is right."

The wraiths had gathered closer to her. They shifted back and forth along the black stones, hissing and growling like feral dogs. Apparently she'd irritated them.

Then his former master began to laugh, a sound that doubled Halina's fear. "She even speaks for you," Shemel said, derision filling his voice. He reached past the stone barrier again and gestured toward Gethen as he began a string of incantations that twisted like night crawlers inside Halina's ears and made her want to run fast and far away.

Gethen jerked, but instantly he raised his hand and his sword and began a series of counter curses.

Between the living shadow mage and his dead master, a black, writhing cloud of shadowy vapor arose as if being pulled from the air itself. Sound, reedy and whispering, a ululation of death and things dying, filled the air. It moved toward Halina, but then, as if striking some invisible barrier, it folded back upon itself, roiling and screeching. Then the other two wraiths reached across the barrier and joined their power with Shemel's.

Gethen cursed as Volker pointed at him and spoke a different incantation. Ranith's lord jerked forward like a string puppet and stumbled out of his protective circle.

As he did, the dead shadow mages crossed the ward stones.

"You won't have him," Halina said. Sword swinging downward, she too lunged from her circle, and hacked off the third mage's left hand at its bony, shriveled wrist. Volker's mummified flesh smoked and curled back upon itself as the wraith roared. His companions turned their magic upon her.

Choking terror clutched her brain and body. Halina stopped mid-swing and stumbled blindly backwards. Helplessness and horror surged through her as icy water filled her lungs. She was drowning again; she was six years old, her head ached where it had struck stone, and Waldram's high-pitched, cruel laughter mixed with the low, masculine droning voices of undead sorcerers.

"That's not real." Halina jerked upright, turned, and raised her sword. Immediately she ducked as Olegário reached for her with his scraggly, yellowed fingernails. His thin voice intoned. Halina coughed. Liquid filled her mouth. Blood. Phlegm. She spat. "No-no-no. That's. Not. Real."

Again she brought her sword up in a vicious slash and sliced the second mage's jaw from his face. Swinging back, she finished the job by removing the remainder of the bastard's head.

But two wraiths remained, and the twisting black cloud they'd summoned had grown and threatened to engulf Gethen. Ranith's mage brought his own sword around and buried it in the chest of his former master, even as Halina lunged at the other wraith and slammed her shoulder into the bag of bones.

Volker tumbled back across the line of black stones but grabbed Halina as he fell. She hit the ground within the warded mausoleum's circle and cold sank into her bones. The world had turned dark and dismal. She stood. Her movements we're clumsy, and the wraith laughed. Halina looked up and spun away from him, as he grabbed for her. But she couldn't move fast enough. The mage, who now appeared as a man intact, though gray and sickly, seized her with inhuman strength and threw her toward the dark, open maw that led into the mausoleum.

Halina shouted and twisted, somehow managing to change her course, and struck the stone column to the left of the entry. Her sword clattered and skidded across the marble, coming to a stop halfway into the darkness. Pain stabbed through her skull as she pushed up to her knees.

Then feeling rather than hearing the movement of the wraith behind her, she lunged past the mausoleum's opening, grabbed her sword, and rolled free of Volker's grasp.

Where's Gethen? She had only a second to wonder as the wraith continued his pursuit. She couldn't defeat him. She was on his cursed ground. Here he was faster and stronger.

She had to escape the stone circle.

Halina dived off the raised portico of the mausoleum. She turned in midair to land upon her back, her sword upright and poised to thrust through her attacker. The third mage lunged into her trap, and her blade sliced upward through his gut to emerge out his back near his shoulder blade.

But instead of falling still, her undead attacker straightened and jerked to the side as he grabbed the hilt. Volker would pull it free and be doubly armed. Halina's grip tightened on her weapon. She shoved him back and used the force of his weight to pull her to her feet. Then she put all her strength into yanking the sword sideways and cleaved the mage's body nearly in half.

It was a great enough wound to hamper his movement, and Halina took advantage of his imbalance. She swung her sword back and through his bony knees.

With a curse the mage fell.

But Halina wasn't free. She scrambled toward the black stone circle, even as Volker began uttering another incantation. She had one chance at this. She dived across the stone line as something black and nebulous surged up and slammed into the invisible barrier behind her. It shrieked and grabbed for her, but it couldn't cross the ward. She turned to find Gethen and his former master facing off.

They hurled curses and incantations at one another. Shemel poured malice into a black inky form that oozed toward Gethen like a puddle of death. It tried to rise. Gethen's incantations knocked it back each time. But Ranith's lord shook with the effort and his voice rasped.

Halina charged Shemel and thrust her sword into his back even as he let loose a tremendous, roaring spell.

It lifted Gethen and threw him toward the black stone circle. But he wasn't undone yet, and his counter curse dropped him just shy of the ward.

Shemel turned on Halina, reached toward her, and uttered a curse that knocked her to her knees. That same horrific sensation of drowning overwhelmed her. The laughter of a heartless boy filled her ears.

Illusion. It's illusion!

But Halina choked and gasped for air, drowning in memory rather than the flooded oubliette's icy water. Once again on her knees, she struggled to breathe, dragging in bubbling breaths and coughing up blood, mucus, and a thick, chalky liquid. She shook and tears streamed down her face as the world blackened. Then a shout rose over the imaginary laughter. Suddenly her vision cleared and the sensation of dying stopped. Halina arched back and sucked in a deep, cleansing breath.

Shemel's incantation had failed. The shadowy figure he'd been summoning collapsed into nothingness as Gethen thrust his sword into his master's throat, twisted the blade, and yanked it sideways, severing the wraith's neck almost through. His skull dangled to the side, but his body didn't fall, and he grabbed Gethen's throat.

Once again Halina was up. Two strides put her close enough to sweep her longsword up and across, splitting Shemel from hip to shoulder. The wraith toppled, pulling Gethen to his knees.

The Shadow Mage pried his dead master's boney fingers from his throat and straightened slowly. He whispered another incantation and, with a sharp gesture, sent the bodies and limbs of his predecessors back across the line. "Find the ring," he said, rubbing his throat.

Halina gaped at him. "What ring? The black stones?" She gestured toward the circle that marked the ward around the mausoleum.

He shook his head and began searching the trampled snow. "The ring that fell from Shemel's finger."

"Oh, bollocks." Halina joined his search. Snow flew around them, and periodically Gethen sent another incantation toward the barrier as the fallen wraiths slowly regained form and thudded forward. Halina's gloved fingers found icy rocks and scraggly grass, they grew numb and painful with the cold, but still she couldn't find the ring.

She straightened and scanned the area. Where had it fallen? She turned a circle then remembered that Shemel had been leaning across the ward-line. She scrambled toward the black stones and dug into the trampled snow at their edge, cursing the burn and ache in her hands. Finally, her fingers found something regular and smooth. She brushed away the snow and pried it from the frozen ground. "Here!"

With a crow of triumph, Gethen snatched it from her hand and hurled it through the open door of the mausoleum. As he did so, he uttered a final incantation and his three predecessors were sucked back into the black maw. The thud of the closing iron doors cut off their howling protests.

Halina remained on her knees, aching and trembling as the effort of the battle overwhelmed her. She scooped clean snow into her mouth, swished it around, and spat. It was pink with blood, and its iciness made her teeth hurt.

Gethen's shadow fell upon her, and she looked up as he offered his hand. She hesitated for a heartbeat then accepted it. She gasped with the surge of desire that blazed from her palm to her heart. Gethen's grip tightened and he pulled her up and into his arms.

"My thanks for your aid, Your Ladyship." He gazed into her eyes.

His pluming breath warmed her cheek, and his body felt solid and so very good against hers. Halina's lips parted; she smelled him, almost tasted the heady combination of spices and sweat rising off him. Gods, how he heated her desire. "My pleasure, Master Sorcerer." She licked her lips and the cold air stung them when she inhaled.

Careful. He may be the trap.

With that thought, Halina yanked her hand from his then pushed him away. Chilled to the bone in the absence of his heat, she shivered. Frustrated and twisted around by desire, she snarled, "I thought you said the blood magic on my sword and armor would protect me."

Gethen cursed beneath his breath then replied, "You're alive, aren't you?"

She offered him a gesture that was universally unfriendly.

He ran his hands through his hair, turned, and pushed through the snow toward their waiting horses.

With a last glance at the quiet mausoleum, Halina followed. As they began the long, cold ride back to the citadel under a lowering silver moon, she pulled her hood up and studied the man from deep within its folds.

If the confrontation with the dead mages had been a trap, she'd easily sprung it. But the tension building between Gethen and her was the real danger. That fire was growing hotter. She'd thought she could ensnare him with his own desire but, truthfully, if he was baiting a trap for her with his charms, she'd willingly climb into that cage.

Don't let him distract you. Bend him to you. Or break him.

TWELVE

"Evil cold's taken hold of the tor," Magod muttered as he entered the kitchen, blowing on his gloved hands and stomping the frost from his boots.

Snow had begun falling before Gethen and Halina had reached Ranith's front gates and hadn't stopped.

Gethen had slept like the dead, finally emerging, groggy and sore, to take his midday meal in the kitchen. Halina had not yet appeared. He was relieved not to see her; their foray to the mausoleum had left him feeling as bitter as the weather. And her heated rejection of his embrace still burned. They'd fought well together, but apparently that would be the extent of her favors for him. *She'd as soon gut me as tup me.*

"Capsicumel's what you need, Master," Noni said as she placed a dram of mead before him.

Gethen downed the fiery drink in one gulp. "Another." He held out the cup and glared at Noni's straight-lipped disapproval. She hadn't even corked the bottle yet. Gethen slammed his fist on the table. "You may be *his* mother," he stabbed his finger toward Magod, "but you're not mine. Pour. Another. Drink."

Magod stood with his back to the closed door and stared at Gethen as if he'd never seen him before.

Noni's chin jerked up, then she clunked the bottle and cork down beside Gethen's hand. "Already debilitated. Won't be blamed when you're sick drunk. Want to punish yourself for whatever mistakes happened last night?" She jabbed her finger at him. "Take the blame yourself. *I* won't."

Gethen bared his teeth at the white-haired woman and poured a cupful of mead. "Ride your high horse out of this room," he snarled and, after Noni had left with a *harrumph*, he glared at Magod and added, "Well? Are you going to join her?"

The groundsman removed his heavy cloak and hung in on the hook beside the door. He tugged off his gloves and slipped his feet from his tall winter boots. Then he retrieved another cup from the cupboard and sat opposite Gethen. He poured a drink for himself and replied, "No. Going to warm up, too."

Gethen downed the capsicumel and watched snow drift lazily into the bailey. "How are the animals?"

"Fine." Magod took a healthy gulp of his mead, grimaced, and sucked cool air between his teeth. "Am worried about grain and hay stocks, though. Won't be able to get supplies if this keeps up another fortnight."

"How about the hives?"

"Don't want to open them. Should be all right; left them lots of honey and syrup."

Gethen nodded. His head ached. The capsicumel was unlikely to aid that.

Both men drank and watched the snow. After a few quiet moments Gethen said, "My wards are damnably weak."

Magod refilled their cups.

With another sip, warmth suffused Gethen's body and the tension he'd carried across his shoulders since the previous evening finally eased. He pointed at the bottle. "Stopper that before I prove your mother right." Magod did and returned it to its shelf in the larder. When he settled opposite Gethen again, the Shadow Mage drained his own cup and turned it upside down on the table. "We reached the clearing as the moon turned red. I summoned only Shemel, but he brought that prick Olegário and Volker the Whiner. Her Ladyship and I were forced to fight. The bastards nearly escaped, and Volker tried to drag the margrave into the catacombs." He pointed towards the ceiling and continued. "That woman battles as fiercely as any man."

"Her reputation precedes her." Magod sipped his drink then said, "Lucky she's our liege."

"She's a marvel, Magod. Saved my skin last night, no doubt." Gethen's tin cup rattled and hopped as he pushed it across the smooth tabletop between his hands, making a game of not tipping it and watching his distorted reflection dance. Finally, he stopped its slide with a hard grip. "Shemel was hiding something; they all were." Gethen knocked the cup away. It tipped and rolled off the table, hitting the stone floor with a metallic clatter. "They redirected every time I asked who released the witch."

The groundsman cocked his head. "Toying with you?"

Gethen scowled. "You mean evading just for the pleasure of making me suspicious?"

Magod nodded.

"That's as likely true as the possibility that they released her."

The groundsman folded his arms upon the table. "Mummin and I will die to help you, Master."

"You're both better than I deserve."

Magod tilted his head and gave Gethen a sage look. "Hear some advice from your servant?"

"Gladly. My servants are far wiser than I am."

"Don't fight the margrave. Your goals are the same." Magod pushed back from the table, collected the cups and dunked them in the wash water. "The sleeping chambers need more firewood," he said and left the room.

After sitting for a few more minutes and contemplating the

deep wisdom of uneducated servants, Gethen left the kitchen and headed for his library. When he reached it, however, he stopped short in the doorway.

Halina sat beside the fireplace reading a book and dressed in dark blue. She looked up, her finger poised on a word. "Good afternoon."

"I trust Your Ladyship slept well?" The dark shadows beneath her eyes gave him all the answer he needed.

She studied him for a moment then closed her book. "No. Disturbing dreams plagued my sleep. I rose before your servants and came here to read." She put the book on the short table beside her chair. "It appears, however, that I haven't the concentration to enjoy this excellent story." She met his gaze directly, indicated the chair opposite hers, and added, "Perhaps some conversation will enliven me. Sit."

A request or an order? "What shall we discuss, Your Ladyship?"

Her lips twisted into a wry smile as he sat. "An excellent question. There are so very many interesting things that I wish to ask you about."

He wasn't rested enough for this. She was too smart, too fast, and too determined. He couldn't evade her desires for long. Gethen pinched the bridge of his nose. "Ask what you will, Militess Halina. I'll answer honestly and with as much patience as I can muster on this cold and bitter afternoon."

She folded her hands upon her lap and considered him with unflinching eyes, their color made more intense by the hue of her borrowed gown. "Did Shemel free the Rime Witch?"

Gethen stifled a grimace. "Quite likely."

"Why?"

"He must believe that he can use her to conquer Quoregna." He, too, folded his hands in his lap and returned her gaze. "The witch is an ancient power, banished to the Void centuries ago by the previous Sun Mage. The weather was her weapon and she wielded it with more ferocity than any mage before or since."

"Is she attacking you on his orders?"

Gethen shrugged. "Possibly."

"Her magic is greater than yours?"

"Today, yes." It was impossible to keep neutrality in his tone. "Last night's adventure further depleted my strength, and short of taking the lives of the animals and people around me, I've no options available to restore my power." His attention drifted to the flickering fire and he added, "Soon I'll be balanced upon the cusp, and my shadow sorcery will be a memory. I only hope that the strength of the sun empowers me before the Rime Witch becomes corporeal."

Halina shifted her hands to the padded arms of her chair. "Aren't there other mages you can summon to fight alongside us?"

Us? That was hopeful.

He shook his head. "There are other magical folk scattered far between Quoregna's four kingdoms. Many are healers, but their power is a puff of wind compared to the Rime Witch's strength. And the strongest sorcerers practice the dark arcana, but I wouldn't call on any of them for aid. They'd join with our foe. Spite enjoys like-minded company."

Halina went to the window. The silk of her gown swished across the floor and swirled around her legs. Hers was a strong and graceful figure and the ease of her stride belied the bruises and aches she must have gained during their fight. She watched the gently falling snow, the fiery hue of her hair an intense contrast to the white outside. "Only hours ago you summoned and battled three wraiths. That was no easy task, and it confirmed my suspicions." She faced him. "You're lying about your lost power, Master Gethen."

Those were cold words; the next ones were colder. "Your actions make fools of your words. And you think you've fooled me with both. But you're quite capable of serving Ursinum in the coming war."

Gethen knitted his fingers together to keep from reaching for her throat. "How can you ignore what is so obvious? I struggled to control mere spirits last night." He pushed up from his chair and stalked toward her. "You've nearly lost your life and freedom to dark sorcery twice since entering Ranith because my wards are so frail. You mistake minute displays of power for the entirety of my strength. Only months ago I could've dismissed Shemel with a snap of my fingers." His fingers echoed his words. "And the Rime Witch would've pissed herself at the idea of crossing my wards. Can't you see how depleted my magic is?"

She folded her arms and watched him with those cool, blue eyes. "You think you can distract me with spirits and seduce me with your magic. But I'm no addle-brained girl."

Gethen shook his head. "I regret the trick I played on you when you arrived at Ranith, because you've taken that for power when it was mere illusion." His tone hardened with every sentence. "You think magic is mixing a few potions and summoning mage fire. That's child's play. You know *nothing* of the power required to control shadow sorcery, *nothing* of the dangers that lurk beyond the Voidline. Yet you've decided that I'm a liar." He stabbed his finger at her. "You insult me, Your Ladyship. I may be the Shadow Mage, but I'm not a deceiver or a coward."

Halina accepted his spleen with absolute control. "I would never call you a coward, Master Gethen. But we have an agreement. My aid for your fealty. I helped you last night. Now you will fulfill your half of the accord. Come down from your tower, kneel before King Vernard, and give him your services. Once Besera's aggression is curbed, I will gladly join your campaign against this witch."

Gethen snorted. She had bigger bollocks than any man ever could. "You jest. It's the only explanation for such twisted logic. I refused your proposal and the king's agreement."

"I don't jest." She folded her arms. Her right hand caressed the thin stiletto in its sheath upon her forearm. "You owe your allegiance to the country in which you've dwelled, not the one you left behind as a boy. I won't permit you to aid Besera." Her eyes held a killer's cold malice. The militess wouldn't hesitate to gut him. "King Vernard has been made aware of your brother's demands for your loyalty or your life. 'Bring Ursinum to Besera.' Does that sound familiar?"

How did she learn of that? He rubbed his jaw.

"Clearly your servants have forgotten that walls have ears, especially those of your guest's quarters." Her fingers drummed on the misericord's hilt.

Damnation. Gethen gripped the arms of his chair. "Your bird carried the message yesterday morning."

"Yes. His Majesty will have issued a death mark by now, with a reward so great that every dog and yaldson will be at your door." She shifted and firelight flared in her blue eyes. "Not that you'll be alive when they get here."

"So the refusal I sent to my brother means nothing?"

"Your words aren't proof. If you wish to have the mark lifted, accept King Vernard's offer. Then I'll have no doubts and will gladly protect you."

Gethen sat back and the tension in his shoulders eased. "Vernard's offer?" His lips twitched, and a particularly wolfish smile slowly spread across his face. "Very well, Militess Halina, if that's what *you* want."

Her eyes narrowed and her fingers froze on the misericord. The hunter sensed a trap.

Gethen turned his head and bellowed, "Magod!" but his gaze never left her face. She saw everything. She was like Kharayan's wolves, a beautiful and deadly hunter.

The thud of feet echoed in the hall, then his groundsman appeared in the library doorway, a load of firewood under his arm. "Yes, Master?"

"Go to my office, find the letters from King Vernard and King Zelal on my writing desk, and bring them here. Be quick." He watched Halina as Magod's footsteps receded. "You're welcome to read my brother's messages. I keep no secrets from you now." Ignoring her and her knife, Gethen stood. "Would you like a glass of mead while we wait?"

"No."

He shrugged and poured a drink from the decanter that Noni kept full for him. Crystal rang and the fire sighed. She dissected him with those beautiful, keen eyes. He knew she'd sensed the situation twist from her control.

Gethen leaned back against the sideboard, openly considering the woman, her face, her hair, her curves. Her dagger. Militess Halina could be his. Sign the agreement and take the woman. An enticing thought.

Magod delivered the letters and was smart enough to flee. The woman had filled the library with tension.

Gethen tossed his brother's parchments on the table beside her chair. The letter from Vernard he handed to her as he returned to the chair opposite hers. "Enjoy your father's offer first. Halina. It holds some surprises."

Her expression hardened at his too-familiar use of her given name. "I was present for the discussion and creation of this document, *Master Gethen*." The paper rustled between her fingers. "Do you believe that I'm ignorant of its contents?"

He looked down his nose at her. "Read it."

She unfolded the parchment and scanned the document. He saw the moment when she realized that her father had thrown her into the bargain like a brood mare. Rage crossed her face — there and gone in a blink — narrowing her eyes, tightening her mouth. But instead of tossing tables or stabbing him in the heart, she swallowed and her expression turned to stone.

He was disappointed to see her restraint. No woman accomplished what Halina had without possessing a deeply passionate nature. Gethen wanted to scrape away some of that self-control and experience the fire that drove the militess. Instead, her hands were steady as she folded the parchment and returned it to him.

"It seems that you have the advantage, Shadow Mage."

Her admission collapsed his smugness, and Gethen grimaced. "No. I have a death mark, the Rime Witch, failing powers, and an angry guest."

Halina nodded. "Ursinum needs your aid, especially if this Rime Witch is as powerful and spiteful as you claim."

"You have doubts?"

She ignored his question. "If you accept Vernard's offer, I will uphold its terms. For Ursinum. For Khara. I offer to you whatever aid and power I have to protect you and replenish your strength, if you will protect my king and country."

Gethen had never wanted or needed a wife. He knew a few hedge witches who were all too happy to rut when the mood distracted him. But Halina Persinna was a prize that kings would kill for.

He looked away from her then stood and went to the windows. Halina's fate was in his hands, and his was in hers. He stared at the featureless, white world outside. "If I take you and your lands, I'll always be your warden, never your husband. You'll never come willingly into my bed or lay contented in my arms. Ours will be a bitter marriage."

He resented Zelal for receiving the life that should've been his. In one afternoon, Gethen had gone from future king to monster's apprentice. He wouldn't disrupt Halina's life in the same way, change her fate to suit the needs of a king who was being driven to war by an undead witch's dirty magic.

"I would never force myself upon a woman, even with her father's permission." His gaze strayed to her reflection in the window and he added, "Especially a woman I so greatly admire."

Halina's expression softened, and Gethen added, "I'm neither a traitor to Ursinum, nor willing to betray Zelal. However, you gave me your protection last night, so I'll return the favor. I won't leave Ranith with you, but I will write to my brother on behalf of Ursinum and do my best to avert war."

He downed the rest of his mead and turned to refill his glass. "Our negotiations are over, Militess. I don't want your freedom. Perhaps you can convince your father not to steal mine."

She retrieved Zelal's messages and scanned them. Understanding and regret crossed her face as she read his threats. When she was finished, she closed her eyes and whispered, "I've misjudged you."

"As often occurs."

She stood. The papers rustled and hit the floor. He looked at the crystal decanter instead of her as she came to his side, but their reflections were there, distorted and almost unrecognizable.

Halina said, "I'll return to my father's camp, explain that your efforts must be confined to negotiating with King Zelal, and pay off the death mark from my own coffers."

"Halina, I—"

She pressed her hand over his mouth. "I'm sorry." She held his gaze for a long moment. "Goodbye, Gethen."

Then Halina turned and strode from the library, and he was colder for her absence.

"The margrave took Idris, thankfully," Magod said as Noni slammed down a meager meal before Gethen. "But even he'll struggle; those snow drifts reach my chest, Master. Insisted upon leaving. Said she needed to warn the king about the Rime Witch." Magod's expression was grave. "What could I do?"

Gethen scowled at the bowl of cold, curdled porridge, the crusted cheese, and the shriveled apple on his plate. "What's this?"

"Supper," Noni said. "I'll not waste effort on a fool." She

stomped from the great hall before he could complain, and returned a moment later with a glass of pale, vinegary mead.

"I loath oxymel," Gethen grumbled but the look of disgust Noni turned on him shut his mouth. Halina may not have stabbed him, but his housekeeper seemed determined to poison him. He sighed and shoved the food away as she disappeared back to the kitchen.

Magod slid a stack of coins across the table. "Insisted on paying for the replacement cloak, tunic, and trouzes."

Gethen gritted his teeth. "Tell your mother I did what I must. I face a fight with my own demon. It's better that I draw the witch's attention away from Ursinum's troops and keep her battle with me. That's the only way I can aid the militess."

Magod stood. "Dumbest thing you've ever said, Master." He rested both hands upon the table, and leaned over Gethen. "I said not to fight that woman. Guess battling those mages addled your brain last night."

Gethen massaged the back of his neck; his head pounded and the weakness that had started after he'd left the mausoleum hadn't improved with the day's passage. "I couldn't accept the terms she put forth in our negotiations. No one should trade their freedom for my pitiful sorcery."

Magod shook his head. "She can help you battle the witch. You need her protection. Mummin and I see how weak you've become, but we can't help. The militess can; she *did*. Bring her back to Ranith, Master. Let her help you beat your enemy."

It was tempting, but that way only led to their deaths. "No. Let the militess return to her king."

"She protected you against the the dead shadow mages," Magod insisted. "Now she's alone in Kharayan. Something wild lurks in those woods; even the wolves sense it."

Gethen slammed his fists upon the table. The cutlery and coins jumped. "Enough! You forget that she was born with a sword in her hand. Don't underestimate her; she can handle a few errant beasts in that forest." He was at his wit's end, and his servants' censure wasn't helping. "I'll hear no more of Margrave Khara."

He stood and the groundsman stepped back. "You and your mother have served me well, but I can't guarantee your safety in Ranith anymore. Take the animals to Etherias. When all of this is over return here. If the citadel still stands, Kharayan will be yours."

With those orders he strode from the room, ignoring Magod's open-mouthed astonishment. He couldn't think through the pounding in his head and the aching of the muscles in his shoulders and back. He took the stairs two at a time, but when he reached his stillroom he stopped and stared into the infirmary. The entire wolf pack was lying on the floor around Halina's empty bed.

"What you ask is impossible. The woman serves Ursinum, not Ranith. She doesn't belong with us. She asks too much of me." The wolves stared at him. They weren't interested in his arguments; he'd assigned them to guard her, and they continued to do so. "And she gives too much of herself."

Gethen pulled a tincture from one of his cabinets. He slopped some into a dram cup, mixed in a small amount of great mead, and knocked it back in one gulp.

"That damnable woman; she'd pay too high a price." He stared at nothing. The warmth of her fingers on his lips had stayed with him like a curse. And her scent — she smelled of honeyed soap, leather, and horses. Not even the stag wraith's stench had obliterated Halina's scent from his memory.

Gethen replaced the tincture bottle in its cabinet then paced the room. Perhaps if he drew power from all the wolves he'd be able to cross the Voidline and battle the Rime Witch.

"That'd kill the animals." And there was no guarantee that their sacrifice would bring the desired result. "Noni and Magod are right, I'm an idiot." Like it or not if he wanted to defeat or even distract the witch without Halina's help, he'd have to sacrifice the spirits of a lot of animals, not just the pack but all of Kharayan's beasts.

Gethen circled the room. He touched his worktable and the boxes of spices, set the dangling sprays of herbs swinging gently to and fro, and made the small, dark glass bottles clink with a touch. Finally, he dropped upon the worn, red sofa below the window. His eyes closed. He'd be able to think clearly and formulate a plan once he'd rested and his aches had eased. "I'll search the books," he mumbled. There had to be something he'd missed.

When he awoke evening's darkness and chill had arrived. His first unbidden thought was of Halina. *She'll have crossed my wards and left Kharayan by now.* Outside the window Ranith was white; the storm raged, stronger and colder than ever. Icicles as long as his forearm hung from the citadel's downspouts.

Gethen frowned. He hadn't sensed any change in the wards. But that meant nothing; he hadn't known when she'd entered the woods. Why would he know when she'd left? He stood and stretched, grimacing as the ache across his shoulders continued unabated. At least the headache had eased.

The wolves hadn't left the infirmary. *She's like one of their own,* he thought as he returned the animals' unrelenting stare. The margrave had faced down the dead mages' mental onslaught with a ferocity reserved for a predator. She'd coughed up blood and fear yet kept battling. She'd offered him far more than he ever would've expected from her or any other member of Ursinum's ruling class.

He'd never known such a woman as Militess Halina and, like it or not, he missed her already.

He scrubbed his hands over his face. He regretted her loss but was too fond of his life to recall her and hoped she was too fond of her freedom to come.

He meandered across the room to stop beside the bed. The gown she'd worn that day was tossed upon the covers. Gethen reached out. His fingers hovered over the dark blue velvet. Then they brushed it. The fabric was cold without Halina's body to warm it.

He went to the window. How many times had he looked up from the bailey to see her looking down from above? He pressed his hand against the glass, just as she had, then he worked the window open and leaned out into the stinging, frozen air.

Some sound carried to him from the edge of the forest. Some high, thin sound like an animal suffering. Behind him, the wolves snarled and jumped to their feet. Their nails scrabbled on the floor, glass and pottery shattered, and a chair crashed against a wall as the pack bolted from the infirmary, through the stillroom, and into the hall. Their growls, barks, and howls echoed throughout the citadel. Gethen knew that sound; he'd never forget it. It was how they'd called to each other when they were trying to stop him from running off the cliff.

"Halina," he whispered.

She was one of them. And she was in trouble.

He charged down the stairs after the wolves. "Magod! I need you now!"

The man appeared in the great hall his eyes wide and his large figure tense. "Master?"

"Fetch my sword. Arm yourself to guard Ranith. The margrave is under attack and—"

Gethen knew every shadow that lurked in his woods. He'd brought them across the Voidline to patrol Kharayan. But as his power had failed, so too had his command of them. He'd dispelled all but one. Now the creature of his own making but no longer under his control haunted the margrave. His own shadow had turned upon the militess.

"And she faces a losing battle." Gethen continued across the hall and into the soaring foyer. The wolves snarled and snapped around his heels. His groundsman joined him and together they put their shoulders and all their weight into pushing open the front doors. The mass of snow blocking the inset door forced them to strain, though Magod had cleared it every day since the storm's arrival and Gethen mustered what heat he could to soften the ice. Finally, when they had it wide enough the wolves charged into the blizzard and disappeared behind a white curtain of blowing snow and ice.

As the men turned from the door Noni appeared, her frail, boney figure stooping beneath the weight of armor and swords. Wordlessly, Gethen donned chain mail and plate armor, pauldrons, vambraces, and his heavy winter cloak as Noni helped her son dress for battle. Then all three forged through the snow-packed bailey to the stables.

While Magod and his mother blanketed and saddled Remig, the Shadow Mage drew power from his small herd of goats. It was a hasty and sloppy effort, and one of the poor animals paid with its life. "I'm sorry." He stroked the creature's still, brown flank, but there was no undoing what had to be done. And the magic coursing through his veins gave Gethen the strength to weave his shadow armor and summon a bright, hot ball of amber mage fire to burn away the snow in his path.

"Bar the gates and postern and set the heights ablaze," he ordered Magod as he lit a torch with his orange flame and handed it to the man.

"I should come with you, Master," the groundsman protested, but Gethen slashed the air with his hand.

"No! I can't be certain of my senses, and there may be more than one invader. Keep the ward fires burning until I return with the militess. Keep the shadows at bay, Magod. They no longer respect the scribed wards, but they still fear mage fire. Set Ranith's perimeter ablaze, and they'll stay clear."

A sound made them turn. Idris galloped into the bailey, blowing hard and foaming his bit. His saddle was empty and fear widened his eyes. Noni captured the horse's loose reins as the animal tossed his head.

With a leg up from the groundsman, Gethen mounted Remig. He pulled the horse's head around and urged the gelding to charge through the snow and onto his stablemate's path.

Riding low upon the horse's neck, Gethen stretched out his reinvigorated senses to find Halina, searching beyond what his eyes could see. Scattered snow and a deep furrow showed the way of the wolves past stark, black trees. Gethen directed Remig and his own awareness to follow it.

He stretched and hunted. Waves of rage emanated from the militess as she fought for her life. They rolled over him like hot summer winds, a maelstrom of determination and fury.

And finally, there! He found her. She fought at the very edge of Kharayan.

Ahead, the wolves charged through the snow, dark bobbing shapes moving through white, hampered by the deep drifts but determined to reach the militess.

"Hurry," he urged his horse and the wolves. He stretched his call out to the bears and boars and all the creatures of his forest. "Hurry or she'll die." Gethen couldn't imagine anything worse, even as he cursed himself for caring.

THIRTEEN

"**V**ernard! You lying *coward*!" Halina had stood at the edge of Kharayan's ward circle, her toes touching the black cobblestones while she'd cursed at the place where King Vernard's camp should've been. She'd raged at the empty acres with their pristine drifts of shimmering snow until her ears had pounded with her own blood and fury. Her bastard father's abandonment had combined with her rage at his scheme to use her, *again*, and an unexpectedly bitter sense of loss.

In the moment when she'd left Gethen, she'd realized just how much she wanted him. And she'd known it was too late. He'd rejected her. She didn't blame him. She'd never hate him. And she'd set herself the task of ensuring his freedom from the death mark that she'd wrongly set against him.

But the damnable king had left.

Blind to the approaching danger, she'd been unprepared when something had struck her side, knocking her off her feet and into a tree. Her body had glanced off the trunk, and she'd landed like a rag doll in a snow-covered thicket.

Now breathing made her cough and shot sharp pain through

her body. Her lungs bubbled, and she couldn't fill them. "Skiron's bones," she gasped.

Turning pain into rage, Halina got to her hands and knees, crawled to the path's edge, and drew her sword and dagger. She blinked the relentless blowing snow from her eyes and searched the woods for her attacker. "Where are you?"

Wolves howled in the distance.

Whatever had hit her had fallen back to see the damage its attack had done.

Halina clenched her teeth. "Come on, you swine!" A coughing fit crippled her and droplets of her blood splattered the snowy underbrush, brilliant crimson that made the hoarfrost steam and melt.

There was movement on her right. Something dark shifted. Its inkiness stood out against the snow. A black wolf? Halina squinted and tried to identify her attacker. It moved like a shadow not an animal. Another wraith. "I don't fear you." She raised her sword. She had her weapons and armor. And Gethen said they held blood magic.

Halina bared her teeth in a rictus of pain and rue. She still bore the aches and bruises from the fight with the shadow mages, but they were whispers compared to the new agony spearing her ribs and gut.

More movement came, this time on the other side of her. Was there more than one?

Something lifted her off her feet. It hurled her backwards into the forest. Again she hit tree trunks. Branches snapped. Bones broke. Blood filled her mouth and ran into her eyes. Everything turned red.

She lay still for what felt like forever, fighting to keep blackness from tunneling her vision, gasping for air. Her head rang. Three trees overlapped in her vision where there should've been only one. Finally, Halina rolled to her side and moaned with the effort of pushing upright. Her life bubbled from her lips and drooled onto the white snow in a long line of crimson spittle.

Her fingers spasmed painfully. Three on her left hand were broken. And she'd lost her dagger. Halina tried to pull up to sit on her knees, but her left leg wouldn't cooperate. She peered at it.

"Blood and bones."

No, she hadn't lost her misericord. Its blade was buried up to the hilt in her thigh. She blinked and laughed even as pain and nausea twisted her gut. She choked on her own blood, and then vomited.

A shadow fell across her. "I've had worse," she slurred. Before she could look up, a blow to her face cracked her jaw and knocked her onto her back. Something cold seized her left ankle and dragged her through the snow and broken branches. Pain stabbed straight from her thigh to her brain, and a high, thin scream escaped her. She twisted and swung her sword. It struck her attacker. The thing released her but made no sound. That eerie silence was worse than the dead shadow mages' hissing, growling, and whinging.

"Damnation." Panting, she lay on her back and squinted into the forest. "Where is it? *What* is it?"

More wolf howls — close now — snarling, whining, and crackling underbrush. The pack was all around her. They'd finish what her attacker had started. Maybe that's why it had released her.

No. It wasn't through. The wolves growled and barked but didn't attack as a shadow blotted out the sunlight and cold, unseen hands constricted Halina's throat. It lifted her from the ground. She slashed with her sword but hit nothing. She grabbed for a hand, but there was only frigid air. How could that be? Her feet kicked. She twisted.

Cold.

Black.

Then a shout. Hot amber light flashed through the darkness.

Words Halina didn't know bent the air around her. Something roared like a bear.

Pain stabbed through her as she hit the ground. The world was white and cold again.

Wolves snarled and attacked, but they weren't after her.

Then strong arms wrapped around Halina. Warmth suffused her. Yet another shout, and the arms were gone. She was cold again.

"Khotyr, take me," Halina mumbled and opened her eyes. She lay in the snow. Gethen stood over her cloaked in his dark, living armor. He faced a massive, twisting shadow. Within its mangled folds faces snarled and screamed, hands reached, teeth gnashed, and things writhed — cold, grotesque abominations, tortured souls and the demons that consumed them.

The largest black bear she'd ever seen leaned against Gethen. The mage clutched the animal's thick fur with his left hand. Silver light rose from its body to wrap around the sorcerer's arm. He used the light to weave fiery spells in mid-air with his right hand. Wolves and boars circled the combatants, snarling, lunging toward the shadowy thing but unable to get close.

Gethen's deep voice reverberated off the trees. With each command the wraith twisted and shrieked but didn't diminish. It darted forward only to be repelled by another incantation. It was a deadly dance that slowly, slowly the shadow was dominating.

The wraith lashed out a tentacle of darkness and struck Gethen. Shreds of his incorporeal armor twisted and fell away, steaming in the snow. He staggered back a step but remained upright. His droning incantation continued. The bear groaned and swayed. Gethen's grip on its fur tightened.

The shadow spun forth a dagger of darkness that skewered a boar. The creature screamed as it was lifted and thrown at the mage. The bear roared and swatted the carcass away. But the monster moved closer. Again it struck Gethen. Again the bear blocked it. Again the mage lost some of his shadowy armor, and stepped back.

Three more times the demonic wraith attacked, and always Gethen droned on, his words unknown to Halina. They demanded, commanded, but the wraith disobeyed and edged ever closer.

Then the bear swayed on shaking legs and groaned. It turned its dark brown eyes upon the Shadow Mage and, with a deep moan, collapsed into the snow.

Gethen staggered. His armor disintegrated. But he didn't stop his incantation. The wraith was close; its tendrils snatched and clawed at his legs and stretched toward his hands.

Halina looked up at him. She blinked to clear her vision of blood. "Bollocks," she rasped. He was becoming incorporeal, like a shadow himself. He was using his own spirit to battle the wraith, expending the last of his strength.

The shadowy beast speared a gray wolf and hurled the wounded animal. Gethen spread his stance to brace for it, but this time, the shadow struck its target. The wolf knocked him back. His incantation faltered. The wraith surged forward.

Instinctively, Halina reached up to steady Gethen. She caught his left hand. Strength and heat filled her. He gripped her fingers in turn, tight, tighter. He shouted another spell and heat scorched her from the inside out.

The entity shrieked and exploded into a whirlwind of amber fire. The Shadow Mage pivoted and shielded Halina with his body as the burning column shot through the treetops then collapsed into a white-hot ball and exploded into cinders and ash. The massive release of heat melted the snow around and above them. Water cascaded from the canopy of leaves overhead.

Gethen groaned, convulsed. He released Halina's hand and straightened. He looked at her with dull, glazed eyes, and then collapsed beside her, cold and unconscious, a pale shadow of his former self.

Halina struggled to breathe. Blood pooled around her leg and soaked her trouzes. But she laid her hand upon his back. It rose and fell slowly, shallowly. Gethen wasn't dead. Yet. She pulled his fur-lined cloak around him and dragged her own over her battered body.

The black bear stirred, raised its massive head, and sniffed the air. It stared around the clearing, paused as it noticed them, then rose and lumbered into the forest. As it departed, Ranith's wolves approached and settled around their master.

Halina found Gethen's hand and curved her unbroken fingers around it. She stared up through the blackened treetops. It had stopped snowing and stars winked at her through a break in the thick clouds.

Her eyelids were too heavy to keep open. Her chest was too heavy for her lungs to push against. She was drowning, and the water was dark. She'd never felt so tired. But, for once, the water was soft and warm, its weight reassuring as it lapped around her body and cushioned her battered and broken bones. It lifted her and carried her away from the cold and the pain.

———

Something was clicking.

Halina opened her eyes, blinked, and then squinted against candlelight and a cheery fire burning upon the grate. She peered around and recognized Ranith's infirmary.

Noni said, "There you are, Your Ladyship. Knew you'd come back to us." The clicking emanated from her thin wooden knitting needles. Gethen's housekeeper sat in a chair beside Halina's bed, buried by a green-and-gray blanket of wool, the needles and yarn a blur in her hands.

Halina tensed to sit upright and winced; the room swam. She inhaled and gasped as pain knifed her chest. A rolling wave of nausea followed.

Noni stood and set aside her knitting. "Don't move too fast. Your body's still a ruin." She wrapped her arm around Halina's shoulders, gently eased her upright, and propped two more pillows behind her back and shoulders.

Halina endured a round of wet, agonizing coughing. Noni helped her turn to her side and spit blood and mucus into a bucket. The fit subsided. She held her ribs and whimpered at the pain. Sweat dampened her forehead and tears traced paths down her cheeks. There was no shame in suffering. Halina had learned that long ago.

The housekeeper wiped her face with a cool, damp cloth. "Easy, Your Ladyship. It'll be a while before you're fully mended."

Halina took slow, careful breaths then whispered, "Did your ... master ... survive?"

"Oh, yes, thanks to your protection." Noni beamed down at Halina as if she was one of the old gods reincarnated.

"I didn't ... help." Halina labored for breath. "I couldn't ... protect myself ... or help him."

Noni went to the fire and lifted a kettle off an iron bracket. She poured the hot liquid into a cup and added something from a dark brown bottle. "That's not what Master Gethen says." She perched upon the side of the bed and held the cup to Halina's lips.

Reduced to a babe and dependent on the good graces of the Shadow Mage and his servants, the Margrave of Khara relinquished control to the woman, whose hands were gentle and soothing. This wasn't the first time Halina had been injured in battle; her body bore many scars, some thick and ugly enough to make her lovers — and enemies — blanch.

The drink was spicy and sweet, and its warmth flowed through her, dulled her aches, and made breathing easier. After five sips she was spent.

The housekeeper sat back and traded the cup for her knitting. "Master said if you hadn't given him your strength, he would've been pulled into the Void and trapped forever, a shadow too weak to return to his body." Noni cast on a new stitch and added, "And you'd be dead, Your Ladyship."

Whatever was in that cup made Halina languid. Her eyes slowly closed and she sank into a deep, dreamless slumber before she could share her version of the story.

When next she awoke, Noni's chair was vacant. Dim gray light cast heavy shadows across the floor and walls. The fire had been banked for the night and the candles had been snuffed. Gentle snores filled the room. Halina looked around. The housekeeper slept in a cot between the bed and the fire. And it took several seconds of squinting before she realized that the large lumps spread all over the floor were wolves. The pack had returned to Ranith Citadel, and they were guarding her.

Halina's smile was stiff and painful. She lay for a long time, gathering the courage to move, but when she finally turned onto her side, the pain wasn't blinding. She exhaled — slowly — and found the cup of liquid that Noni had prepared for her. She spilled some, and her body and hands shook from her efforts when she finally settled back into her pillows, but she'd had five more sips of the draught and felt better for it. Whatever magic Gethen had infused that drink with it was miraculous.

This time she remained awake and her smile was stronger when Noni awoke and sat up, her yellow nightcap askew.

The woman yawned and stretched. "Your Ladyship has some color this morning."

Halina's voice was stronger, too. "I think I'll live to fight by your master's side again."

"Not without some food in you. Be back soon with hot broth." Noni handed the cup of metheglin to Halina and added, "Meanwhile, you finish this." Dutifully, Halina took it and drank as the woman wound her way through the hills of wolves to the door muttering about "fur everywhere, even in the knitting."

After broth and help with her toilet, Halina returned to bed, weak and shaking, and fell asleep again.

It was dark when she stirred. She was shivering. Her head swam from dreams of heat and thirst, of hands pinning her down and pain knifing her leg. "Noni?" Her eyes were too heavy to open.

"Here." A cool cloth gently wiped her face. "Got a fever and the shakes, Your Ladyship. Infection's taken hold in that knife wound."

Strong hands held her thigh and burned her skin. Fearing the restraint, she lashed out, and her fist knocked someone away.

"Skiron's bones, she's strong," Gethen said. "Hold her hands, Magod. I've got to reopen the wound."

Delirious with fever, Halina strained against the hands that had captured her wrists. "No! Don't cut!" She thrashed and twisted.

Noni's gentle hands caught Halina's face. "Shhh, Your Ladyship. Master Gethen's just pulling out the stitches." The cool cloth wiped her face again. "Needs to drain the wound. Hold still now."

But fear from childhood fevers and bloodletting bubbled up from a place in Halina's brain that usually remained firmly locked. "No! *No!* I'll take the draught! Don't cut me!" She kicked and fought. "Don't! Don't cut! Let me *go!*"

Weight settled across both of her legs. "It's no use. She'll hurt herself and undo the healing of the last five days. Noni, fetch the somnifcrum ether."

Her arms were released. Halina tried to sit up, but a firm hand held her against the pillows.

"Here, Master."

A cloth covered Halina's mouth. Some cloying scent filled her nose. She snatched at the fabric, but that firm hand now held it in place. She inhaled to scream. But, instead, her mind went numb and time slowed to a stop.

The room was still dark. Halina ached all over, but the hot pain in her thigh dominated her mind. She tried to shift her leg to alleviate the discomfort, but agony knifed her and she cried out.

A muted amber glow lit the room, followed by movement. Then Gethen leaned over her. He held something beneath her nose. "Breathe this in. It'll ease your pain."

It was the cloying scent again, but fainter this time, a weaker compound. Halina inhaled. Her head swam. The room skewed strangely and the amber of his mage fire intensified. But just as quickly it all faded, including the pain and heat. "Thank you."

He capped a little clay pot and set it upon the bedside table then took up a roll of linen and another pot. He placed these upon the bed beside her leg.

"Since you're awake, I'll change your poultice and bandages." He folded back the blankets to expose her wounded thigh. Gently he unrolled her bandage, removed a poultice of pungent herbs, and washed her wound with an astringent liquid. Halina shivered as her skin cooled. With great care, Gethen applied more unguent, another poultice, and fresh linen bandages.

Neither of them spoke as he worked, but every time his fingers brushed her skin a small shock flashed from her leg to her belly and he gave a little start. Yet, despite their reactions, Gethen didn't hurry. His hands were careful, his touch respectful, his actions methodical. When he'd finished, he returned the linen and pots to the table and dropped the soiled dressings into a bucket beside the infirmary door. He returned to the chair beside the bed. "Better?"

"Yes."

"It's my duty, honor, and pleasure to serve you, Margrave."

Margrave. Halina plucked weakly at the weave of her yellow blanket. "What happened to our inappropriate familiarity?" She swallowed. Her throat was cottony. "We almost died together in that forest. Doesn't that warrant the use of given names now? Gethen?"

He stared at her, and then he smiled. It wasn't the smirk or wolfish grin she'd come to expect, but an astonishingly wide and beautiful smile that revealed laugh lines at the corners of his eyes. As dark and dour as the Shadow Mage was when he was serious, he was equally bright and charming when he really smiled. "You're right, Halina." He leaned close and his expression turned secretive and seductive as he added, "Let's be allies and forget the bickering of kings."

Halina sobered. "I can't. Too many people rely upon me."

Gethen sat back. His cheer was gone, too. "Your king?"

"My tenants. They trust me to protect them and to be their voice. Families with children, old women and men past their fighting days, fishermen and merchants and farmers and cooks and-and all manner of people who just want to live and trade with each other *and* Besera. They leave the bickering of kings to me." She caught his wrist, shuddering as her body reacted, but forging on nevertheless. "Don't you see? You're my tenant. It's my duty to protect you, too. I shouldn't have forgotten."

Gethen eased his hand back until their fingers were clasped. "You're right."

"Not that I've done that very well," she muttered.

His fingers squeezed hers. "Some fights even you can't win, Militess."

They were quiet, and he held her hand between his palms. The fire hissed and popped. Wind shrieked around Ranith's gray walls. One of the wolves stretched and sighed in its sleep.

"What news of Khara? What of Zelal, Vernard, and the witch and her storm?"

Gethen stroked Halina's broken and battered fingers. "Nothing. You've been abed for nine days, and the blizzard has continued. There've been no messages from either Vernard or Zelal, and no other manifestations from the witch, though her ceaseless snow continues to bury us."

Halina frowned and exhaled frustration. At least the pain in her ribs had eased from stabbing to aching. "I don't like the quiet. It means everyone's waiting for someone else to act."

"The witch possessed one of my own shades to attack you. Or perhaps I was the target. Her stag wraith never returned to her, so she sent something subtler but more dangerous to spy on me."

"That was subtle?"

His smile was rueful. "She's capable of far worse. But summoning another mage's creatures and controlling them from within the Void drains strength quickly. So does weather work. I suspect she's still recovering, just as we are."

It was intimate knowledge of their enemy; exactly what Vernard had come to Kharayan for, except that he'd been looking at the wrong enemy. Halina sighed. "He left too soon."

"Your father?"

"Yes. He and Crown Prince Ilker should know where the real battle lies. They should be giving you *their* aid, not demanding your fealty or surrender."

Gethen studied her blunted fingers. "My brother, too. I'll write to both kings." He sandwiched her hand between his palms. "They face a rude surprise and certain death, and I fear that their animosity could fuel the witch's power."

Halina looked from their hands to his eyes. "Are you siding with Vernard?"

"I'm siding with Quoregna. The Rime Witch will suck the warmth from the world, gaining power with every death. She'll swallow the shadows and the sun." He touched her cheek and added, "And she's starting with us."

Whatever his reasons were, Halina rejoiced that he was joining her in the coming battle. "Thank you." She pressed her cheek against his palm.

Gethen stroked her skin. Slowly he bent until their faces were so close that his breath tickled her. "You're welcome, Halina," he murmured.

Her lips parted, and his gaze went to her mouth then returned to her eyes. Her breathing hitched, and then Halina lifted her chin, bridging the small gulf between them. She pressed her mouth to his, and her eyes closed.

Gethen exhaled as she inhaled. He deepened the kiss and responded as she parted her lips. Their tongues touched, the kiss intensified, Halina moaned. He slid his hands into her hair and tilted her head.

Pain flared across her left shoulder. She stiffened and a little, "Ow," escaped her.

Gethen froze then eased away. "I'm sorry." His voice was hoarse. He cleared his throat then disentangled his fingers from her curls. "I — need to send those letters." Instead, he pressed his lips to hers again. Then he broke the kiss, stood, and strode from the infirmary.

Halina touched her lips and smiled. She quite liked this kind of dark sorcery.

FOURTEEN

Gethen paced the library, sidestepping precariously piled books as he contemplated the shadow's attack. It had exhibited far more aggression and power than he'd instilled it with, so much so that it had pushed him to the brink of the Void. Yet the margrave's mere touch had empowered him to obliterate the beast.

How? he wondered. *She's not magically gifted.* Aside from her acquired blood magic, the militess had no knowledge of any magical arcana and no gift for wielding it.

He exhaled a slow breath. *Halina.* Gods, he wanted her. Her kiss had bound him. Desire warmed him. She was fierce and fearless, foul-mouthed and headstrong, and more compelling than any woman he'd ever known.

"Focus on the problem, not the woman." Gethen tapped his fist against his forehead with each word.

But the woman was part of the problem.

Many a man had been ruined by desire. Maybe that was the witch's game, to drive him mad with distraction at his most vulnerable hour. If so, why had she tried to destroy her own weapon?

He looked out the window and saw the postern door, now nearly buried in snow. He snorted. "You thought you were sending me a seductress, but you chose poorly, Witch."

Halina was no concubine, and treating her injuries had revealed their powerful connection. Her touch conveyed heat, longing, strength. She hadn't distracted him. Just the opposite, she'd empowered him.

A slow smile curved his lips. "She isn't your weapon. She's mine." Something the witch hadn't anticipated, and when she'd realized her mistake, she'd possessed his shadow wraith and sent it to kill Halina.

But how did the Rime Witch know his affairs? How did she know he hovered on the cusp of shadow and sun magic? Why was she so determined to weaken him before the change?

He scanned the library. Books occupied the floor, the tables, the chairs. He'd looked through every dusty, crumbling tome but had found only dark and malevolent magic. Perhaps answers to his questions required different source material, something unavailable in books.

Gethen had largely ignored the library once Shemel had died. He'd devised his own incantations and found his own methods of summoning power. He'd neither wanted nor needed grimoires filled with invocations meant to cause suffering, death, and violence.

But not all the library's books contained dark magic and one in particular contained no magic at all. It was a register of every mage who'd made Ranith their home and it spanned centuries.

Shemel had stored it with the reliquary. Gethen went to a cabinet in the far corner of the library. He opened its hinged doors. Inside was a black metal box the size of a man's torso and tucked beside that was a registry with a cover the color of dried blood.

Careful not to touch the reliquary, he retrieved the large book and settled into one of the chairs before the fire. Shemel had opened it only once in front of Gethen, to force him to add his name to its lists using his own blood mixed with black ink.

He swiped at the layers of dust coating the cover, then began the laborious task of searching for the identity of the last Sun Mage.

Few shadow mages survived past thirty years. Magic, particularly the dark arcana, was a harsh mistress. So he thumbed through ninety years' worth of history — atrocities Shemel, Olegário, and Volker labeled triumphs — and began searching the entries backward from there. Three hours later, he rubbed his eyes, stretched, and thanked Noni for the tray of food she'd brought to break his fast.

"What has you bleary-eyed, Master?" She set down a bottle of mead and a bowl of porridge and cocked her head to consider the old book open in his lap.

Gethen picked up bowl and spoon and shoveled warm porridge into his mouth. He swallowed and replied, "Ranith's mage registry. I need the name of the previous Sun Mage."

She frowned as she scanned the writing on the open page. "What makes the Sun Mage different from the rest of them?"

He indicated the book with his spoon. "He or she will be the only one who's written of something other than brutality. The rest of this is all bleakness and malevolence." He took a large gulp of the golden mead she poured into his glass. "How is the margrave this morning?"

"Resting. The fever's eased but not broken. Pain's lessened, too, I think. Fetch you when she wakes?"

"Yes." He turned back to the book and continued to eat and drink even as he searched the lists, complaints, and dark boasting until his stomach churned.

The timepiece upon the mantle had chimed three times to indicate mid-afternoon when Gethen paused his finger upon a name and mumbled, "Sulwen," as he read, reread, and translated a passage of Quoregna's first written language: "I triumphed in the battle and defeated the witch. She is trapped forever and the garment of winter snow is a river of life once more. The sun shines upon Kharayan today and forever." He nodded. "Yes. Sulwen."

He'd carefully scanned entries that spanned almost eleven hundred years before finding the only description that didn't include death, mayhem, torture, and elaborate descriptions of how to remove the entrails from people and animals while prolonging their lives and suffering. His predecessors were, on the whole, a bloodthirsty and brutal lot.

Sulwen had imprisoned the Rime Witch in the Void. But someone — probably Shemel — had freed her and given her the strength to reach across the Voidline. He closed the book and stood.

He needed to speak with the Sun Mage before his magic failed completely. Though he'd received a gift of power from both the animals of Kharayan and from Halina, that strength wouldn't last. But, unlike the dead shadow mages, Sulwen wasn't imprisoned in Ranith's mausoleum and catacombs. Her body was entombed somewhere in the citadel, and if he was to have any hope of summoning her, he needed something of hers — a bone, a lock of hair, a tooth.

Gethen glared at the open cabinet. Just thinking of the reliquary made his skin crawl, but today he'd have to open it. He returned the register to its hiding place then passed his hand over the hinged face of the metal box. Like the citadel and the mausoleum, the Reliquary of the Mages bore grotesques of every kind carved into its surface, and there was no question that within the black box he'd find death. He uttered a spell and its doors clicked open.

The must of the grave wafted out and Gethen stepped back to let the air clear. Inside were thin, fabric-lined shelves that slid out with a gentle tug. Arrayed upon those shelves were bone fragments, teeth, and fingernails all wrapped in curses and black magic.

With a calculated guess, he moved down from the top, finding the century he wanted, and then slid out one of the little shelves. He grimaced as the tainted sorcery that lingered on the remains filled his mouth with the metallic taste of blood and whispered murder inside his mind.

It took two more tries before he found the correct shelf. Unlike her fellow mages, Sulwen had left a thin braid of shiny, black hair. Gethen fingered the silky strands, getting a sense of the power, warmth, and authority that Sulwen had commanded in life.

He returned the braid and closed the reliquary and the cabinet. Then he headed back to the great hall, wiping his hands upon his tunic. His destination was the basilica. Sulwen's body was buried there; the trace of magic he'd absorbed from handling the Sun Mage's relic was directing him to her grave. From there he'd contact her spirit.

His footsteps echoed off the arched ceiling and high walls as he passed through Ranith's largest room. Glancing at the windows, he stopped mid-stride.

Magod had cleared the snow from the glass, but he'd had to tunnel through the drifts to reach the sills. Ranith was being entombed. These were siege tactics at their finest, and soon enough the witch wouldn't have to send her creatures to destroy Gethen, because he and his companions would starve. He could summon fire to light and heat the citadel, but he couldn't conjure food from nothing.

Shaking his head, he turned down the low, narrow hallway that led beneath the bailey and into the basilica's narthex.

"Master."

Gethen stopped at Magod's call. The man had descended the main stairs.

"The militess has asked for you."

"Very well." The basilica and Sulwen would have to wait.

As Gethen reached the second floor, Noni's harsh laughter carried down the hallway. Upon entering the stillroom, he was greeted by wolves and their pups growling and scampering beneath the table and around the chairs. Bundled herbs and dried flowers were strewn across the floor, and a parchment bin had been upended, its contents tattered and scattered.

"Stop!" he commanded and all of the animals obeyed. Gethen strode through the room, saying to Magod over his shoulder: "The wolves have been housebound too long. Get them away from my ingredients and materials."

Magod bowed, clapped his hands, and then dodged the thundering wolves as they charged past him and into the hallway. They were as anxious to escape the citadel for the fresh air as Gethen was to have them away from his equipment.

Halina was upright among her pillows when Gethen entered the room. She watched him, direct and unflinching. Clearly she was un-embarrassed by the kiss they'd shared that morning. The bruises and cuts that had marred her face now were healing, but left a sickly greenish cast around her eyes and mouth. Still, it was a vast improvement over the swelling and brutality that had distorted her skin when Gethen had found her in the woods.

"You wished to see me, Your Ladyship?"

"Yes. The pain in my leg is much reduced, and my breathing has vastly improved thanks to your servants' diligent care and your excellent medicine."

"I'm glad to hear that. Noni, have you checked her leg?"

"Thought you should see it." The housekeeper watched him with avid, unblinking eyes. Shemel had followed his movements that way, judging, looking for weakness and an opportunity to strike. It was unsettling and strange. She'd never made him feel uneasy before. Then, again, he was acutely aware of Halina — her warmth, the scent of honey and metheglin coming from her skin.

Perhaps it was proximity to the militess, and not the housekeeper's stare, that made him edgy.

"May I touch you?" he asked Halina, his hands hovering above her blanket.

Her lips curved into a slow, sensual smile. "Please."

Khotyr, take me. He watched her mouth even as he folded back the blankets to reveal her bandaged thigh and braced for the inevitable heat and desire that would flood him with his first touch. Yes, King Vernard had known exactly what he was doing when he'd sent Halina across Gethen's path.

"Noni, make me a pot of tea," Halina ordered.

The older woman started as if she'd been deep in thought. "Tea, Your Ladyship?"

"Yes. Tea. There's a whole room full of herbs over there," Halina waved her hand toward the stillroom door. "You must be able to brew a pot of ebonberry tea. Do it."

"Yes, Your Ladyship." Noni curtsied and left.

Halina leaned forward and deliberately wrapped her fingers around Gethen's wrist.

Fire surged through him. He almost jerked away, but she held fast, and he relaxed.

She closed her eyes, blew out a breath, then met his gaze and swallowed, her eyes darkening. "Whatever this is between us, I don't want it to interfere with the responsibilities we have to the people of Khara and Ursinum. We're not young and inexperienced, easily swayed by notions of love or driven to distraction by lust. If you wish for it to be a source of strength for your magic and nothing more, I'll accept that. But I want to know now. And I want it to be clearly understood by both of us. I'm not amused by games."

"All right." He moved closer. "What if I want more?"

"Do you?"

"Yes." He cupped her jaw and kissed her hard, deep, demanding and challenging.

Her grip tightened on his wrist. Her other hand caught the front of his dark blue tunic and held him captive.

Aware of her wounds, he released her jaw and planted his hand against the wall behind her, stopping himself from climbing onto the bed and tearing off her thin, white nightgown.

Halina moaned and tried to pull him closer, but Gethen locked his arm. If he gave in to desire, he'd push her healing body too hard. And he smelled somniferum on her breath. He'd wait until she was well, until he knew her thinking was sharp. He'd wait. But, gods, she tasted sweet and she was the only thing in his world at that moment. The storm, the witch, the war — all were buried beneath the softness of Halina's lips, the sweetness of her tongue, and the smell of earth and fire on her breath and skin.

Gethen pulled back, pressed his lips to her hair, and said, "I came here to check your leg." He was hard for her and backing off was agony, but one of them had to be sensible. Clearly, it wasn't going to be her.

Halina sighed and stretched languidly like a cat until some muscle or nerve protested, and then she grimaced and went limp against the pillows.

"Semele's blood, do you know what you're doing to me, woman?" he said, his voice husky.

She smiled up at him through half-closed eyes. "Of course I do."

Gethen laughed and returned to the stillroom for his medical supplies. He downed two drams of oxymel to cool his fires then mixed another healing tincture for Halina. He returned to her side and gave her the metheglin. "That'll speed your recovery and deepen your sleep."

The wind howled outside and the fire on the grate flared and fluttered. "Damnable witch," he muttered.

Halina downed the mead then said, "Indeed. She's dampening our pleasure."

"She's using you against me."

"What? How?"

Gethen straightened from re-bandaging her leg. "She ushered you across my wards. She thought she was sending me a damsel she could distress, and she certainly didn't expect this." He bent over her and slid his fingers from her cheek to her jaw to her chest, leaving a trail of heat and an amber glow. Halina gasped. He smiled. "You strengthen me. And when the witch realized that, she attacked you, which forced me to expend my own dark sorcery in your defense."

"That fen-sucking troll."

He nodded. "Indeed."

"But why hasn't she attacked you?"

"I don't know."

"Before this cusp thing happened, you were stronger than her, right?"

"Yes. She couldn't have matched me."

"But now you're vulnerable and you think she's trying to weaken you?" Gethen nodded and Halina continued. "Well, if my enemy has a superior weapon, I want to take it from their hands and use it myself. So, I'll chip away at their defenses until they're weak and tired. Then, when they're vulnerable, I'll move aggressively to break them and take that weapon. My guess is that she doesn't want you dead. She wants you weak enough that she can use you the way she used the stag and your shadow."

It made sense. He nodded slowly. "You're right." He stood beside the bed, his hands clasped tightly. "The good news is that the Rime Witch was defeated before, so we can do it again."

"How?" The word came slowly; the draught was already working.

"I'll explain after you've rested."

Her eyelids fluttered closed. "Good." And then she slept.

A shadow fell across the doorway that led from the stillroom into the hallway. Gethen turned expecting Noni to enter with Halina's tea. Instead, she hovered just out of sight.

He returned to the stillroom, closing the infirmary door behind him. "Come here."

"No tea, Master," she said from the hall, and her footsteps retreated from his doorway. What was wrong with the woman? She'd never been sly or disobedient. Overbearing, mothering, and opinionated, yes, but it wasn't in her nature to skulk behind doors.

Magod must have told her I'm sending them away. He blew out a slow breath. That was probably what had upset her. He didn't have time for this. He had a sun mage to summon from beyond the grave.

Gethen left for the basilica, lighting the dark passages with mage fire. He'd expected it to return to its normal green hue — it had only ever been green — but the amber light persisted. It burned hotter and brighter, too. It was a good omen. He reached the basilica's massive doors and laughed at himself as he wove the spell to unlock them. Apparently, the Rime Witch was making him superstitious; he'd never believed in omens.

His footfalls echoed through the enormous, empty room. Wings fluttered and rushed as pigeons and songbirds took flight. He paused just past the doors, allowing the birds and their debris to settle.

Gethen gritted his teeth. He hated the place. It had been the site of much of his physical and mental suffering. Shemel had enjoyed torturing his apprentice so much that Gethen had finally murdered him in the basilica after one particularly long and brutal night.

He strode down the center of the massive space, pausing only when he'd passed through the transept and reached the edge of the apse. This was where he'd gutted the bastard. The master mage had lured two wolf pups into the basilica, and then summoned an ijiraq — a demon that hunted animals — to chase and slaughter them. It had been one of Shemel's favorite amusements, because it tortured his apprentice. Gethen had been so raw after eight years of suffering, of being belittled, beaten, and neglected, that he'd seen red when he'd realized what his master was doing. Noni had found him hours later, writing incantations on the floors and walls with Shemel's blood.

He looked up at the round stained glass window in the center of the apse's head wall. "If that window remains intact when so many others in this building have fallen to ruin, then there must be a reason." Something had given him the strength to challenge and destroy his older, stronger, and far more powerful master.

"Are you here, Sulwen?" He stepped upon the dais and began studying the marble and tile floor. "Have you been beneath the basilica all these centuries?"

In the middle of the apse a rectangle of honey-colored marble disrupted the white pattern that covered the rest of the floor. "Is this your tomb?

He knelt upon the golden-hued marble and contemplated the basilica. He'd assumed it was built by former shadow mages, the same men who'd erected Ranith. But now that he considered the stained glass windows, it was clear that those depicting depraved scenes were newer, and their quality was not so fine as the one featuring the Sun Mage. The basilica was older than the tower and the keep.

Shemel had hated the place. "Every shadow mage despises the basilica, boy," he'd said often enough. Gethen had presumed it was because every apprentice had been tortured there.

After Shemel's murder, he'd locked the basilica and not returned. Magod had used it for storage until the rats made that impossible.

Shemel had only brought Gethen there at night, often leaving him alone after blocking his ability to summon light. "You need to embrace the darkness and its cold, hungry dwellers," he'd snarled.

Gethen peered into the shadowy aisles and coves. He'd never seen it fully illuminated. "What does this place look like?" With a whisper, his mage fire rose, swelled, and brightened until it filled the tall, long room with its amber light.

"Khotyr, take me," he murmured.

The white marble ceiling shone with golden sun symbols and geometric patterns — lines of shining gold leading the eye. There were swirled circles of golden marble, like tightly-petaled flowers, decorating the corners of all the windows and the apexes of the ribbed arches. Dust and filth dulled every surface, but the beauty of the space was unmistakable. And it was unquestionable that the basilica had been built not for the shadows but for the sun.

"This building was yours first, Sulwen." He flattened his palms against the golden marble upon which he knelt and began the incantation to summon her spirit. As he did, the mage fire slowly faded to a dull glow. Gethen's muscles cramped across his back and shoulders. His fingers and feet grew numb. Still he intoned and spent more of his waning strength in summoning the Sun Mage. His power ebbed. His voice faded to a whisper. And his head sank until his forehead touched cold, yellow stone. Finally, he was silent, his eyes closed, and his body trembling, cramping, cold.

Then light shot up through the cracks between the great golden slab and the surrounding white marble into which it was set, forming a cage of golden light within which Gethen knelt. Warmth suffused him, like the warmth he felt upon touching Halina but even more powerful, and a mellifluous voice filled his mind, its words spoken in the old common tongue.

"I have long awaited your call, Shadow Mage."

"You know me?"

"Of course. Shemel spilled much of your blood upon my gravestone. It seeped through the cracks and onto my dust and bones. Though I had no tears, I wept for you many nights and yearned to comfort you, the boy who would become the second sun mage."

"How did you know?"

"Have the acolytes forsaken the sun so quickly?" She took the form

of a golden orb, and Gethen shielded his eyes as she floated around him.

"The old ways die. Our gifts have been forgotten and the new religions convince the kings that we are as much threat as ally."

"Has the telling of my war with the Rime Witch become so diluted that Quoregna's kings do not know the signs of her return?"

"Much has been lost. There are only disjointed tales rarely told. I've neither heard nor read the true and complete accounting of your triumph."

"Yet you knew to recall my spirit from the Void."

"A lucky guess led me to you, driven by my need for information about the Rime Witch."

"She has crossed the Voidline?"

"She's reached across to cover Kharayan with ice and start a war between Ursinum and Besera."

"Then Ranith and Kharayan are not secure."

"Agreed. Already the witch has turned my own wraiths against my champion. I fear she knows my thoughts before I do. How did you defeat her?"

"It matters not how I fought her. It is through you that warmth must flow so that change may come. Harness the fire of the heavens. Use that power to imprison the Rime Witch in the Void."

"I only know how to harness the shadows."

"Not true. You were not born to be in the shadows, Beseran. You belong under the sun. But your strength comes from your knowledge of both the darkness and the light."

Gethen raised his hands, palms up. "I'm powerless."

"No. You are balanced upon the apex of night and day, and you are at your weakest as your dark sorcery fails. But soon the sun will rise within you as your protector empowers you. The time for warmth has come."

"I understand."

"If the witch captures you during your weakest hour, she will consume all your sorcery, destroy the Voidline, and unchain the shadow mages. Your champion must protect you when you cannot or darkness, murder, and

madness will rule the world. The more you struggle against change, Gethen, the longer you will remain vulnerable. Harness the sun."

"How?"

"Trust its magic within you. Embrace the change it brings and discover your true potential. Until this day you have witnessed only the shadow of your power. Leave Ranith and Kharayan. Take only your protector and do not reveal your destination to anyone but her."

Gethen frowned. "I trust my servants with my life."

"As the Rime Witch knows. She uses anything and anyone to her advantage, and your trust in them may blind you to deception."

"They are loyal—"

"And she will use them against you." Sulwen's voice softened. *"Trust me. Leave them, so that they may be spared the witch's attention, and you may be spared their blood upon your hands. Go where you can be protected by your champion and where you can safely welcome the sun's warmth, light, and power."*

Gethen stood and bowed to the golden orb. "Thank you for your advice, Sulwen." He then quickly unraveled the spell that had reached well past the Voidline to snag her spirit. The orb dissipated and the basilica returned to silence and mystery.

With dim mage fire to lead his way, Gethen staggered from the basilica and closed the great copper-clad doors, perhaps for the last time. The metallic sound of those massive doors clanging shut and the locks sliding and clanking home added finality to his departure, and he leaned heavily upon them, his muscles aching and his head pounding from the draining spell he'd maintained.

He'd be leaving Ranith, and he might never return. Gethen straightened his shoulders. He couldn't afford self-pity or doubt. His world was changing, he was changing, but his old self remained. He strode toward the living area of the citadel. It was time to embrace the sun's magic. To turn away from this new role was to invite enslavement, suffering, and death — for all of Quoregna. "That's a cheerful thought," he muttered, "and a lot of weight for one man to shoulder." As if feeling that weight, his muscles shuddered and his feet slowed.

"Where'd you go?" Noni stood on the first landing of the great stairwell, her hands on her hips. "Been searching the citadel for two hours. Thought you'd gone off into the storm without telling me."

He reached her side but looked past her toward the second level and the stillroom. He sucked in a deep breath and straightened, banishing exhaustion and aches. "Does Her Ladyship require aid?" Had the Rime Witch struck while he was speaking with Sulwen and feeling sorry for himself?

"No, no. Just wondered where you'd gone. Don't like you wandering off without saying anything."

Those words slid under Gethen's skin and worked his patience loose. "What I do is not your business. Keep to your own work and stay out of mine, unless I invite you into it." He headed up the stairs, ignoring the little curse she sent after him. Clearly she disliked his tone. But her obedience would keep her alive.

In the stillroom Gethen considered all the tinctures, bottles, herbs, and pots, wondering what to pack. Deciding it depended upon Halina's needs, he knocked on the infirmary door. Her voice was strong when she called for him to enter.

She was standing beside the window, wrapped in a blanket, as she combed her hair. Gethen closed the door and went to her side. "I'm glad you're well enough to be out of bed." He slipped the comb from her fingers and took over the task. He made quick work of it, starting at the ends and moving upward in small sections.

Halina shrugged. "I couldn't sit on my arse any longer." She closed her eyes. "How do you know how to work out the snarls so adeptly?"

"Shemel made me grow mine for eight years. After I cut his throat, I cut my hair."

Halina snorted. "Prick."

"Him or me?"

"Both."

"Quite right." Her hair fell in long, thick ringlets past her shoulders. "You have beautiful hair, Halina."

"I suppose you won't want me to cut it."

"I'm not Shemel," he said as he handed her the comb. "And I know you'd slit my throat if I tried to tell you what to do."

She smiled. "Smart man."

Gethen separated several sections and began braiding her hair in the soldier's style that she preferred. "Does your leg hurt?"

"Some, but it's holding my weight. I won't be winning any races or dancing a rondel in the weeks to come."

"No. But you *will* be traveling." She turned from the window, her brow furrowed, as he continued. "You and I are leaving Ranith. We're doing it quickly, and we're not informing my servants of our destination."

"How long will we be gone?"

"As long as it takes for my power to transition from shadow to sun." Noni's shuffling footsteps caught his attention, and Gethen turned to see the woman in the doorway. "Fetch Magod." And he turned away as she curtsied and said, "Yes, Master."

Halina's gaze slid from the housekeeper's retreating figure to the Shadow Mage's face. "You don't trust her?"

Gethen lowered his voice. "It's not a matter of trust. For everyone's safety they can't know our destination. She won't understand and will be upset with me for years to come — provided we have years — but sometimes we must hurt those we care for." He indicated Halina's chain mail shirt. "Do you need help?"

She considered the armor then said, "If I can't dress myself then I can't protect you. I'll be fine but for some of the buckles." He nodded and excused himself from the room.

He was assembling a kit of unguent and herbs when Magod and Noni arrived. The housekeeper came straight to his side, distress pulling her mouth down at the corners and furrowing her brow. "Don't send us away, Master. Let us help. We've always helped."

Gethen touched her wrinkled hand. "Plans have changed. You're not leaving Ranith. The Militess and I are. I require clothing and two bedrolls, as well as food for three days, packed and provided to Magod to be added to my saddle." To the groundsman he said, "Ready Remig and fetch my longsword."

Magod nodded, but Noni clutched Gethen's arm. "Going where? How long? Don't you trust us?"

"I trust both of you with my life. But I can't answer any of your questions. This silence is for your protection. Now, quickly do as I've asked. If all goes well on this venture, the Militess and I will return soon, and I'll have the strength to lift the Rime Witch's curse from Khara and restore peace between Ursinum and Besera."

Noni opened her mouth as if to argue, but Magod grabbed her elbow and steered her away. Gethen frowned then returned to his medicinals. When he was satisfied that he'd packed everything he'd require, he knocked on the infirmary door.

Halina opened it. She was dressed and armed but said, "I need your nimble fingers to check all these straps and buckles." She held her arms away from her sides.

He schooled his hands not to stray as he tightened the side buckles on her plate armor. It followed the curves of her figure, and he was reminded of the taut muscles and pale skin beneath the leather and metal. Gethen flattened the strap that crossed her back, adjusted the pauldrons capping her shoulders, and tightened the metal tassets that protected her hips and thighs — one of them damaged by her own dagger.

She affixed her sword frog to her belt, and he tightened it at her waist. She'd managed her left vambrace and had it buckled, but her mending left hand prevented her from tackling the other. This he took and buckled on over her gambeson's sleeve and the cuff of her gloves. Finally, he held open her demi-gauntlets and Halina slid her hands into them. Gethen lowered his hands to his sides, but he didn't want to leave the space she occupied.

Halina met his gaze, her blue eyes steady even as they grew dark with the same desire coursing through his veins. "Well done and quickly, Master Gethen," she said.

"In this," he moved his hand as if stroking her body, "I know what I'm doing."

Her lips slowly curved. "We shall see."

Gethen placed a finger beneath her chin and gently tilted her head back. This time she didn't complain as he placed a long, slow kiss on her mouth. He only stepped back when the sound of wolves reached them from the stillroom. "Do you want help gathering your belongings?"

"I'm ready to leave." She indicated her haversack on the chair beside the bed.

Noni appeared in the doorway. "Your bag and horse are waiting, Master." Her expression was unreadable as she held out his tarnished, silver Beseran coin. "Take this, please. It'll be like I'm with you."

"If that old token will help ease your mind, Noni, I'll gladly carry it," Gethen said. Her fingers were cold as they brushed his. "When did you become so sentimental?"

She turned away with a shake of her head. "I've always seen you as another son, though I know it's wrong."

He smiled and squeezed her arm. "All will be well. I'll gather the information I need and will return to Ranith before you've grown accustomed to my absence." He turned to Halina. "Are you prepared to ride?"

"Always. Bed rest never suits me."

Gethen stepped aside and beckoned her to precede him. "Then let us act, Militess Halina."

FIFTEEN

"Doubtless Vernard ran as the first snowflake slapped his face. And I'm certain he sealed the passes through the Valmerians behind him." Halina gazed above Kharayan's snow-topped trees to where the towering mountains were hidden by the storm. Their height and the thick snow blanketing them would prevent the king's enemies from following. She clenched her fist. "He's abandoned Khara." It was the first time she'd been out of the citadel since the attack; the first chance she'd had to comprehend the enormity of what Vernard had done.

"He's abandoned you," Gethen said. They were standing in the stable while Magod secured her haversack to Remig's saddle.

She waved his words away. "He did that before I was even born." She stared at her armored hand for a moment then said, "He abandoned my citizens." She let her hand fall to her sword grip. "I'm sure he took my troops, too." Her lips pressed into a thin line. "Khara stands alone."

Gethen emerged from the shadows. "I'd cut off his bollocks, but the bastard hasn't got any."

She laughed without humor. "I wish that were true, but the

snow is the only reason Khara isn't burning from border to border right now."

Noni stared at her. "What do you mean, Your Ladyship?"

Gethen answered. "If he could've, Vernard would've burned the entire holding rather than allow my brother to obtain any resources from the land and tenants.

"I'm sorry to remove you from Khara, Margrave. But I can't return until the power of the Sun Mage has filled me and I've learned to wield that magic."

She stood with her hands on her hips and both feet planted. "I've committed my sword and strength — such as it is — to protecting you, Master Gethen. There's a larger battle to be won than that which disturbs Khara's borders." Her chin lifted and resolve set her expression. "My tenants have faced war many times and still survive. Give them warning and they'll fight to the death. Of that I'm certain. But if we're to help them survive, it'll be in discovering whatever knowledge or magic you seek on this journey then returning quickly to Khara with the power to destroy the Rime Witch."

The snow outside the bailey was as high as Halina's eyes. They were fortunate that Magod had been diligent in keeping the area cleared. But mountains of white were piled around the gates and obscured the trunks of the trees. How would they get anywhere beyond Ranith?

"I'm leaving my wards in place around the citadel and Kharayan, though I'm unsure they'll hold in the woods," Gethen told Noni and Magod. "Keep the animals warm and well fed. I'll do what I can to be back before you run out of food and fodder. And light the warning beacon atop the citadel, Magod. Khara's people need to prepare for attack."

"Of course," Magod said.

"Why are we taking only one horse?" Halina asked as Gethen mounted Remig and offered his hand to her.

"Because I can't transport two people and two horses; I'm too weak. But I don't like to travel to parts unknown without an available mount." He helped her swing up onto the back of the horse.

"And that destination is?" she asked.

He pulled the horse's head around until they faced his servants. "Leave us now. I don't want you to know where we're going." Noni looked as if she would object, but Magod grabbed his mother's hand and pulled her back into the citadel's great hall, closing the massive wooden doors behind them. "You tell me, Militess," Gethen said.

She shook her head. "I don't understand. I'm only along to swing a sword."

"Yes, and this is one of the ways you're going to keep us both safe. I don't know if the Rime Witch has breached my mind. It seems unlikely, but if she has, then it's better that I not go somewhere familiar. So I'm leaving the choice of our destination to you. Someplace warm, if possible."

It was a surprising but logical decision, and she knew immediately where they should go. "Have you ever visited the Abbedei of Gurvan-Sum in Or-Halee?"

He shook his head. "I've never even heard of the place."

"Then it's perfect, except that it's on the opposite side of Quoregna." Halina's gesture took in the mountains, forest, and snow around them.

"Ah, that's not an insurmountable distance." Gethen touched her leg. "Do you trust me?"

"Yes."

"Good. Take my hand and describe the abbedei to me in as much detail as possible. I'll summon the last of my strength to weave an incantation around your description. Whatever you do, don't panic and don't stop describing every detail you can think of."

"I never panic." Halina clasped his hand, bracing against the ever-present spark that happened when they were united. "Do you want to hear of the people as well?" He nodded and she began.

"The abbedei is built of red and beige stacked stones, some ancient and some newer. It's an ever-changing cluster of tall buildings that are set into the stony, pinkish mountainsides of the Gurvan Range where the Sumum Spring first emerges from the rocks and drops over two hundred feet to crash into the mouth of the Sum River. The Gurvan Pass is dry much of the year, a cold desert during the winter and blistering when the sun is high in the summer. Few plants or animals live there, and those that do are tough, spiky, and more than willing to make a meal of you and me."

As she spoke amber mage fire swirled around them, lifting bits of snow with it, creating a cloud of glittering golden light. Gethen intoned his spell. Their palms grew warm. Her memories sharpened.

"It's spring there now, so yellow and purple matad flowers cover the ground at the base of the falls and spread through the valley, and white thistle globes stand as tall as my waist. The abbedei consists of many towers and squat buildings, and it hugs the mountainside. You'd think it was built by spirits and giants rather than a single man and his large family." She smiled at the memory of Appa Unegen and all of the children, grandchildren, and great-grandchildren who chased each other up and down the precipitous stairs and winding paths that made up the abbedei.

She closed her eyes. Despite Gethen's grasp, she was colder than she'd ever been, colder even than after the Rime Witch's attacks. She shivered against his wide back. His fingers tightened on hers. She opened her eyes again.

The snow and amber light swirled around them faster and faster, a dizzying dance. She'd be sick and fall off the horse if she kept her eyes open, so she closed them and remembered: "Inside the abbedei the paths are worn smooth with time and the passage of so many feet. The building is older than Or-Halee, older than

Quoregna. The walls bear brightly colored murals — red, blue, yellow, green, orange, purple — the most beautiful colors you've ever seen painted within a building. The pictures tell the story of Khotyr's creation of the world and of the struggles between Skiron and Semele to control the light.

"Sound echoes from the bottom of the abbedei all the way to the top, and if you close your eyes in the middle of the day and turn a circle you won't know if you're in the kitchens or outside standing above the precipice with the whole desert spread out before you. In some places, you can whisper and someone on the other side of the abbedei will hear your words.

"Appa Unegen is one of the kindest men I've ever met. He has a narrow face, a bald scalp, and he's so tall that it's a miracle he never bludgeons his forehead on the abbedei's low passages. He has a deep, mellow laugh but sounds like a donkey when he sings." She laughed.

"What do you smell when you're there?"

"Dirt and the damp spray of the waterfall. The delightful, warm scent of teff bread baking, chingis spices mixed with rice and amsoth beans. Sweet matad flowers. The honey the appa's sons collect from the bees that feed upon those flowers. There's the sharp scent of fire, fueled by the oils of the songin bushes; the smoke makes my nose itch and I always sneeze the first time I smell it. It flavors the breads and meats. Everything smells like it."

"Open your eyes, Halina." Gethen's grip upon her hand eased. "Have we arrived?"

Shouts and ululation answered his question. Remig stood in the middle of the abbedei's yellow-clay bailey, and a crowd of adults and children surged toward them. Or-Haleean greetings filled the air. Halina laughed at the traditional welcome.

"Militess! Tavta!"

"Tavta morgitun!"

"Tavta!"

"What's the meaning of this?" A thick voice echoed back and

forth across the bailey, rising to the heights of the abbedei and sinking to the plains below. It was the appa. Halina smiled, warmed by the sight of the man and the sound of his resonant voice. She hadn't realized how much she'd missed the abbedei and its residents.

Gethen swung his leg over the horse's head and slid to the ground. He caught Halina and steadied her as she, too, came off Remig's back quickly, forgetting the weakness in her leg. She staggered, grabbed hold of the mage, then stepped away hastily.

She was enveloped in arms and hands, passed from grandmother to mother, sister to aunt, brother to uncle, and finally landed in the arms of the appa himself.

"So, it's fierce Halina," he said and planted two large, wet kisses upon her cheeks. "What brings you back to Gurvan-Sum, and where are all your soldiers?"

She turned to introduce Gethen but was arrested by the sight of him. He trembled uncontrollably, held up only by leaning against the horse. His eyes were closed, circled by darkness. His face was gaunt. She'd seen him look so depleted once before, and she reached for him with a steadying hand. "You may not die on me, Shadow Mage," she said as she draped his arm across her shoulders and caught him about the waist.

Gethen mumbled, "Trying not to."

The appa's grandson, Qulan, went to his other side, and Unegen led them into the warm shadows of the abbedei.

They were taken to one of the topmost rooms, a place of warmth and sunlight. It was Halina's turn to play nursemaid to the sorcerer, and he could do nothing but shake and sway while she pulled his cloak from his shoulders, eased him down to the bed, and removed his boots. She opened the wooden shutters to flood the space with sunlight and warmth.

Gethen closed his eyes and mumbled, "It's gone." He'd spent the last of his shadow magic escaping Ranith. "All of it."

The Sun Mage's time had come. Halina wanted nothing to

stop that transition. Whether he was asleep or near death she couldn't tell, so she sat beside him, their fingers entwined as she gazed out the window and watched the shadows change as the sun climbed slowly toward its zenith.

The appa and his wife came to her room hours later.

"I owe you an explanation," she said.

Amma Xana bowed, took a chair beside the cold hearth, and folded her hands in her lap. "Why have you brought the Shadow Mage here?"

The appa's brows were deeply furrowed. "Were it any other person who had endangered my family thusly, she and this man would have been driven from the abbedei." Anger made his voice shake.

Halina nodded. "I understand. And I wouldn't ask you to provide hospitality for a man such as the Shadow Mage, if it weren't of the utmost importance and urgency that I keep him safe and secret." She removed her sword and armor as she explained their presence. "Gethen was the Shadow Mage when we left Ranith. But he depleted his dark sorcery with the incantation that brought us here and is now crossing the cusp into sun from shadow."

Xana peered intently at him. "Is it so? The time of the Sun Mage has finally returned?"

Unegen folded his hands and exchanged a look with his wife. "Xana has portended this. The stories reaching us from Ursinum, Besera, and Nalvika say winter has come too soon and too fiercely. Are they true?"

"As true as I'm a woman and a warrior. Snow blankets Khara, taller than I stand. My father has closed the passes and withdrawn his forces from the shores of the Silver Sea. And that vast water nears freezing."

The appa's expression darkened as he considered Gethen. "You're certain this man is not the cause of such misfortunes?"

"I'm his protector. Of that there can be no doubt."

Xana stood and went to Halina. She touched the fading bruises upon her face and hands, bumped her fingers over Halina's damaged knuckles and said, "It is as I foretold. This is why we saved your life after the Battle of Sum."

Halina gaped at her. "You foresaw the rise of the Rime Witch?"

"No, only that you were meant for some great task, and if we failed to twice shelter you, the world would fall to darkness and ruin." She pointed at Unegen and added, "I told you so."

The appa shrugged. "You know how these things go, Militess." He waved his hand. "Smoke, sweat, and too much oxymel, and my wife fancies herself an oracle."

Xana returned to his side and slapped his arm. "I must not be too bad at it. I certainly earn enough coin from the Emirs of Or-Halee to keep you fattened with bracket and fried fish." He laughed but quickly sobered as his wife continued: "You're right to keep the shades up while the sun travels the sky's great arc, Militess. But close them before sunset and don't open them before sunrise. Your mage will be most vulnerable in the night and the dark. That's when you must remain at his side, vigilant, and ready to destroy the Rime Witch's servants."

"Will she find us here? He thought to go someplace from my memories rather than his own."

Xana squinted and slowly nodded. "That'll test her abilities, but the longer his transition takes, the more time she'll have to scry his whereabouts. Do what you can to hasten his change."

"I will," Halina said. "I know we're endangering you with our presence." She slipped off the bed and bowed to her hosts. "Thank you again for your hospitality."

Unegen said, "I'll have some of the boys move a pallet and bedding in here."

Halina nodded. "It's best if I stay here. I don't know what to expect from the Rime Witch or the mage's transition."

"Agreed," the amma said.

A pallet bed with a straw-stuffed mattress, thick wool blankets, and furs was brought into the room, along with their haversacks and Gethen's sword. The room faced east and the morning sun warmed it until, sweating in her gambeson, Halina stripped down to her white chemise and pulled on the only front-lacing kirtle Noni had found for her, a wine-red one. She'd borrow clothing from their hosts, if they remained longer than a few days.

The whole process of changing was awkward and painful, and she kept glancing toward the sleeping mage, knowing what she'd do if he woke and saw her undressing, unsure if he'd go along with it. She shoved the thought from her mind. The heat it evoked went with it. She fumbled to get the gown laced then donned her belt and longsword. She unpacked her haversack and emptied his, pausing on the tarnished silver coin Noni had pushed into his hand as they were leaving.

On one face a bee perched upon a liminth flower. The other side had a gold circle struck into its center. A jagged and angry *X* spanned from edge to edge and passed through the circle; it had been scratched into the surface. The coin was cold and heavy. Dread made Halina frown as she held it. She shivered and dropped it on the windowsill where the sun could warm it. She brushed her hands upon her skirt as if to rub off something foul and dirty.

Gethen stirred and turned away from the window, murmuring something in his sleep. As he did, the coin flashed in the sunlight.

The mark was strange. The coin troubled her. Perhaps Xana could tell her more about it. The woman was scholarly and versed in many languages and cultures.

Baichu, the appa's youngest daughter, brought a tray of food to Halina. She stared wide-eyed at Gethen's unmoving figure and Halina's sword. "Is it true you're guarding the mage, Militess?" she asked as she sat down to share the meal.

"You've not become less forward in the years since I left Gurvan-Sum."

"No." Baichu scooped up magluba — a dish of amsoth beans, rice, vegetables, peppers, and goat's milk — with a piece of the dark brown teff bread baked daily in the abbedei's clay ovens.

The food was spicy. Halina sucked air over her burning tongue and wiped her running nose with a napkin. "That's not information I want leaving the abbedei."

Baichu smiled. "Of course it won't. We love our secrets, and you and your mage have become our most beloved one. Nothing makes Amma Xana happier than to have a good secret. It makes her feel wiser and worldlier than the most experienced travelers who cross our gates. She knows something they never will, no matter how many stones pass beneath their feet."

Halina laughed. "Indeed she does."

Baichu's smile turned just as quickly to a scowl as she added, "Except she won't share all the secrets with us. Only she and Appa Unegen know the whole story of you and your mage." She eyed Gethen, then her attention slid like oil on water to Halina. "Unless you'd like to whisper it in my ear. Then I'll have something to hide from Amma. So you see, it won't go any further."

Halina pressed the back of her hand to her lips, the Or-Haleean sign for *silence* and *secret*.

Baichu shrugged. "It was worth trying." But her interest continued to stray to Gethen as they ate and she nattered away about the activities around the abbedei and her younger daughter's prospects of marriage to a sheep merchant who regularly went between Sumum and Gad-Dargan. "Handsome and smart, with keen eyes for Vachi. I think he'll make a fine husband, but Amma's getting the stories about him from the other wives in the caravan. That's how you know if a man's really as good as he wants you to believe, eh?"

Halina nodded and glanced at Gethen, too. He hadn't stirred since she'd removed the coin. When her focus returned to the food and bracket before her, she caught Baichu's knowing look. "What?"

"Does he know how you feel?"

Her face warmed. "Our situation isn't as simple as a passing trader and the appa's granddaughter making eyes at each other." She waggled her eyebrows at Baichu.

"But you've been injured for him."

Halina stared at her. "Who told you that? Because it's not exactly correct."

Baichu ate an olive, swallowed, and said, "You're guarding him and your limp is obvious. So is that injured hand, your bruised face, and the stiffness of bones his magic only recently fixed. You've been with him for weeks, so you must have gained those injuries in his service. Why?"

"Because Quoregna will pay a high price if his safety is compromised. He's not just some small healer."

"No. He's the Shadow Mage. He's your tenant, right?"

Halina licked magluba from her fingers. "So?"

"I doubt you go so far to protect all your tenants like this." She leaned close and her voice deepened. "And this one's danger- ous." Her right eyebrow rose as she asked, "How does he hold you, the Margrave of Khara, in thrall?"

Halina sniffed and shoved bread into her mouth. She washed down the large bite with bracket, glanced again at the unmoving mage, and said, "He doesn't. I've agreed to protect him until he no longer requires me."

"*Requires*. And if he *desires* you?"

"*What if I want more?*"

Halina still felt Gethen's mouth on hers and his fingers on her jaw, holding her, demanding she match his passion, his body daring her to deny him. She shoved another piece of bread in her mouth and waved the question away, chewing hard. The bread formed a lump. She swallowed it with more bracket, grimacing at its slow, painful progress down her throat. Finally, she said, "Baichu, you're as salacious as a whoremonger and an embarrassment to the appa. How is it that you have *any* unmarried daughters at all?"

She laughed. "Vachi is my shame. I wanted her married off years ago, mule-headed thing. She's as stubborn as you." But her broad smile and bright eyes spoke only of adoration for the girl. Baichu relished love and rumors. She only wanted happiness for everyone she cared about, including Halina.

Hours later, when they'd finished eating and chatting, Baichu hugged her and took the tray. "Do you want a light meal after the sun sets? I can bring enough for both of you."

Halina shook her head. "I doubt he'll awaken until tomorrow. The incantation that brought us here drained an already taxed mage. I'll come to the kitchen for my own supper; I want to ask Amma Xana a question."

Baichu nodded and left, the tray balanced on her head and her sweet voice echoing through the halls as she sang a song about love and death.

Halina went to the window and stared out at the desert valley. It spread toward forever from the feet of the abbedei's precipice.

Gethen stirred as a warm late-afternoon breeze filled the room with the sweetness of matad blossoms and the thick scent of magluba from the kitchen. The sunlight had changed from bright yellow to the golden hue of late day. Heavy iron bells rang. Lowing carried on the wind, cattle destined for the market at Or-Halee Cid. On the road above the abbedei's cliffside location, passing travelers made camp for the night and restocked their water from the spring. They'd trade goods for food with the abbedei and bring news from other parts of the world.

Gurvan-Sum stood near a crossroads on a heavily traveled and dangerous trade route that served Or-Halee Cid, Sumum, and Gad-Dargan. There were many opportunities to trade knowledge and goods between the travelers and the abbedei's residents.

Halina glanced at the prone mage then shuttered the windows, plunging the room into shadow. "I wish I could ward this place." She went to the bed and took in Gethen's drawn face. She reached out to touch his cheek, paused, retreated. She drew her sword and placed it upon the floor across the doorway. It wasn't much protection, but he'd said it held blood magic. "That's better than spit," she said.

She'd forgotten to ask Baichu to inquire after news of Khara and Ursinum from the travelers. If she hurried, she could catch her before the woman was too busy serving the evening meal to the traders. Halina snatched the coin from the windowsill and left Gethen to sleep as she trotted down the gently sloping hallway to the abbedei's bustling kitchen.

She could've found Gurvan-Sum's kitchen with her eyes closed. It was the noisiest room in the complex and emitted the most delicious aromas in all of Or-Halee. Teff bread baked in banks of clay ovens. Its sweet, earthy aroma filled her nose and made her mouth water. Another wall of the expansive room held four hearths, two with grates large enough to hold four enormous iron cooking pots, and two with double rows of spits. Thick stews, savory rice, hearty porridge, and flavorful vegetables bubbled away in the pots. Fish, beef, coney, and chicken turned on the spits, dripping juices into the fires beneath them and creating a chorus of hisses and pops.

Halina stopped in the doorway to inhale, then inhaled again. Her stomach rumbled. "Hush, gut, you just got full."

Qulan looked up from a long wooden table where he was filling a basket with fresh bread. "You look lost, Margrave."

She went to stand beside him. "Do I?" She accepted the chunk of warm bread he offered. "Strange, because I always feel at home in Gurvan-Sum."

Baichu turned from one of the spits. "The militess is searching for answers. Her heart and her mind are playing games."

Qulan leaned close to Halina. "Don't discuss your troubles with Baichu. She'll have you tied in knots so confusing not even a fisherman could help you unravel them." His wife threw a rag at them. Halina laughed as she caught it.

"Are you taking those up to the crossroads?" she asked, jerking her chin toward the basket of loaves. When he nodded, she said, "Would you inquire about news of Khara, Ursinum, and Besera? I've been a few weeks away from my hold and war was brewing between the kingdoms when I last saw King Vernard."

"War?" His eyebrows rose. "But Ursinum and Besera have always traded peacefully."

"Times change, Qulan."

"Not for the better, if there's talk of war." With an easy swing, he hefted the wide basket up to balance upon his head. "I'll ask for news, Militess." He strolled from the kitchen, ducking beneath the entry's low lintel without breaking his stride despite the weight and girth of the full basket.

A bowl of stew appeared before Halina. She looked up to see Xana offering it and a spoon. "You're too thin, Halina, and wan. Join my table, eat some more, and tell me what's drawn you from your mage's side this late in the afternoon."

As the amma spoke the coin in Halina's pocket gained weight and lost warmth. She followed the slender old woman through the crowd of men and women, girls and boys working in the enormous kitchen. They crossed the room to reach a table in a corner. It had been carved from the abbedei's stone and had three-legged stools tucked beneath it.

Halina sat and dug into the stew as Xana poured bracket into two tin cups. The food warmed her with spices and deliciousness. She swallowed three heaping spoonfuls before stopping to pull the coin from her pocket. She handed it to the amma. "Do you know anything about the marks on the back of this?"

Xana's smiling eyes darkened, her expression grew somber. "Did the mage give you this?"

"No. It's his from his housekeeper; they both come from Besera. I'm puzzled by the mark on its reverse."

"This is an evil omen," Amma Xana said as she pointed to the jagged X. "The circle is the sun, but it's been blotted out. And the cross through it means more than night, it means death." She dropped the coin upon the table, then spat on her hands and wiped them on her apron. "Whoever gave your mage that coin wants him dead."

SIXTEEN

G ethen awoke on his stomach. Sunlight streamed through an open window to fall across his face. He was too warm, and what a strange sensation that was. He couldn't remember the last time he'd been made uncomfortable by the sun's heat.

Halina slept on a pallet beside his bed. His hand hung over the side, and she'd propped her arm on two pillows so that her fingers could twine with his.

He studied her face. It was turned away from him. Her loose hair trailed across her shoulders and chest. She'd fallen asleep with his longsword at her side, waiting to spill blood for his sake.

He looked around and spied her weapon on the floor barring the doorway. It was a primitive sort of ward, effective enough with its blood magic to give them warning.

Gethen took in the curve of her high cheekbones, the splatter of reddish-brown freckles trailing like a constellation across her cheeks and over her nose, a few on her forehead. They dappled her chest, her shoulders, and her thighs; he'd noticed when he'd helped her after her injuries. Maybe they dapple her breasts. He pushed that tantalizing image away.

Halina's place in his maze of shadows was unclear. The militess had been offered up as goods at too steep a price. She'd proven to be a protector but also needed protection. She'd kissed him like a lover and he desired her above all others. She made him want. She made him want to survive, to win. She made him believe he could.

Halina was strength and hope.

She was his sun.

But how was he to harness this power? Certainly not by yoking her. She'd never submit to a man's control, and he wouldn't desire her if she did. That wasn't the woman he admired.

And he did admire her; there was no denying that. She'd given him strength and support. She'd been true to her word in coming along and protecting him, providing him a place of sanctuary that was closer to the power of the sun and filled with people who understood the strength and the warmth that came from daylight.

Gethen squinted at the window. How long had he slept? The sun hadn't reached its zenith, but it was past early morning. So Halina had awakened, opened the shutters to let the sunshine into the room, and returned to bed. She may have stayed up all night, sitting vigil at his bedside.

He slid his fingers from hers, swallowing a curse at the loss of her warmth and the coursing desire for her that he relished. As quietly as possible he slipped from the bed and ran his hands through his mussed hair. His mouth was pasty and tasted like mud. He tipped water into a cup from the ewer beside the bed, downed that, and drank two more cups before he felt human again. He stretched his arms toward the rough stone ceiling and scowled. He smelled worse than his breath tasted.

"I need a bath." But he hesitated to turn away from the sunshine and warmth spilling through the window. He was bliss-fully warm in a way that he couldn't remember ever being before, certainly not since he'd gone to live at Ranith.

He tried to summon his sorcery. But though fire stirred deep within him, he couldn't bring it forth anymore than he could draw up the shadows. "Still on the cusp," he muttered. He just needed time and knowledge. He squinted at the window. And more sunlight.

He moved to the sill, meaning to lean out and inhale the desert air, but his palm fell upon something round, metal, and cold. He looked down and yanked his hand away. It was the coin. The metal was colder than a witch's tit. He picked it up and immediately dropped it. It felt cursed.

He'd always kept the coin on the mantle above the fireplace in Ranith's solar until Noni had pressed it into his palm as he and Halina were preparing to leave the citadel. He turned it over and stared at the symbol on the back. Someone had cut a death cross through the sun.

"Militess, wake up."

Halina stirred in her sleep, murmured. Her eyelids fluttered open, closed, open again. She looked around with the puzzled expression of someone who'd fallen asleep and expected to awaken someplace else. She saw him and sat up. "How are you feeling?" Sleep thickened her voice and she yawned, hiding it behind a hand and a mumbled apology.

Gethen held the coin between his thumb and index finger. "I was feeling better until I saw this.

"That's how I found it yesterday." She rubbed her hands over her face then stood, grimacing as she limped around the bed and tried to stretch her leg, her back, and her arms. "I asked Amma Xana about it and hate what she told me."

Gethen dropped the coin on the sill. "It's a death cross put through the sun. Somebody wants me dead."

Halina looked down. "Who was the last person to have it in Ranith?"

His voice was fierce when he replied. "I know what you're thinking, but I trust Noni with my life. You expect me to believe she serves the Rime Witch?" He slashed the air with his hand. "Impossible."

Halina shook her head. She poured a glass of water and drained it before answering. "I don't expect you to believe that, no. But something's happened. Somehow the Rime Witch has cursed that coin."

Gethen ground his teeth as he gathered clean tunic, britches, and surcoat. "I want to bathe. I can't think past the smell of myself."

"I'll show you the way."

She led him through the sloping hallways and deeper into the mountain. As they descended, the air grew moist and the sound of falling water echoed against the walls. At last, they took a wide tunnel and a series of deep steps and came out into an area where the running Sum River had seeped down through cracks and created a broad, natural pool. A wool screen stretched across the cavern to separate the large bathing hole into two private areas, one for the women and one for the men.

Halina pointed him to the brushes, soap, and towels, then made for the women's side of the pool. Her sigh echoed in the room and the water rippled as she slipped into the bath. Gethen suppressed the urge to look around the curtain. Instead, he stripped off his own clothing. The water was surprisingly warm. "How is this heated?"

"The vents from the kitchen run beneath the pool and around the walls before emerging at ground level. There are more natural pools there. Travelers pay a penny to the abbedei to bathe and relax. It's five days from the closest inhabited town, and that one lacks baths, as well as anything civilized."

Their voices echoed throughout the chamber. Water dripped from the ceilings, condensation on the cooler stone above from the steam rising below. Lanterns lit the area, casting strange dancing shadows across the walls and over the shimmering water.

The stone was worn smooth from centuries of feet, hands, and arses.

Gethen found a natural shelf upon which to sit. He stretched his arms across the stony lip of the pool and laid his head back. He'd never been so content in his life. "I'm warm, Militess," he said.

Her laughter was light and held a note of puzzlement as she replied, "You say that as if it's a new experience, Mage."

"It is."

Water rippled beneath the divider as she moved around. She was swimming. Just beyond the curtain her auburn hair was sliding through the water, and her pale body was bare. *Think of something else before all the blood in your brain heads south.*

Halina asked, "Being the Shadow Mage kept you cold?"

Her question squelched his desire. "Being the Shadow Mage was a curse and, yes, kept me cold, even on the hottest summer days." Gethen grabbed the hard bar of honey soap he'd brought to the pool's edge, inhaled its clean scent, and set to work on his scalp and skin. "I'm sure I was warm as a boy in Besera, but it's been so long I don't remember." He dunked beneath the water and rubbed the suds from his hair then came up and shook his head like a dog. He leaned back against the pool wall again. "I feel reborn." It was good to be clean, warm, and with Halina. And *damnation* he wanted to see her.

The curtain was only an arm's length from him. Her dark silhouette moved behind it, looming as she came close. Very close. He held his breath as her hand caught the edge of the curtain. She drew it aside and crossed over.

"Welcome to the world, Sun Mage Gethen." She stood naked before him, close enough to touch, her gaze steady. Water rippled against the curve of her ribs. She was pale and imperfect, her breasts firm but scarred and, as he'd hoped, dusted with freckles. A thick, jagged scar cut from beneath her right armpit to cross her breast. Silver with age, it distorted the symmetry of her pale, pink areola.

Gethen traced the scar, his gaze following his fingers then going to her face as his thumb caressed her nipple.

Her smile softened, her breathing deepened, she pressed forward. "I never properly thanked you for saving my life."

But his answer and explorations were interrupted by light laughter and young female voices. Halina sank and pushed backward beneath the water, slipping to the other side of the curtain as two girls entered the women's area of the bathing chamber.

"Good afternoon, Margrave Khara," one of them said while the other giggled.

"Good afternoon, girls," Halina replied, her voice strong and even.

"Baichu saw you and the mage heading for the bathing area. She told us to hurry here and help you dress, Your Ladyship."

The ripple of water accompanied Halina's voice as she slipped from the pool. "Your grandmother is very *thoughtful*, and it's good of you girls to offer your aid. I find ties and buckles almost impossible to work with these wounded fingers."

Their voices moved away from the divider. Gethen stuck his face in the water and released a long, low, bubbling groan. Then he took advantage of the solitude to haul himself out of the water, dry off, and dress in his clean clothing. Apparently, Halina's thanks and his desire would have to wait.

He needed to get her alone again. Soon. For hours. And her wounds were a perfect excuse. "Militess?"

"Yes, Master Sorcerer?"

"If you'll join me in my chamber after you're dressed, I'll provide you with some metheglin and check the healing of your wounds." Halina agreed, and Gethen made his way through the maze of stairs and tunnels, trying to block the sight and feel of her from his mind as he went. "One more interruption and I'll be testing this new sorcery on an undeserving victim," he said under this breath.

He emerged into the sunlight on a balcony that overlooked the desert and the abbedei's bailey. "Skiron's bones." He was two levels below his chamber and in an adjoining wing. "This isn't where I wanted to be." Somewhere he'd gone astray.

There was a stairwell to his right, and he descended to the level of the bailey. He spied another stairwell that looked like a promising route back to his room and struck out across the bailey.

"Good day, Master Sorcerer."

Gethen looked around. The appa sat in the shade of a blue-and-white striped awning, strumming a stringed instrument and humming quietly as a cluster of kittens rolled in the dirt around his large feet and beneath his wooden chair.

Though he wished to, Gethen couldn't ignore his host. So he composed his expression and his thoughts, crossed the bailey, and bowed to the older man. A quick greeting and then he could quietly excuse himself back to his room and Halina.

"You look much improved, Sun Mage."

"An improved version of myself, thanks to your fine hospitality, the desert's warmth, and Her Ladyship's diligence. Already my strength grows with the light and warmth of the sun. The Abbedei of Gurvan-Sum is swiftly becoming a beloved place to me."

Unegen smiled and pulled a little stool away from the shadows. Gethen sat, resigned to be a good and patient guest, as the older man said, "I hear that from every visitor who comes and goes from these stone walls. The desert can be a gentle and loving mistress, as well as a harsh and evil witch." He studied Gethen with knowing eyes. "I understand you have your own woes because of a witch, and that we are reliant upon you to prevent those troubles from becoming ours." Gethen nodded, and the appa went on. "What can we do to aid you in this transition and speed the increase of your sun magic, Master Sorcerer?"

Despite the yearning that wouldn't be satisfied until Gethen slid inside Halina, he smiled as the kittens rolled around his feet, hissing and spitting at each other. They scrambled over his legs, their little sharp claws catching on his boots and gray trouzes. He chuckled and captured a little buff-hued, striped one. It chewed his thumb and then closed its eyes and purred with contentment as he scratched the top of its head with his thumb. The kittens were much like Ranith's wolf pups. "I need information about sun magic. Does the abbedei have such knowledge in its library?"

The appa set aside his lute, scooped up two black kittens, and deposited them upon his lap, mesmerizing them with his long scratching fingers. He thought for a moment, his eyes half-lidded as if he was seeing every book on the shelves in his library, and then he shook his head slowly. "I don't think I have any of that information upon my shelves, Master Gethen. However, I know some people who can aid you."

He summoned, and then sent, three of his great-grandsons to the Dargani nomads who lived in the desert not far from Gurvan-Sum.

The sun had climbed over the edge of the abbedei's ridges and now shortened the shadows in the bailey. The appa rose. "Midday meal is being served, and you look like a man who could use some abbedei cooking. Come, sorcerer. My wife will curse me if I don't let our kitchen fatten you up."

Though his hunger wasn't for food, Gethen followed Unegen into the building's great hall. It was larger but cozier than Ranith's, noisy and crowded with all of the children, grandchildren, and great-grandchildren of the appa and amma.

A place was cleared at one of the tables for Gethen and Appa Unegen, and they were served a meal of warm bread, butter, dates, nuts, and roasted vegetables. A kind of meat stew was served to the appa, but Halina must've told the women that Gethen didn't eat meat, as none was set before him. It was a relief not to have to have that conversation. More than once it had raised eyebrows and confusion; people didn't understand why a man with the Shadow Mage's evil reputation refused to sacrifice animals to fill his own gut.

Unegen's young messengers returned with word that two of the Dargani men, including their shaman, would be honored to meet with Gethen and the Militess. They were welcome to come to the tribe's encampment the following morning.

"How do the Dargani know Halina?" Gethen asked.

"She is well known throughout Or-Halee," the appa said. "When, as a mortally wounded girl, she stood over her fallen brother and rallied his retreating troops to face an unwinnable battle, Arik-bohk noticed. Our great king saw the blood aglow on her upraised sword, put down his weapons, and called for peace between our kingdoms. He, himself, carried her to my doorstep and demanded that I save her life."

Gethen knew this story, but not the heroine's name. "Margrave Khara is the Red Blade of Or-Halee?"

"You didn't know?"

"No. I thought that was a myth told to bolster Ursinum military pride."

Unegen chuckled. "Perhaps you've been a bit too isolated in that dark tower of yours."

"Perhaps."

Halina sat in a corner with a gathering of women and girls who were sewing and knitting. Her back was angled to him, and Gethen stared, amazed by this new information and arrested by the sight of her. She wore gold and gray, and the appa's granddaughters had pulled her thick, wavy hair into twists and braids secured with golden ribbons. She sat upon a padded stool beside a roaring fire, her head down as she bent over a task. The curve of her neck — ivory skin and dark copper curls — enticed him to come closer. He swallowed. He wanted to taste her not food.

"Will you excuse me, Appa? I see the margrave, and you've reminded me that my duty to tend her wounds and speed her recovery mustn't be shirked another day."

"By all means, Master Sorcerer, see to the militess. If she's willing to permit any man to attend to her needs, then I bow my head to that man. I know how impatient a patient she is."

Gethen returned his bow and headed for the corner beside the fireplace, his attention fixed upon Halina. He came up behind her and quashed the urge to kiss the place where her neck curved down to her shoulder.

Beside her, Baichu stitched an apron and Qulan darned socks. Halina shifted, and Gethen swallowed a laugh. She was dressed as prettily as a princess while she wrapped new cord around the grip of her longsword.

"You present an ironic picture, Your Ladyship."

She looked up and slowly smirked. "One should always look her best before she stabs a man through the heart."

Baichu began to laugh, and Gethen matched Halina's lopsided smile. "Should I be concerned?"

"Every man should be concerned if he spends too much time in my presence." She tied off the cord, cut its ends, and returned the sword to its scabbard. She eyed him and added, "Why do you think King Vernard sent me into battle in Or-Halee when I was barely more than a girl, granted me rights to rule *distant* Khara, and dropped me into the Shadow Mage's lap in the hopes that he might murder me?"

Gethen cocked his head. "So His Majesty considers his daughter a great danger to his rule?"

She folded her hands upon her lap and looked up at him, wide-eyed and innocent. Rather than answer his question, she smiled sweetly, though it was a cloying sweetness like the kind that came with metal poison. "Have you come to foist one of your foul tinctures upon me, Master Mage?"

Gethen bowed. "It is my duty to torture you thusly, Margrave Khara."

Halina snorted. "And your pleasure, I think." She stood, excused herself to her companions, and led him back through the maze of hallways and stairs to his chamber. Once there, she sat on the bed and gazed out the window, the orange-gold sunlight of late afternoon setting her hair alight like a fiery halo, while he prepared a healing tincture and sorted through the unguents and herbs he'd brought from Ranith. He retrieved the damaged talisman and dropped it into his haversack while she drank the tincture. She made only the slightest face as she drained it, and he pretended not to notice.

Then Gethen knelt before her feet and gazed up at her for a heavy moment. She pointedly studied the desert beyond the window.

How can anyone not see that she's beautiful?

"How does your leg feel?" He was delaying touching her, not because he didn't want to, but because he very much yearned to lay his hands upon her skin. He craved that rush of heat and desire that came with their contact. And he intended to finish what she'd started in the bath.

Halina gazed down at him. She licked her lips. "Much improved thanks to your ministrations." Slowly she lifted and folded the fabric of her surcoat and kirtle, revealing smooth, freckled skin and a shapely, scarred leg.

Gethen swallowed and cleared his throat. "I, ah, think it looks very good."

Halina began to laugh. Gethen smiled and shook his head. She only laughed harder until she was panting and gasping. "Oh, my stomach hurts from laughing." But that only made Gethen chuckle and her laughter continued until she was wiping tears from her eyes. And every time she looked at him she started to laugh again.

Finally, Gethen grabbed her ankle. Halina gasped and

clenched the folds of her skirts, all laughter gone. What before had been warmth flowing through his hands and body when they'd touched now blazed like an inferno. He held her gaze and slowly, so slowly, slid his hand up her calf. Her eyes darkened with the same desire he felt. His fingers glided over her knee and brushed the fabric of her bandage. He stood and Halina's breath slowed as she leaned toward him. Her muscles tightened beneath his fingers. He paused upon the bandage. Her hand covered his.

Gethen swallowed again. She was so close that her breath warmed his cheek. He parted his lips and tasted the scent of her — honeyed soap, chingis spices, and matad flowers. His voice was husky as he said, "You were thanking me when we were interrupted."

She leaned even closer. Stray wisps of her hair tickled his skin. "Yes. In the bath."

"So disrespectful." Gethen tilted forward and his lips found hers. They moaned. His hand moved past the bandage, guided by hers. Their lips parted, their tongues touched, and their kiss deepened. His fingers found fabric, skin, and warmth. She groaned and pushed against him. Then her hands slid into his hair. She pulled him down as he lifted her up. Their bodies came together. Pressing. Needing. Yearning. The heat and desire overwhelmed logic, propriety, sense, and safety.

"Halina," he murmured into her mouth. "Let me have you."

"Oh, yes."

So many laces between her bare skin and his hands. But Gethen knew where to tug, what to pull. He didn't rush. First the gold and gray silk surcoat. And she had his brown one off too. Her hands pushed under his tunic, fingers hot and strong, kneading the muscles of his back, nails dragging across skin. Then the white kirtle; its laces down her back took time, but he was happily distracted by the soft mounds of her breasts as they swelled above the dress's low-cut, square neckline. She had his tunic off and was pulling at the ties of his trouzes when she suddenly stopped and pushed him aside.

"Now what?" Gethen said through clenched teeth. She was killing him.

"The shutters," she replied calmly. She stood and closed them as the last rays of the sun slipped below the horizon, turning the desert sands purple and rose and setting the sky and her skin aglow.

"Would anyone notice us?" He couldn't decide between bemusement or frustration. The heat and tension inside him were becoming unbearable.

Halina shot him a look that said he was being an idiot. Then her expression softened and she cocked her head. A lascivious smile curved her lips as she turned and let her loose kirtle slip off her body. "Night has fallen," she said, her voice husky and sensual. He was on the edge of the bed, and Halina placed her knee between his legs. She caressed his face. "You're most vulnerable when the sun disappears." She leaned down and, just as their lips met, she said, "Gethen."

He wrapped his arms around her, turned, and lay her on the bed. Her chemise came up and over her head, and Gethen's mouth explored hers. He relished the taste of her tongue, the softness of her lips. And she matched his lust, biting, licking, sucking his lips and tongue. He cupped her breasts, his thumbs rubbing her nipples, and then he moved his mouth to them, tasting her skin and making her moan.

Halina surged up and pushed him over, rolling with him to come up straddling his hips. Her hair fell like a curtain around his face, tickling his skin. He bucked against her, hard and aching to be inside her, aching to feel her, warm, wet, and soft around him. He marveled at the beauty of her body again. Fair skin and a dusting of freckles over taut muscles. And so many scars. But there was strength, determination, and ferocity in those jagged lines. He intended to trace every one of them with his tongue.

Halina shifted back on his hips, tugged his trouzes down, and freed his erection. Gethen moaned as she gripped him, stroked her hand up and down the shaft, and teased the sensitive tip with her thumb. She kissed him, hard, and her hand and her tongue moved in rhythm.

The burning ache became a fiery demand. He captured her hips, and pulled her forward. Their eyes met, an unspoken question between them; Gethen sought permission, Halina granted it. He nestled between her legs, found the place that was slick, hot, and yielding. He thrust up as she moved down. They both moaned and moved, sliding, stroking, caressing. She rode him slowly, tortuously, arching back and moaning, until sweat slipped between her breasts and fell upon his skin.

Then Gethen rolled over, taking her with him. He held his body above hers, staring into her luminous blue eyes. Her pulse pounded against him, her body pushed for more. He kissed her mouth, sucked her tongue, and began to move forward and back, in and out, slow, then hard and fast.

The heat they shared stoked his internal fire and sorcery exploded within him, a conflagration of power. It sparked, yellow-orange-red off his fingers, skated across her skin, and enveloped them. Halina gasped and arched. She clawed his back and rose up to meet his every thrust until a shudder gripped her from belly to back. She came, moaning and biting, her face pressed into his shoulder. And Gethen, unable to hold back, released his seed, his desire, and his magic into her.

And then, as had happened once before, a fiery spark blazed from his feet, up his spine, and through the top of his head. Gethen's muscles locked as he held himself over Halina, eyes shut, teeth gritted. Pain and pleasure surged through his body as power threatened to tear him apart at the seams.

Sun sorcery set him aglow and lit the room like an explosion, defining the edges of the shadows, and throwing him across the cusp. It receded as quickly as it had surged, a ball of immense power that nestled within his chest and waited to be called forth and wielded. Gethen collapsed upon Halina, spent, satisfied, warmed from head to toe, and empowered.

"Khotyr, take me," Halina said, awe filling her voice.

"Oh, no, she can't. You're mine," Gethen said as he rolled to his side. She threw her leg over his thigh, keeping him inside her still, even as she continued to shudder with her own orgasm. He tugged the blankets over their bodies and pulled her close. Halina was his hope, his sun, and the fire that now burned bright and hot inside him. He cradled her head upon his arm and kissed her forehead, cheeks, nose, and lips.

"You're beautiful, Militess Halina." She smiled. Then Gethen added, "Do you think it's too late to accept the terms of your king's offer?"

She laughed and rubbed her face against his arm, then peered at him and said, "I belong to no man, woman, or god, Sun Mage Gethen. But if you're fortunate and don't anger me, I may decide to make you mine."

The room had darkened from purple to black. Gethen sketched a ward above their bed, his fingers trailing golden light that lingered in the air and gave off warmth. He pressed his lips to Halina's hair, her forehead, and her soft mouth. "Thank you for helping me find the sun."

"Thank you for saving my arse. Twice." There was a smile behind her words and upon her face.

They closed their eyes and slept, the cold and the dark forgotten.

SEVENTEEN

G ethen was already up when Halina awoke in the morning. He'd opened the shutters to allow the early sunlight to flood the room and chase away the night's shadows. She lay still and studied his wide, bare back, admiring the planes and hills of his muscles, and fascinated by the Beseran stripes that darkened his spine and banded his ribs and arms. Despite being a mage, he had the build of a soldier, broad shoulders and back over a narrow waist, and muscular arms.

The air before him glowed with red, gold, and white lines. He turned his head slightly, revealing his profile, and said, "Good morning, Militess. I apologize if I awakened you."

He had a nice arse, too. She rolled onto her side, reached out, and pressed her fingers into the two divots at the base of his spine. He had a dusting of freckles across his shoulders and upper arms. Funny that he didn't have them on his face like she did, though he was full-blooded Beseran and she was only half.

"You didn't wake me, and even if you did you're a pleasant sight in the morning." Languid from the long rest and the evening's pleasure, Halina stretched her arms above her head and reached down toward the edge of the bed with her toes, twisting her spine and hips until her bones and joints crackled and popped. Everything moved back into place, and she sighed with satisfaction, then laughed when Gethen's hand found her belly. His fingers skated across her skin and scars leaving heat and a trail of red and orange magic. He cupped her breast, leaned down, and kissed her mouth, slowly and deeply.

"I do hope to repeat last evening's pleasure often," he murmured against her mouth.

Halina smiled. "I encourage you to do so." But as he shifted toward her she pressed her hand against his stomach. "But not this morning, Master Gethen. We have a shaman to meet."

He captured her wrists, held her tight, and kissed her hard before pulling back with a low growl. "I hate that you're right." Then he pushed up from the bed and gathered their discarded clothes.

A pitcher of fresh water and a clean basin and rags sat on the floor outside the room, and Gethen brought them in. He gestured for Halina to stand, and then sponged their combined scent and sweat off her body, smiling when she shivered from the cold liquid. His fingers traced the puckered lines of scars that criss-crossed her skin, pausing on one that covered a hand's breadth of her lower abdomen. "This should've killed you."

"It's thanks to the healing skills of Appa Unegen and Amma Xana that it didn't."

"I'd forgotten that you fought in the Battle of Sum, Red Blade." He kissed the scar.

"My first, and nearly last, battle." She snorted, and added, "I'm only called the Red Blade because I survived and Arik-bohk is a very superstitious man."

He laughed and tugged a lock of her hair. "I thought it was because of your fiery hair and temper."

Halina snatched the rag from his hands and dropped it into the cold water. "My turn."

She got her revenge by returning the slow, cold bath and he cursed. "Hurry before my bollocks shrivel up and fall off."

She smiled and her hand lingered. "Later I'll warm them." She flicked her tongue across his lips.

He growled and grabbed for her, but Halina evaded his grasp. "I see your leg's better," he said as he caught the trouzes she tossed to him.

She sobered and dropped the rag into the basin. "Thanks to you." Halina ignored the feminine clothes from the previous evening, opting instead for her armor. If she was well enough to tup Gethen, she was well enough to protect him.

Baichu arrived with a tray of food and mead, gave Halina a knowing look, and left without saying a word. Halina shook her head. "Within ten minutes the entire abbedei will know that you and I enjoyed each other's flesh last night."

Gethen handed her a bowl of porridge and a small pitcher of goat milk. "I'm sure they already do."

Halina laughed. "True."

Gethen sobered as he ate.

"What's wrong?" she asked.

He looked at the last bite of porridge on his spoon, frowned, and dropped it into his bowl. "How can I, as the Sun Mage, master in days what took me a lifetime of lessons to perfect as the Shadow Mage?"

"You're strong, Gethen, shadows, sun, or nothing. Learn the ways of the Sun Mage. I'll protect you while you do."

"I know you will, with your sword and blood. But this magic is foreign. As opposite to what I've practiced as the sun is to the moon."

She drained her cup then asked, "Are the sun and the moon so different? Both give light. Both own the sky and travel the same road. Both move the world — the moon pulling our tides, the sun controlling our path. Sorcery is sorcery."

"Spoken like a neophyte."

She raised her fist. "No. Spoken like a soldier. We stand on a field of battle and see our enemy approaching. Our weapons are limited. Do we open our arms and await death? Or do we use what we've been given?"

"I don't even know how to lift this weapon."

Halina's hand fell to her sword hilt. "Try or I'll murder you now and return to King Vernard's side to face my death like a soldier."

He laughed. "Of course I'm going to try. I've no desire to give up and become the teat upon which the Rime Witch suckles for an eternity." He pulled her hand away from her sword, kissed her scarred knuckles, and added, "Nor do I wish to be run through by your blade, Militess."

But what was expected of him seemed unattainable in such a short period of time. He'd spent twenty-two years perfecting his dark sorcery and still had only scratched the surface of his abilities. Ranith and Khara were freezing and the Rime Witch would spread her winter to every kingdom as she sought Gethen. Now that he'd crossed the cusp, she'd move even more aggressively to possess him before his strength grew too great for her to defeat.

After breaking their fast, Halina quickly plaited her hair to keep it off her face. Then she and Gethen returned to the bailey where the appa already awaited them with two of his youngest sons, Ogotai and Juchi.

Gethen's horse and another had been saddled. Metal jangled as Remig shook his head and pawed the ground. The small group set out riding across the blanket of purple and yellow flowers that insisted upon growing through the dry dirt and pink sand of Or-Halee's deserts. Though the sun had risen, the moon still hung low above the horizon, a pale, imperfect globe that soon would be swallowed by the day.

"How far is the ride?" Gethen asked. He sat easily and comfortably in the saddle.

The appa indicated distant mountains that were purple at

their base and brown at the top where sunlight struck them. "We're riding for that range. Our advisors are camped at the foot of the mountains where water flows freely and strangers rarely go. It'll take us until zenith to reach it." He swept his hand across the expanse of flat, open desert, and smiled. "Enjoy the warmth and beauty that Or-Halee offers, and allow the sun to fill you with its magic, young mage."

Gethen stared toward the mountains and the white dunes that spilled their sand. The winds mixed it with the desert's red soil to create the pink that was so typical of Or-Halee. The sky was still soft blue and cloudless. The air was crisp. He raised his right hand. The air around it shimmered. The appa and his sons exchanged glances but said nothing. Again he warded the air with red, gold, yellow, and a bluish white light. He uttered incantations then frowned when he got unexpected results.

The horses' hooves were muted by the sand and dusty soil. Wind whistled lightly through the bushes and bent the flowers that bloomed so brilliantly in the desert sunshine. High above a raptor called and circled lazily, riding updrafts and looking for its breakfast.

Juchi began to hum and his brother and father joined in. The humming turned into words, a song about love and lust and the trouble it brings. Halina smiled; she didn't doubt that their song was for her. *Nosy bastards.* The horses picked up their pace, perhaps inspired by the music, and the jingling and creak of metal and leather added a counter chorus to the song.

Gethen had looped the reigns over his pommel and now held both hands out in front of him at chest height, palm to palm with a fist-sized opening between them. A blue-and-orange ball of flame danced between his hands, and his eyes were alight with a glee that she'd not seen on his face before. It was the kind of delight she expected to see from a small child who'd received an unexpected gift.

The sun was high when they slowed their horses. Two riders

on small, dark ponies trotted toward their group hands raised, palms open. Ogotai rode ahead and greeted the men with an upright palm and a wide smile, and then brought them back to join their small party. Introductions were made and both men bowed deeply in their saddles pressing their palms to their foreheads in a greeting of the deepest respect for Halina. They wore long coats that flowed loosely from their shoulders down to their ankles and covered their arms completely. Their heads were wrapped with brightly colored turbans in orange and red hues. Their coats were sky blue and almost as beautiful as their smiles and their dark brown eyes.

Halina returned their respectful greeting with her right palm, and then introduced Gethen. The implication was clear; he was under her protection, he was her companion, and if challenged she would defend him. She leaned over and tugged on Gethen's sleeve. "When you meet their chieftain, show respect and acknowledge her position by pressing both palms to your forehead like they did for me. With everyone else, including the shaman, use only your right hand." She raised her left hand and added, "Never use your left hand alone."

"It's insulting?"

"Very. I don't want to battle one of their champions because you called someone a goat turd."

He didn't laugh, and that meant a lot to her. Instead he nodded and said, "Right hand only for everyone except their chieftain who gets both. Got it."

The nomads accompanied them along the ridge to where goatskin tents were pitched in a large circle. The greeting that welcomed Halina, the appa and his sons, and Gethen went up loud and long with increasing enthusiasm as all of the members of the tribe surrounded the visitors. Hands were pressed to foreheads, smiles and eyes were bright, there was clapping and laughing, hands shaken and kisses given.

Gethen watched Halina with an expression of amusement and

wonder as the Dargani chief, a heavily armed woman named Mahish, exchanged greetings and kisses with her. Again Halina introduced him. Mahish took him in slowly, her keen gaze roaming his body from head to toe and back again. She bowed and welcomed him, offering him her respect as she pressed her palm to her forehead. Gethen returned the gesture with both hands.

The horses were led away to be fed and watered, and their small party was escorted into Mahish's wide tent. Dark brown and simple on the outside, the inside of the tent was lit with lanterns and offered brightly colored and elaborately patterned pillows and blankets upon which to sit. Plates of rice, beans, and more teff bread were offered. Pink wine made from songin berries was poured, and Halina leaned close to Gethen. "The wine is sweet but don't let it fool you; she's a bitch of a mistress if you abuse her."

He arched an eyebrow at her and inclined his head. "Probably not the only one in my life." This time Halina was the one wearing a wolfish grin.

After they'd washed their hands and thanked the gods for food, drink, and shelter, they relaxed and spoke in the common tongue of the chaos back in Khara, the quiet desert, and the ever-changing faces that passed through Gurvan-Sum from the crossroads.

Two men entered the tent. They made obeisance to the chief, and then offered their respects to the appa, Halina, and Gethen. This was the shaman Balaad and his apprentice.

White-haired and wrinkled, the shaman was the oldest man in the entire Dargani community. He sat opposite Gethen and stared at him with wide green eyes, disconcerting in their color and intensity. "Shadow cloaks you, mage, yet you wish to understand how to manipulate the sun?"

Gethen inclined his head. "It's true that there's much of the shadow about me. I've been the Shadow Mage since boyhood. But

I've just crossed the cusp to become the Sun Mage. Like a baby learning to walk, I'm untrained in this new magic, and my home," he indicated Halina, "and Margrave Khara's lands, are under siege from the Rime Witch."

All of the Dargani shifted and exchanged wary glances. Muttering filled the tent and the atmosphere grew tense. They weren't using the common tongue now, and the snatches of conversation that Halina understood made her uneasy. She stood, bowed to Mahish and said, "Tell me what troubles you, so that I can help."

The chieftain lifted her hands and the harsh murmur quieted. She gestured to the pillows. "Please sit, Your Ladyship." Halina did and Mahish drained her wine cup then began.

"Of all the creatures that dwell between the four kingdoms and the Void, the Dargani loath the Rime Witch most. Because she was one of our own, and she began a war that nearly destroyed us."

Halina frowned and glanced at Gethen. She didn't know this story. Did he? His expression was intent but revealed nothing.

"Her name was Yisun. She was a powerful but inexperienced shaman who drew magic from the winter. She was also the younger of two daughters of a Gad-Dargani chief, and to prevent war she was offered to a Sum-Dargani chief. Their marriage was to unite two powerful clans that had been battling over land for a decade.

"Yisun's older sister, Sulwen, should have been the first to marry, but the Shadow Mage had already chosen her as an apprentice over Yisun, and she'd long dwelt in Ranith Citadel. Rather than complete the union to save her people, Yisun ran away to her sister."

Gethen was watching her; he knew she understood the girl's objections to being bartered.

Mahish continued. "But her story doesn't end happily. When she reached Ranith, Sulwen turned her away. 'Go back to Gad-

Dargan,' she said. 'You are being childish and cold-hearted. Go back and save our people from war.'

"But Yisun didn't return to the desert. Instead, she cursed her sister, her family, and all the Dargani. She swore to bury them beneath ice and snow.

"As Yisun surrendered to these evil wishes she became the Rime Witch. Though more powerful, Sulwen couldn't bring herself to destroy her younger sister. So she imprisoned Yisun's spirit within the Void.

"But the witch vowed to return and destroy the Sun Mage, the Dargani, and the world."

Mahish sipped her wine and said, "Because of Yisun's betrayal, our people were plunged into a war that lasted three generations and nearly destroyed the Dargani as it swallowed the tribes like a storm."

Halina touched Gethen's knee. "Did you know the story of Yisun and Sulwen?" He shook his head. *Bollocks.* If the Dargani decided that the Rime Witch's return was his doing, then she'd be forced to fight her way out of that tent. She stood again. "This is my responsibility." All the nomads' attention went to her. "I chose to bring Sun Mage Gethen to Or-Halee. I endangered your people by bringing him to Gurvan-Sum."

As she spoke Gethen's expression grew grave. He pressed his fingers to his lips and slowly nodded. Then he stood and took Halina's hand, squeezing her fingers as the heat surged between their palms. "I understand your anger and fear. But even if I'd known the Rime Witch's story, I would've come here. Because she *has* escaped, and I'm the only mage who can stop her. But I need help understanding how to control the sun. All records of this magic were destroyed by my predecessors. My library is useless."

Voices rose around them as arguments flared. The Dargani spoke in their own tongue, their words too fast for Halina to follow. But it was clear that the tribe was divided.

Mahish said nothing as debates ebbed and flowed around her. She nodded and shook her head in response to questions, ate her food, and studied Gethen and Halina, who remained standing. Finally, Mahish finished eating, raised her hands for silence, and stood. She circled her visitors then gripped their joined hands.

"I've listened to our guests and to the arguments their presence has brought. It seems that storms arise with even the mention of Yisun." She faced her tribe. "And I believe that this new sun mage seeks to destroy that which Sulwen could not. We'll give him our knowledge of the sun and its magic."

Gethen bowed to her. "I thank you and your people. All my years as the Shadow Mage, I've sought a different path than that of my predecessors, and so have been led into the sun. It's because of my change that the Rime Witch has returned. And it's because of my change that she'll finally be destroyed."

Approving whistles filled the tent, and heads nodded all around. The Dargani were with him.

Balaad stood on scrawny, weedhopper legs, and raised his hands before his chest, his palms facing. Silence spread around the tent. He intoned several words and a fiery orb grew between his hands. He sent the growing ball of heat and sunlight to the tent's ceiling where it flattened and spread, like a massive bubble of golden light caught beneath a pond lily's leaf.

"It's not only the manipulation of the light and the heat that gives power to the Sun Mage," he said, his voice high and reedy with age. "It's the weight, the pull of the great burning star, that's now at your fingertips, Gethen of Ranith." He snapped his fingers, and the light crashed down around them. It passed over their bodies weightlessly, yet the ground shuddered beneath their feet, the tent poles rocked, and dust rose around them. "You have the greatest magic of any man dwelling in the four kingdoms. It is a power that comes not only from our day star, but from all the stars in the night, all the fires on our earth, and even the lightning that splits the sky."

Gethen bowed to the man. "You practice sun sorcery."

The shaman grinned a toothless smile and spoke quietly, his shaky hands gesturing in all directions and his eyes bright. "I heal. I destroy. I use wind, soil, water, and fire. But I cannot leash the darkness or the cold. Only you, the mage of the cusp, can control both the darkness *and* the light."

Gethen shook his head. "I've lost my power over the shadows and only toy with the light. I perform the simplest tricks, but I can't control it yet. Quoregna will fall before I have enough mastery of the sun to confront the Rime Witch."

The shaman leaned forward and touched Gethen's forehead with his bony, brown finger. "You have all the knowledge here." He coaxed another ball of light from Gethen's skin — smaller but brighter than the first — and sent it up to the ceiling. "Shadow magic is difficult to master. It's sly and erratic, because it originates from your heels." He pointed at Gethen's feet. "It follows. It leads. And always it seeks to topple the one that stands upon it." He squinted at the bubble of light undulating overhead. "The sun's magic flows around and through the mage. It's life. It's alive. It's ever-changing but never lessening." His focus returned to Gethen. "If you wish to harness the magic of the sun *and* find the power to control the shadows again, you must surrender."

Gethen frowned. "I don't understand."

Balaad grinned again. "Surrender to change, Master Sorcerer, and you will find your strength. The shadow is most intense where the sun is strongest." He shuffled toward the tent flap but paused before pushing through it. "Within the shadows dwells possibility. And *that* is illuminated by the sun."

The other man who'd accompanied the shaman hadn't said a word while Gethen and the elder tribesman spoke. Now, however, he raised his hand. "I'm Samar. I've been apprenticed to Balaad since I was just old enough to walk. I'll help you to feel and harness the weight of the sun, Sun Mage. With this knowledge, you'll have the power to control lightning, harness fire, draw molten earth from the rocks, and make a man's blood boil in his veins."

Halina looked from Samar to Gethen. *What a terrible power. What price will he pay for wielding it?*

Mahish, her advisors, the appa and his sons, and Halina left the tent. Not wanting to stray far from the man she'd sworn to protect, Halina sat cross-legged upon the rug outside the entrance, drew her sword, and laid it behind her. It was a show of support for Gethen at the same time that it demonstrated her trust of their hosts.

The chief returned a short time later and crouched before her. She offered a cup of tepid water, and knowing how precious such a gift was from a people who dwelled in the desert, Halina drank every drop, and then pressed her palm to her mouth — a gesture of gratitude.

Mahish lit a smoke stick and proffered it, but Halina shook her head. The nocoli leaves the Dargani smoked were hard to harvest, acrid, and twisted the mind. The chieftain shifted to sit beside her and downwind. A stiff breeze pulled the blue haze of the burning stick away from them.

Dark gray storm clouds gathered in the northern sky. Halina wondered if they were Gethen's doing. The wind lifted her hair in a ghostly dance around her face and partnered it with wisps of Mahish's black, silky locks. Lightning forked the clouds and gray bands of rain dropped to the earth forming a hazy curtain over the distant desert.

"You've chosen a powerful companion, Militess."

"Chosen isn't the right word. Paired by need, is closer to the truth."

"Yet you care for him."

Halina peered at the woman who'd once been her enemy. "Do I?"

Thunder rolled across the desert. The storm was still far off.

Mahish smiled and exhaled a thin stream of smoke. "You're

sitting here rather than guarding Khara's shores with men who are fated to die a quick and violent death."

"Doesn't that make me a coward?"

She bumped her shoulder against Halina's. "It's a wise leader who knows where and when to seek a great weapon."

Halina shivered. The cold wind had sharp teeth. No wonder the clouds crackled with lightning. "True. But the wisdom of my actions remains to be proven."

The Dargani woman stood. "Often such things aren't revealed for many years after a battle, Red Blade." She meandered away, her attention on the gathering storm clouds. Lightning made their insides glow and laced their surfaces with blue-white streaks.

A rider thundered into the camp, his clothes soaked and dripping and his horse dancing and wild-eyed. "Shelter the animals and the children!" he called.

"Why?" Mahish dropped her smoke stick and crushed it into the sand with her bare, callused heel.

"Hail is falling. The size of my thumbnail."

It was a cold and violent storm.

With a curse and a glance at Halina and the tent, the chief strode off to gather her fighters and warn her people.

"Skiron's bones." Halina stood and stepped into the tent, expecting it to be dim. Instead she had to shade her eyes from the golden-white glow that filled the space. It seemed to emanate from Gethen, from the space between his upraised palms, from beneath his skin, and behind his closed eyelids.

Samar looked at her, and Gethen collapsed the light into a single pearl-sized point then closed his hands around it. The expression on her face must have been grave as both men stood quickly. Samar's focus went to the sky beyond the tent flap, but Gethen's pinned her. "What's happened?" he asked.

"Storm's coming. Cold and fast. Full of lightning and hail. Did you summon it?"

He shook his head and said, "We have to lead it away from the Dargani."

Appa Unegen, Juchi, and Ogotai appeared at Halina's shoulder. "I agree," the appa said and turned to his sons. "Fetch the horses. We'll ride hard for the abbedei."

As Gethen exited the tent, a cold, white flake swirled around him and Halina, landed upon his brown surcoat, and melted.

Within minutes they were mounted and had offered thanks and farewells. They raced across the desert, their hoods raised and cloaks pulled tight to the bruising hail and stinging sleet. The horses snorted and tossed their heads; they disliked the storm, but they were pointed toward home and knew the shortest and safest route to warmth and safety.

But it was only a matter of minutes before the hail and lightning gave way to swirling eddies of fat snowflakes.

"Can you ease this?" the appa shouted to Gethen.

"I'll try." He peered at Halina from deep within the folds of his dark cloak. "The coin," he called above the wind and clatter of hooves.

"What about it?"

"It must hold more than just a curse. She's tracked me." Bitterness deepened his voice. "She's been watching me, maybe for years. She knew I'd lose my power and leave Kharayan eventually. I made it too easy."

Halina shook her head. "You assume too much about her."

"I've dealt with darkness for decades. I know how it's manipulated and how it manipulates the mind of the one who wields it. I should've known she'd use the talisman in more than one way. I should've destroyed it yesterday when I saw the death mark. And we shouldn't have stayed."

Unegen said, "It doesn't matter how the witch found you, Master Gethen. Increasing your knowledge has been our priority. Without you, Quoregna is lost." He pointed toward the horizontal screen of blowing white flakes that had replaced the desert.

"Without you, the four kingdoms will be enrobed in this, and all will die."

Halina nodded. The appa's wisdom wasn't lost on her, but the bitterness didn't leave Gethen's eyes. She hoped he wouldn't hate himself for bedding her and ignoring the warning signs.

They rode in a close line. The appa's sons took the front and rear positions with Unegen followed by Gethen, and then Halina. The horses forged on, shaking the snow from their ears and blinking it from their eyelashes. Steam billowed from their nostrils and mouths, white against a white world. They moved steadily forward at an easy jog, keeping warm, and determined to reach home.

EIGHTEEN

The abbedei's mountain appeared out of the white, an indistinct form against nothingness. Time had slowed to a standstill as they'd traveled through the whiteout. Gethen had tried again and again to clear the weather, to send the storm back across the horizon, to merely create a pocket of warmth and clarity around their small group. He'd possibly succeeded in the last; all of them remained alive despite the freezing temperatures and bitter, howling wind.

Unegen's horse whinnied and the other four horses responded. The animals quickened their pace as the fenced opening to the abbedei's stable appeared before them, a darker maw against darkness. Ogotai swung out of his saddle and opened the gate. All five horses trotted into the shelter, and everyone, horses and people alike, exhaled with relief.

Gethen dismounted and moved from horse to horse, stroking their noses and murmuring, "Thank you for bringing us back safely."

The animals were rubbed down and blanketed, fed grain and hay, and watered. The work warmed stiff fingers and frozen bodies.

An echoing shout was the first sign that their troubles hadn't stayed outside. As one, they turned toward the stairwell that led up to the abbedei's many levels of living space. The horses shifted and whinnied. They pawed the floors and kicked the walls of their stalls, tossed their heads, and paced.

"The horses say something's wrong." Juchi's breath billowed out, a sudden brume as the temperature in the stable plummeted.

A cracking, squealing sound, like ice breaking apart, echoed down the stairs. More shouts and now the screams of children joined the chorus.

"Blood and bones." Halina bolted for the worn stone stairs, the men on her heels. In the lead, she came to a sudden halt on the third level but slipped on its icy landing. Gethen's closeness stopped her from tumbling down the stairs. The appa's sons charged onward toward the bailey, slipping and sliding but determined to aid their family. "Wait!" she rasped. But they didn't. She grabbed Gethen's arm and pointed at a small unmoving lump on the landing. "What did that?"

Appa Unegen paused beside them, gasping for air in the frigid stairwell. "It's one of the cats." It was covered in hoarfrost, stiff, and dead. He began to reach for it.

"Don't touch it." Gethen knocked the man's hand away. A high-pitched, eerie shriek echoed from the top of the abbedei and back again. He took in the sudden icy stairs and the rime-coated animal then said, "Hoarbeast." He glared up the shadowy stairwell.

"Hoarbeast?" Halina wheezed. "Made of ice and hoarfrost?" Gethen nodded, and she said, "Burn it." Another ear-piercing roar echoed through the stairwell. A chorus of screams and shouts joined it. As Gethen pulled Halina to her feet, she pushed him ahead of her. "Go!"

He took the slippery stairs on hands and knees to keep from falling. Finally, he emerged onto the bailey. Fog and snow swirled in a strange, blinding miasma. Blood and bodies littered the snow.

Ogotai, Juchi, Qulan, and Baichu dodged and feinted, swords in hand.

A human-like creature coalesced from the blizzard itself. The size of two men, it captured Ogotai as his sword passed through it harmlessly. The beast shook the man until his bones snapped and blood spattered the snow then it tossed him across the bailey.

"Don't let it touch you!" Gethen shouted. His sense of cold and time's passage slipped away, replaced by screams and shouts, howling wind, the eerie shriek of the beast. Pure white snow. Bright red blood. An incantation built in his mind like the hum of bees.

Then Halina pushed past him, sword in hand. He watched her, seeing every movement creep through time. The creature lumbered toward Baichu and Unegen. The militess shouted, "Protect the children!" and threw one of the appa's wooden stools at the beast. The monster roared and batted it aside. The chair splintered against the abbedei wall. Wooden shrapnel flew everywhere.

Halina dived beneath the monster's grasp. She used the icy ground to her advantage, slashed at its form, and skidded out of reach. She came back at it fast, sliced through its legs, lopped off its clawed hands. But the creature regained its form. She wasn't killing it, but she *was* stopping it from injuring anyone else.

Gethen's incantation grew in volume and power until he was shouting. Time caught up to him. He formed the spell between his hands, and molded it into a glowing orange orb. It burst into flames and grew brighter, turned blue-white with heat and strained his muscles as it took on the weight of his rage. Fire licked his fingers. It wrapped around his hands and arms. But no heat burned him.

The Rime Witch's monster suddenly turned away from Halina. It slashed at Amma Xana as the woman ran across the bailey with two of her great-granddaughters in her arms. The woman fell. The children tumbled free. Qulan lunged toward them.

Halina shouted and leaped between the children and the beast, her sword poised to strike.

Gethen shouted, "Get down!" Halina crouched. He hurled the mage fire. It knocked the raging beast off its feet and encased it in flames. But though the monster twisted and roared, losing form and size, the hoarbeast doused the fire and stood. It turned on the Sun Mage and became corporeal — jagged, blackened, and deadly. It shrieked and charged, shedding ash and cinders as it came, shaking the ground, and hell-bent on Gethen's death.

Halina shouted.

The beast thundered closer.

She sprinted toward it.

Closer.

The bailey shook. The monster spread its arms. It meant to crush Gethen. Halina couldn't stop it. People screamed.

The beast reached him.

Gethen smiled and burst into flames. Enrobed with fiery armor, he was a human conflagration. He enveloped the monster, evaporated its frozen flesh, and was unharmed by its icicle embrace.

Water doused his flames, but the heat of his magic turned liquid to steam. He lowered his arms, his flesh and clothing damp but untouched by the fire. His gaze found Halina's. She stared at him, her bright blue eyes shining. A mixture of wonder, fear, and awe played upon her face.

"Amma!" A child's cry broke the moment, and Gethen strode across the bailey to see what could be done for the stricken woman. He knelt beside her in snow, ash, and blood. Her body was stiff and covered in frost, her lips were blue and her eyes saw nothing. But her soul hadn't fled yet. Its warmth remained at the core of her being, but it would be expelled soon. Guided by instinct, he placed a warm hand upon her forehead and one upon her stomach. He leaned forward and exhaled a warm breath of life into her open, frozen mouth.

"What's he doing?" someone asked.

Unegen said, "Have faith." A little girl whimpered and clung to the appa.

Warmth spread from Gethen's hands as Xana's soul surged. Color returned to her skin, pink to her lips, a blush across her cheeks and down her throat. Her heart stuttered then found its rhythm. Her lungs pushed against the paralysis that had frozen them and they slowly expanded. She moaned. Gethen stood and stepped back as her family surged forward.

Halina was glaring at him. "You set yourself on fire."

"You said to burn it."

"With pitch, dunderhead!"

"I frightened you? That's fear? For *me?*"

Suddenly she yanked him toward her and kissed him. Hard. He reveled in her warmth and ... concern. She pulled back. "I didn't know you could do that."

"Neither did I."

Halina sighed. "I can protect the Sun Mage against monsters, but I'm not sure I can save him from himself."

Gethen smiled, but his pleasure died quickly as he looked around. The abbedei was a ruin. Bodies littered the once-peaceful bailey; blood and ash stained the snow. Moans and cries drifted down from the heights. The travelers had been attacked, too. "We can't stay."

"No." Halina stepped back.

He immediately longed for her strength. The battle and healing had drained him. "Let's do what we can to aid the injured."

She touched his hand. "Have you more strength to heal others?"

"I'll give what I can to the most grievously wounded, but I need to retain some strength to weave a travel incantation."

The appa appeared beside them then. "The Rime Witch sent that beast for you?" When Gethen nodded, he asked, "But why did it come here when you were away?"

"I left that cursed coin on the windowsill in my room. She tracked it here."

Unegen said, "Leave now."

"I can heal more people."

The older man shook his head. "I won't risk the arrival of another beast. Only Xana survived the monster's touch. The others are dead." So many of them were the appa's family.

Gethen bowed his head. Halina took the appa's hand between hers. She closed her eyes, bent over it, and said something too low for Gethen to hear.

Unegen touched the top of her head. "Don't seek forgiveness for evil acts that you didn't commit, Red Blade. Death followed you and the Sun Mage, but you both saved many." He met Gethen's gaze. "And there are many more to be spared." He released Halina and offered his hand to Gethen. "Find the Rime Witch and stop her from destroying Quoregna. This is your task, Gethen of Ranith. No one else can complete it." He turned to Halina. "You ensure that he succeeds."

Gethen gripped the appa's hand. "Thank you." Halina embraced Unegen, then they left the bailey's carnage for their room. They gathered their belongings into their haversacks and descended to the stable for Remig.

While Halina saddled the horse, Gethen strode to the base of the abbedei's cliff and threw back his hood. Frost stung his skin and clung to his eyebrows, eyelashes, and hair. He held the coin on his palm, uttered a spell, and lowered his hand. The coin floated before him, untroubled by the wind. It began to spin on its axis, slowly then gradually faster and faster until it was a blur. Unblinking, he continued his incantation. The silver flash of the coin became an orange glow, then it heated to yellow and, finally, white. The metal bubbled. He put his fingers below it and pulled down, distorting its shape until it resembled a narrow rod. Then he brought his fingers up and around it, forcing the metal to form a ring. This he continued to enchant, countering the curse that had been placed against him and turning the coin into his own diviner's tool. Finally, satisfied with his work, Gethen released the renewed talisman from his magic. It plunged into the snow at his feet, sending up a little plume of steam. He retrieved it and returned to where Halina waited at the mouth of the stable astride Remig.

Gethen tugged off her demi-gauntlet and glove then slipped the blackened band upon her right ring finger. "I've turned the Rime Witch's curse against her. This'll glow when she's near." He swung up to sit behind her on the horse. "No disguise can fool it."

"Good." She guided Remig away from the stable and into the blustering snowstorm. "Because we're returning to a trap."

He tightened his arms around her waist and pressed his cheek against the rough wool of her gray hood. "I know. But we're not returning feeble and divided."

She covered his hands at her waist, squeezed his fingers, and nodded. "You're right. We're strong. I'll defend you with my life, Sun Mage Gethen."

"And I'll defend you with mine, Militess Halina."

When they could no longer discern the abbedei's pink stone cliffs from the blowing snow, Gethen began his travel incantation. He was taking them back to waiting evil, but he had advantages that the Rime Witch lacked: He knew Ranith and Kharayan, he had the magic of the sun and the shadows, and he had a powerful champion to fight by his side.

Ranith was a dark, frozen ruin. No snow was falling when they arrived in the bailey, but the tower and buildings glittered, the ice and hoarfrost like diamond dust and just as hard.

Halina drew her sword. Stiff and straight in her saddle, she surveyed the bailey, the citadel, and the surrounding woods, all tense muscle and wary instincts beneath Gethen's hands.

No wind stirred the snowdrifts. No animals moved in the stables. No ice melted, dripped, or slid from branches. Even Remig was still but for the twitch of his ears and the plume of his breath.

Slowly, as if he was afraid that he'd disturb the ice sculpture that Ranith had become, Gethen slid off the horse. Halina followed, and he led Remig to the empty stable, put him into a stall, and gave him hay. He removed the horse's bridle and hung it on the stall gate but left him saddled. If they needed to make a fast getaway, Gethen didn't want to mess with the tack. Halina brought a blanket to keep the gelding warm, then they closed the stable behind them.

Idris was missing. As were the goats, chickens, sheep, and pigs.

Gethen scowled. "I don't like this dead home we've returned to."

Ranith was a place of life and noise. Though Gethen had practiced shadow sorcery, he'd always welcomed laughter, conversation, and the sounds of animals — wild and domestic — into his home. The silence that now clung to the citadel was profoundly disturbing. Where was Magod? And Noni? Where were the wolves?

He glanced at Halina, and she nodded. Together they moved forward across the hard, crunching snow, careful to avoid icy patches that shone like glass. The drifts at the front of the citadel had grown so tall and so compact that they blocked the wide wooden doors, and only the arched mouchettes and daggers of the second-floor clerestory windows peeked over the snow — twenty feet above the ground. They followed the curving tower wall to the kitchen. That entry was buried under snow deep enough to swallow them.

Halina scanned the second-floor windows — more exposed on this side of the bailey — and said, "Shall I find a rock?"

"To break my window?" Gethen shook his head then focused his magic on the glittering ice drift that had sealed the door. "You've already forgotten that you're with the Sun Mage?" Carefully he warmed the door and its hinges. Water ran down the stone frame but froze almost as quickly as it thawed. He worked from the lintel down but was hard-pressed to clear the ice without burning down the door.

"Damned unnatural cold." Halina slipped and skidded as she followed the citadel's wall and navigated the snowy lump that was the dwindling woodpile.

Gethen paused and glowered at the door. The top third had been exposed, but the remainder now resembled a frozen waterfall and had gained mass from the water cascading down and refreezing. He stepped back and considered the second floor windows. If they found a drift that was high and solid ....

Halina reappeared carrying an axe. "Save your strength for the real fight," she said then heaved the axe overhead and proceeded to bash the ice wall into flying chunks.

After only a few violent minutes she'd created a gap large enough to squeeze through and had doubled his admiration for her. What Halina lacked in heft, she more than made up for with tenacity. She lowered the axe, wiped her brow, and jerked her chin toward the door. "Would you like to warm those hinges or should I use this?"

Gethen smirked. "I'll handle them, Militess."

After a few moments of heating the door's edges and hardware, Gethen put his shoulder to it and forced it open. The swollen wood and warped metal screeched and fought him, but the door finally gave way, and he grabbed the frame to keep from sliding on the icy stoop. He turned and offered a steadying hand to Halina. She stood, grimacing and rubbing her newly healed leg. He'd forgotten her injury. "Are you hurting again?"

She took his hand and climbed through the opening into the kitchen. "I'm fine. I know my limits." Gethen nodded.

Swords drawn and amber mage light leading the way, they crept through the dark, frozen citadel. Hoarfrost coated every surface, horizontal and vertical, and the rooms were bitterly cold. No fires burned in the fireplaces. No wolves huddled together for warmth in the frosted stillroom. No sounds of Noni shuffling through the halls and complaining about the animals. No responses from Magod, sarcastic and loving, as his mother henpecked him and Gethen like they were ten-year-old boys.

The wards had failed when Gethen's shadow magic had died. Kharayan and Ranith had been violated.

Saying nothing and making as little sound as possible, they explored, and finally returned to the great hall. Gethen surveyed the room and peered into the long dark hall that led to the basilica. That part of Ranith, the oldest part of the building, was the only place they hadn't checked.

He sent amber mage light ahead of them in the passage. It glittered golden against the frost and icicles that coated the low ceiling and hung from the wall brackets. The way was slippery and dark. Gethen slowed, and Halina took the lead, her sword in hand.

Something about the passage down into the basilica bothered him more than the rest of the citadel's emptiness. Something was very wrong. The rest of the building felt cold and abandoned. But this passage and the basilica beyond felt heavy and horrible, full of desperation and death.

As they reached the end of the passage, Gethen grabbed Halina's arm and held her back. His mage light glinted dully off the basilica's massive copper doors. They were ajar, and horror waited behind them. He sent light into the large room and willed it to rise to the ceiling and flare brighter.

"Skiron's bones," he cursed as Halina gasped. The room was full of dead, frozen animals. Wolves, deer, rabbits, goats, bears, pigs — all the creatures of Kharayan and Ranith — bore frosted rictuses of pain and terror. They'd climbed over each other as if to escape some horror. Blood, frozen and pink with frost, coated the walls. Birds, white with hoarfrost and unmoving in death, perched upon the rafters. Gethen groaned and grabbed the doorframe.

Halina offered her hand, and he took it, needing her strength. "Can you save them? Like you did Xana?" Those words echoed off the frozen stones and bodies.

Gethen shook his head. "No. Their souls are gone."

But a noise carried to them. A whine and a high, squeaking howl. "Wolves," he whispered.

"Pups." Halina followed him into the carnage.

They called to the sole survivors of the Rime Witch's genocidal attack. They pried carcasses apart, covering their mouths with their scarves as the heat he carefully employed singed fur, flesh, and blood.

Finally, they found a cluster of wolves — bitches that had sought to shelter their offspring from evil's freezing onslaught. Two pups — one black, one white — squirmed and whined, cold, hungry, and scared. Halina took one, Gethen the other. They slipped them beneath their cloaks, and then made their way back through the dim corridor to the great hall.

They carried the pups to the kitchen. Halina found eggs, bread, and cheese in the larder, frozen porridge in the pot hanging above the grate. Gethen made a fire, and soon the animals were greedily eating, their faces and paws covered in food as they stood in the bowls and gorged.

Gethen melted the snow that blocked the citadel's main doors then, enflamed by hatred for the witch, he thawed the bailey and the tower. Every room and stone, save the basilica. That remained frozen. He stood in the kitchen doorway and stared at the bailey's sea of mud. Anger burned within him, a firestorm rising from his gut. He slipped his cloak from his shoulders. "Take the pups to the stable when they've finished and put them in Remig's stall; he'll keep them warm.

"Where are you going?"

"Outside. I've had enough of ice and snow. It's time to test the power of the sun."

His boots sank into the ooze up to mid-calf when he stepped off the kitchen stoop, but it was no matter. He didn't need to go far. He closed his eyes and felt for the fire that Halina had lit within him. It always burned, waiting to rise from a flicker to a conflagration. He began his incantation, loosing that flame and drawing down the heat of the sun that had been so long blocked by the witch's snow-laden clouds. No more. She wouldn't rule Ranith. She wouldn't kill Kharayan, Khara, Ursinum, Gurvan-Sum, Besera, Quoregna. He bid the sun to burn away the clouds. "Turn water to vapor in the sky, ice to water upon the ground. Thaw the land. Free this place from a winter that shouldn't be."

The sky lightened, black to gray, gray to white, and then blue broke through thinning clouds, pale at first then intensifying, spreading. Soon the sky was more blue than gray. The sun's warmth filled Gethen as it thawed his home and his forest.

The sky was so beautifully blue.

Halina moved past him, her boots making a sucking sound as she tromped through the mud toward the stable, the two sleepy wolves in her arms. The sunlight burnished her hair into an auburn crown. It made her skin glow, her freckles a darker constellation across her cheeks and nose, and her eyes, when she paused to return his gaze, her eyes were the same brilliant blue as the sky. When she returned from the stable, she stopped beside him, looked up at the clear sky, and closed her eyes. She smiled as the sunlight warmed her face.

He stroked her cheek. He would stand there forever watching the sun glinting in her hair and feeling its warmth on her skin. But he couldn't. "We need to look for Magod and Noni."

"I fear for them." She opened her eyes. "Do you think she's the Rime Witch? Or is she just a tool?"

"A tool. But I don't know for how long." He grimaced. "My heart tells me it was only a brief possession, but my brain knows that I could've been a fool for years."

Halina looked out into the forest as creaking and snapping echoed across the bailey. The melting snow was taking weakened tree branches with it as it slipped from upper boughs and crashed down upon the lower ones. It built up weight as it gathered snow and more branches on its plunge to the forest floor. "I hope the trees survive."

"They will. Kharayan is ancient. It has the strength and wisdom of a place that's existed for millennia."

A tree shivered and heaved just beyond the citadel's walls. The oak, apparently rooted shallowly, groaned and cracked, shook off its icy cloak then tipped over upon its neighbors, rolling and falling like a leviathan sinking into the sea.

Gethen had taken a pair of worn, brown gloves from the kitchen before he'd come outside. He pressed them between his bare palms then focused on the gloves and, more specifically, upon their owner. He turned a circle and, from the hard tug that pulled him a step or two forward, he recognized the last path that his groundsman had taken. "Are the wolves settled and safe?"

"Yes."

"Good. We're heading out. We'll find Magod in that direction."

"Alive and safe, I hope. Sheltering with more animals."

Gethen took her hand. "We'll travel more quickly by incantation."

Her fingers tightened on his. She drew her sword. "I'm ready."

Once again golden light enveloped them. In the blink of an eye they arrived at their destination, guided by the waning warmth of Magod's strong spirit. They were facing the stone monolith of the white mausoleum where they'd battled the undead shadow mages.

Halina sucked in a breath. It escaped in a low growl. "Is this a trap?"

Gethen surveyed the open area. All signs of their previous battle were gone, and his wards had failed here, too. Beside him Halina balanced on ready feet, her sword raised, and her eyes searching for their enemy. He still held the gloves, and they continued to pull upon him. It seemed that his only choice was to follow their lead, so he nodded toward the mausoleum. "That's where we'll find Magod."

She moved forward at his side; they were equals, she more skilled with the sword, he with magic. They crossed the black stones and the open space where she'd fought Volker then stopped beneath the mausoleum's portico. A soft, whistling breeze rustled bare tree branches around the clearing.

"Damnation," Gethen said. "The shadow mages have escaped, too."

Halina cursed a long and colorful description of Shemel and his predecessors as her gaze roamed from the doors to the curve of the mausoleum. There was so much to admire about her. She knew what those wraiths could do, and she wasn't afraid.

Gethen turned his back to the doors and raised his hands. He summoned the warm magic from within him and pulled it down from the sky. He focused it upon the stone circle and invoked fiery new wards.

Her focus still roaming, Halina asked, "You're warding us in? What if you're wrong and what's behind that door is particularly unpleasant?"

"If something besides Magod lurks here, it'll be worse than unpleasant, Militess. But I'd rather face it within the confines of a warded circle than allow it to escape. The Rime Witch needs no aid, and I won't release another monstrosity upon this world. If we die here, at least whatever kills us won't be freed."

She glanced at him. "But if you're dead, won't those wards fail?"

"Not the Sun Mage's wards."

"How do you know that?"

"Because the great window in the basilica was warded by Sun Mage Sulwen over a thousand years ago. It remains clear, clean, and intact."

Gethen turned back to the doors, satisfied that his wards would contain anything that could crawl from the bowels of the tor beneath their feet. As he'd done with the door at the citadel, he now focused upon the mausoleum's entrance. The doors soon glowed red along their seams as he heated them. Water trickled down their surface and spread out, a black stain creeping across the marble and toward their feet.

Halina held steady, her sword up and ready to hack apart any foe that should emerge from the mausoleum. Gethen stepped forward, placed his hand against the invisible lock within the doors, and whispered an incantation. A click sounded, the screech of iron against iron vibrated the doors as the locks pulled back, and then there was a sigh as the air from outside the building entered and the air inside escaped. He glanced at Halina. She was tense, focused, and ready for anything. He gestured, and the doors swung open. A pervasive darkness haunted the interior of the mausoleum and sucked all life from its surroundings.

A lump lay upon the marble floor, a body wrapped in gray wool and white frost. Gethen crossed the threshold with Halina at his side. "Magod? Speak to me." There was no response for a painfully long time. But Magod's spirit hadn't fled his body. The man was alive. But whether to live meant to move, to see, to be willing to open his eyes and face the world, Gethen didn't know. And he feared the worst.

Halina glanced at him, and then she stepped forward, reached down, and touched the groundsman. There was a shout. The lump surged up, fists raised, eyes wide, mouth angry. Halina kept her sword between them and Magod. Golden light hovered around Gethen's fingers sparking and arcane, but he too held his power in check, waiting and watching.

The groundskeeper blinked and squinted in the bright light that came through the open doors. He swayed and looked from Gethen to Halina and back again, his mouth wide and his eyes wider. "Are you who you were?" His voice was harsh and gravelly, the voice of a man who had not spoken for days and when last he'd uttered words, they'd been screamed.

Halina lowered her sword. She crouched and placed it upon the ground between them. Gethen drew the magic back into his body so that no light sparked around him. He raised both hands, palms facing outward, and said, "I'm your master and this is your margrave."

Hunched and swaying, his muscles trembling and his face haggard, Magod stared at them. "Prove it."

Gethen straightened and snarled, "I don't have to prove anything to a man who pissed his trouzes like a child." Halina shot him a surprised look, but he continued, "and didn't I promise to gut you a fortnight ago? You were supposed to remind me."

Magod gaped at him then staggered forward and clasped Gethen to him. "Master." It was a shocking display of relief and affection, but Gethen returned the man's embrace. Magod stepped back, stooped and shaking. "Thought you were dead, too."

"No, my old friend. It'll take a lot more than ice, snow, and a foul tempered beast to kill me." Gethen jerked his thumb toward Halina and added, "and even worse to do in the militess."

Halina laughed a little at that then removed her cloak and wrapped it around Magod's shoulders, ignoring his protests. "My armor keeps me warm enough," she said. "Besides, I expect to be fighting soon, and then the cloak will be a hindrance. You need this more. Take it, I insist, and you don't want to deny your liege."

The groundskeeper thanked her and fumbled with the clasp.

The tips of his fingers had developed hard, purplish blisters, damage from exposure to the cold. Gethen frowned. He didn't know if he'd be able to heal those wounds, but he'd try. He gave Magod the brown gloves. "What's become of your mother?" he asked gently.

Agony twisted Magod's expression and tears glittered in his eyes. He looked down at his damaged hands and blinked repeatedly then swallowed and worked at pulling on the gloves. "Left her making bread after you went. Wanted to check the pond hives 'cause that bee yard gets more wind." He stopped fiddling with the gloves and stared at the floor. "Found Mummin trapped under the pond's ice. Don't know how long she'd been there." He met Gethen's gaze and mumbled, "She looked scared."

Gethen swallowed. "I'm sorry."

Magod nodded. "Know you cared about her, Master."

"She was mother to me longer than mine could be."

"The witch stole Noni's appearance?" Halina picked up her sword. "Does she still keep that form?" There was as much steel in her voice as there was in her blade.

Magod shook his head. "Don't know, Your Ladyship. Drove away as many animals as I could before I went into the woods, but there was nowhere to hide. I took refuge under fallen logs with wolves that hadn't been in the basilica when she started killing. Prayed all night to gods I'd never even whispered to and waited to die. Then she came into the woods, so I made peace with the world, sure I wouldn't see another day."

He winced as he grabbed Gethen's shoulder. "The wolves saved me. The pack attacked, so I could get away." He rubbed his arm across his eyes and his sleeve came away damp. "Don't think any escaped."

Gethen closed the mausoleum doors, sent the locks home, and warded them from opening. "There are two pups. They survived the massacre in the basilica and are now in the stable, warm and safe."

Magod's eyes brightened as if that small gift of news was the greatest treasure he'd ever received. "Gods be praised." He wiped his eyes with his sleeve again.

Halina touched Gethen's arm. "We should return to the citadel. We aren't safe here."

"We're not safe anywhere. Not until the witch has been destroyed." He beckoned Magod forward, grasped the man's arm and held Halina's hand. Then he summoned the magic of the sun to return them to the citadel.

They needed a plan to trap their enemy.

NINETEEN

The white walls and arched ceiling of Ranith's great hall formed around them. Halina glanced at Gethen. Shadows had returned to his face and he stumbled as they started up the stairs to the infirmary with Magod held upright between them. "You're getting tired," she said.

Gethen grunted. "I'm stronger than I've been in a long time, but I'm not without limits, and my magic's turned tepid."

"I imagine performing a transportation spell is hard once, let alone thrice."

"Yes, but Magod wouldn't have made it on foot."

"You're no good if you're too exhausted to battle the Rime Witch, and even less useful if you're dead."

He gave her a weary smile. "I recall a time not so long ago when you would've welcomed my death."

"Good of you to help me, Your Ladyship," the groundsman mumbled.

Halina said, "We'll get you warm, fed, and well."

"Then we'll come up with a plan to trap the witch," Gethen added.

Magod winced and groaned with each step as his warming

flesh began to swell and his damaged nerves protested. Their progress was slow, but they finally reached the infirmary and got the groundsman into bed. Halina laid a fire in the grate while Gethen considered Magod's frostbitten fingers and toes.

"I can heal what's damaged, but not even this necromancer can bring life into flesh that's dead."

With the fire roaring and melting what frost remained in the room, Halina gathered blankets from adjoining rooms and covered Magod. The trembling that had begun in Gethen's hands hadn't escaped her notice. He needed sleep and sustenance to renew his strength. She went to the kitchen and prepared porridge, tea, and took a loaf of bread and more cheese from the larder. These she brought upstairs on a large tray. She sliced the bread and toasted it over the fire, added cheese so that it melted and bubbled, and then all three of them ate.

Gethen had brought mead from the stillroom, poured it into a kettle, and warmed it. The whole meal brought life back into the Sun Mage, and even Magod had some color in his face again.

"This may be the finest meal I've ever enjoyed, Margrave Khara," Gethen said as he tore another hunk of bread from the remainder of the unsliced loaf. "My compliments to your cook."

Halina saluted him with a spoonful of porridge. "I'm afraid it's all she knows how to prepare." She, too, felt much restored by the food and drink.

After they'd finished, Halina brought the wolf pups and Remig into the citadel while Gethen mixed metheglin for a healing tincture and sorted through unguents in search of something that would heal Magod's damaged skin. The animals were safest when they were closest to their master, so she snuggled the pups into bed with Magod. She enclosed the horse in a small sitting room off the great hall after pulling apart a bale of straw to cover the floor and shoving all of the furniture into the corners. "Settle down here." She gave him more hay, grain, and water, and decided against a fire in the grate though the room was chilly; horses were more terrified of flames than cold. Remig was blanketed and the straw was thick. He would be fine.

She encountered Gethen as he reached the bottom of the stairs. "How's Magod?"

"Better than expected." He passed through the great hall and toward the long narrow hallway that led to the basilica. "He'll lose some fingers and toes, but not all of them. Not the ones he most needs to walk and work."

Halina's halved fingers twitched. "That's a relief." Fatigue slowed her feet, but she followed him down the gradually sloping path. "Why are you going back to the basilica?"

"Parts of the citadel remain frozen, but I don't want to use my strength for heating so much stone." He paused, discomfort furrowing his brow. He glanced at her and added, "And if I don't deal with the dead animals the stench of so much warm, rotting flesh will kill us."

Halina followed him. "What will you do?"

"Cremate them." He held up his hand to stop her from following him into the basilica. They'd reached the double doors, and Gethen's gesture and incantation already had the locks clunking and squealing. The doors creaked open. He stopped at the threshold, said a short spell, and exploded each stained-glass window outward with a violent punch of magic at them. Only the Sun Mage's great round window was spared.

"But you'll burn down the citadel."

"Wards will contain the flames." He faced her and raised his arms to his sides. Again red, orange, and yellow sparks rose from his hands, trailed across his fingers, and writhed around his arms. The magic rose up, heating the room, and creating a shimmering curtain behind him. It bathed the walls, the floor, and the ceiling.

Halina blanched as a wall of flames rose between them. Its heat forced her back. "Gethen?"

He emerged from the room, a demon walking through flame, his eyes and skin glowing blue-white and his hair twisting and smoking. He turned at the doorway and said another incantation, his voice low and intense. Air whooshed past Halina, sucking her hair forward and pushing her a step toward the room. The light emanating from Gethen was pulled out of him into the basilica, and all the horribly twisted and grotesque bodies exploded into flames.

He clapped his hands together, the sound sharp and violent. The doors slammed shut. The locks clunked and squealed. And Gethen warded them with sharp, angry gestures that burned marks into the metal. No flames, smoke, or unwelcome spirits would enter the citadel from there. "Come." His voice was quiet. "The fire will consume the flesh and bones, and burn itself out. And the smoke will escape through the windows as the conflagration thaws Ranith tonight."

She studied his face. His eyes were haunted and shadowy, and his mouth was set in a hard line. She remained silent as they strode back through those dark, twisting hallways, gradually rising upward from the lowest point in Ranith.

As they reached the great room Gethen stopped on its lush, elaborate rug. "This is the heart of Ranith. The very center of the keep." Once again he raised his arms, closed his eyes, and released the magic that flowed through him from the sun. He wove an intricate but powerful and substantial series of golden wards that encased Ranith and Kharayan.

The hair on Halina's arms stood. Heat shimmered off the floor and walls, and seared her skin. She grabbed the dark wooden banister that curled at the base of the stairs, afraid she'd run from the Sun Mage if she didn't hold fast. Not even the wards she'd walked through when she'd first entered his woods held the strength and threat that these contained.

He turned and looked at her. "Are you frightened of me?"

She swallowed and stared around the room at the glow that touched everything like dust sparkling in the sun. "Of those wards." She looked at him. "Of your power. When you were a shadow mage, you weren't this terrifying."

He went to her, stroked her cheek, and held her gaze. "You're safe from me, Halina." She pressed his hand to her lips. He pulled her up the stairs. "But now I'm tired. Let's hope that those wards hold and are strong enough to repel the Rime Witch through the night."

"Gods help us if they aren't."

―――――――

"Let me remove your armor," Gethen said as they entered his fourth floor chamber.

Halina pulled logs from the firewood box beside the fireplace and stacked them upon the grate then stood to fetch the tinderbox from the mantle. "And my trouzes and shift?" She glanced over her shoulder at him.

Weariness weighed down his smile. "If you wish, Your Ladyship." He caught her sword belt and pulled her backward, slid his hands around her waist, and pressed her body to his. With a small gesture, he sparked a fire on the hearth.

Halina relaxed into him. She rested her head against his shoulder and closed her eyes, sighing as he pressed his face to her hair and inhaled.

"You smell like smoke and battle. And sweaty horses," he said.

Her laugh was low and quiet. "If you're going to stand this close to me, Sun Mage, you'd better grow accustomed to the stink. I don't own any perfumes or powders. Except the kind that stifles lice."

His lips slid along the curve of her ear, and her breath hitched as his teeth nipped her flesh. The leather straps of her armor creaked as he unbuckled them. "That could be problematic; more than once, I've been called a louse."

"Probably by me."

Gethen's hands slid around her hips, found the buckle of her belt, and released it. The sword thudded to the floor. Her tassets, pauldrons, breast plate, and chain mail joined it. "Probably." Starting from the bottom and moving upward, he pushed the metal toggles through the leather loops that fastened her tabard.

She began to tug the buckles free on her left vambrace, but her fingers were slow. "Semele's blood, I'm tired." Languid, she closed her eyes. Warmth infused her from his body. She sighed again as he slipped off each piece of her armor. She always forgot how much it weighed her down.

"Of course you are. I've been using your strength for two days."

That was disconcerting. She turned in his arms to see his expression. "You have? How have I not noticed?"

Contrition joined the fatigue that aged Gethen's face. "Because you weren't fighting it. You gave yourself freely to me." He kissed her then, slowly and deeply.

Perhaps this is what it means to love, she thought.

Gethen broke the kiss and hugged her tighter to him. Halina closed her eyes again, her face against his shoulder and smiled as he added, "Thank you, Militess Halina, Margrave of Khara, for helping a lowly mage defend his remote home."

"Thank you, Gethen, Sun Mage of Ranith, for helping an outcast bastard defend her penniless holding." She leaned back and tugged his sword belt off, allowing it to clunk to the floor beside hers, then pushed his surcoat off his shoulders and tossed it across a chair.

But they were both too exhausted to do much else. Boots came off and trouzes. Gethen checked her leg, ribs, and left hand, and proclaimed them healed. She washed his hands and her own with honeyed soap, though they both winced at the iciness of the water. He removed the braids from her tangled hair, and she dozed in a chair as he combed out the knots. Finally, they slid beneath the bed's heavy blankets.

"Your strength seems limitless to me," Gethen murmured. Sleep slurred his words. "I must remember not to take so much."

"And I must be aware of your need." They were quiet for a while, and the fire crackled in the grate. Halina rolled over and traced the fine lines at the corner of his left eye, followed the curve of his nose to his lips, and then traced the strong bones of his cheek back up to the corner of his right eye. "You were the Shadow Mage. You are the Sun Mage. You have the power of both the darkness and the light. Use it. Use everything. Use me and my strength."

He captured her fingers and kissed them. His thumb found the talisman ring, and he drifted to sleep sweeping his finger across its curve and back again.

Halina soon followed her lover into slumber, and it was many hours of dreamless sleep later when instinct awakened her.

Check Magod, the pups, and Remig. Stoke the fire in the infirmary and throw another blanket over all of them. There was no one else to do these things. She slipped from the bed, wincing at the cold beneath her feet and swirling around her legs. "Blood and bones," she whispered. Though Or-Halee had been cold at night, it hadn't been bone chilling.

"Where are you going?"

She touched Gethen's shoulder and tucked the covers around him. "Just checking on Magod and the animals. I'll be back soon; it's too cold to stay awake long. Keep the bed warm for me." He mumbled, pulled her pillow against his chest, and his breathing slowed and deepened.

Halina dressed quickly but hesitated over her armor. She yawned. The citadel was heavily warded. There'd been no sign of the witch all day. She just wanted to stoke the infirmary's fire and add a blanket to Magod's bed. But what if the pups needed feeding? What if Magod was struggling? What if the Rime Witch had found a way through the wards? Again. With a quiet growl, she donned her tabard and cloak. She grabbed her sword then lit a candle from the grate and headed down to the second floor.

The citadel was dark and quiet. The glowing symbols of Gethen's wards shimmered silver and writhed like living creatures. Their needle chill prickled her skin when she touched them. They reminded her of the wards she'd crossed to enter Kharayan.

Halina moved quickly down the stairs and through the quiet stillroom to the infirmary. The door was open. The fire burned low but warm upon the hearth, and the pups slumbered in the bed. But Magod was gone. "Maybe he went to the jakes." But that didn't make sense since there was a chamber pot beneath the bed.

Frowning, Halina descended to the great hall and paused at the foot of the stairs. She wouldn't awaken Gethen unless she had a clear need, and Magod wandering wasn't necessarily a problem. She headed for the kitchen. Maybe he'd gotten hungry or thirsty.

He was sitting stone-still at the table. A bowl of congealing porridge and a sputtering candle sat before him.

"Magod?" He didn't respond, didn't move or blink. She sat opposite him, leaving her sword upon the bench. "Come back to bed. You need rest." Halina reached out to touch his hand but stopped midway. The ring upon her finger glowed orange and bright in the dark kitchen.

Magod's eyes were white orbs, their pupils missing. "We're not alone, Your Ladyship." He lunged across the table and knocked over the candle as he grabbed for her.

Halina tumbled backward off the bench. The candle was snuffed and her sword clattered away, lost to sudden darkness. She raised her hand, trying to see by the ring's light.

Magod, with unnatural reflexes, climbed over the table like a river crab and leaped at her. She shouted, kicked away from the bench, and rolled as he sought to pin her to the floor. She hooked the bench with her foot and shoved it at him. It struck the possessed groundsman's ankles and knocked his feet out from underneath him. His head cracked against the table then the stone floor. He didn't move.

But she wasn't free.

White mist rose from his body, and the room's temperature plunged. Halina's breath fogged and her teeth chattered. Like a beacon, the ring now glowed white. The mist coalesced into a female form and gained substance.

Halina searched for her sword but found only cold tile. "Bollocks!" Then she was up and running. No looking back. "Gethen! The Witch!"

Cold seized her, a bitter and binding iciness that burned her lungs. Her muscles cramped so painfully that she screamed. She stumbled, tripped over a chair in the great hall, and hit the floor hard, unable to run, breathe, or shout.

On her back, Halina stared up at a gray face and white eyes, frosted brows and bony, icicled fingers. The Rime Witch loomed over her, bent closer, and smiled the coldest, most terrifying smile Halina had ever seen.

Then the witch's fractured, frosted, translucent skin began to slough off, falling like snowflakes upon Halina. The substance hit her skin, burned and stuck. The Rime Witch was disintegrating above Halina even as she reappeared *upon* her, a mask and cloak for Halina to bear. Cold and terror gripped the militess's body, froze her throat, and spread to her heart. And Halina's last thought was: *Gethen won't know me.*

TWENTY

Gethen hadn't gone back to sleep after awakening to Halina's movements. His body had relaxed, but part of his mind had remained alert. And it was that part that perceived her distant shout and jolted the rest of him fully awake.

He was on his feet before he realized it. The fire was out. The room was icy and his wards had turned from gold to silver. She'd gone to check on Magod and the wolves. She hadn't returned. Instead she'd called for him, something she wouldn't have done lightly.

He yanked on his trouzes and shoved his feet into his boots then stumbled into the hallway, slipped, and fell hard. "Blood and bones." He sent up a bright ball of mage light. It illuminated walls, floor, and an arched ceiling that glittered with ice.

The witch had broken his wards.

Halina needed him. Gethen was up and scrambling downstairs, wary of ice on the floor as he pushed his senses ahead of him. He reached, stretched, and searched for her warm, powerful presence in the bone-chilling citadel.

Something responded, but it was strange and erratic, and he wasn't certain it was her. He invoked his wards again, stretched them out and blasted their heat up the walls. The ceilings dripped water as ice melted, and darkness seeped across the floor, a stain brought to his home by the Rime Witch.

"Halina? Magod!"

He went to the infirmary. The wolf pups were asleep, but there was no sign of the militess or his groundsman. He cast his net of awareness as he went down the stairs. And he finally latched onto her, or something like her, and sensed that she was being restrained.

Gethen descended to the first floor. She wasn't in the kitchen, but Magod was.

"Damnation." Unconscious and bleeding from a split skull, the groundsman lay on the floor. Gethen touched his shoulder, uttered an incantation to stop the blood flowing from his wound, but left him when he spied Halina's longsword beneath the overturned bench. "No. No-no-no." He retrieved it.

"Halina!" His senses slipped upward and outward through Ranith's rooms and halls, the broken upper floors, and into the catacombs beneath the tor. There was nothing in the library. Only Remig dozed in the first floor receiving room. Gethen stared with unseeing eyes until his senses crossed the hallway that led to the basilica. His vision focused. "There you are." He bared his teeth, feral and vicious. The Rime Witch was with her. The hunt was on.

He lit the hall as bright as midday and warmed it until the sheet of ice that the witch had left in his path became a river and flowed downward. His boots slapped wet stone, and the sound of rushing, dripping water echoed in the narrow space.

The basilica's doors had been torn open. Twisted metal and splintered planks lay within the confines of the blackened, ruined room. Ash and bones covered the floor in a layer so thick that the white tiles were obscured from view. Moonlight shone through the holes that had once held windows, casting silver beams across everything. Frost glittered upon the entire ruin and even obscured the great glass window that depicted Sulwen's triumph over her sister. Amidst the destruction stood the Rime Witch. An ice carving among ashes, only her fingers twitched.

But there was no sign of Halina.

Gethen drew not only shadows to him but all the light, as well. He summoned up his mage fire and harnessed all the reflections and glimmers that bounced off the puddles and damp walls. He wove his dark, shimmering armor, and then directed the light up to the ceiling. But he withheld its heat and power. He wanted to see what the Rime Witch planned, and he had to find Halina.

He saw no evidence of her in the room, yet Gethen sensed her presence. He surveyed the ash. Along the walls it lay as thick as the snow in the bailey had been. Was she buried alive, struggling to breathe? He shoved that unhelpful thought away and, instead, studied the witch, holding his silence as she held hers.

Yisun had been a young woman when she'd died. Her frosted skin was cracked and fissured. Bereft of pupils and color, her eyes were the white of flesh that had been too long submerged in water. Her tattered surcoat was the same sickly hue as her skin. The Rime Witch had the thick, black hair of the Dargani, but it clung to her shoulders and back, matted and ragged. She'd been beautiful when she was alive and not filled with hate and a cold, dead heart.

Gethen focused on the witch's hands. The control with which she held herself broke at those twitching fingers.

He pushed sunlight into the corners and into the rafters. Halina was there, hidden to him, but reaching out. He opened up to her presence, found her rage, and fueled his sorcery with it. He tapped into her heat, hoping it would guide him to her hiding spot. The room warmed, and steam began to rise off the Rime Witch in little wisps and whorls.

"It's been a long wait for revenge." Her voice was high, brittle, and rang with the strange squealing sound of ice grinding upon ice in the frozen north.

"And you'll have to keep waiting," Gethen said as he eased into the room, his movements swirling ash and frost around and up into the rafters. "Release Her Ladyship. Leave Ranith. And return to your frozen tomb in the Void. You're unwelcome here."

She bared her teeth and hissed. A whirlwind began around her feet picking up ash and frost and spinning it around and around, throwing out little bits of bone and glittering silica. "Ranith isn't yours, Sun Mage, and your power only exists to conquer Quoregna."

The witch raised her arms and uttered a piercing shriek. She was weaving a necromantic spell from the very destruction that she'd wrought. Around Gethen's boots and throughout the basilica, bones skittered and slid, coalesced and took form. Under her command the remains of the animals that he'd sought to protect clattered toward him on ghostly feet and gossamer wings, claws clicked, teeth ground, and talons flexed to tear and rend.

Gethen flicked his fingers, and the same wind that had swirled around the Rime Witch now increased, jumbling the bones and ash of the undead beasts and tossing them into the corners and through the broken windows.

As he worked, the Rime Witch whipped her head from side-to-side and grimaced as if overcome by a fit of madness. She balled her fists and pounded them against her hips. She opened her mouth and white eyes wide and screeched, throwing her head back. And her face flaked into little bits of icicle flesh; blackened, frozen, frostbitten skin cracked and peeled away, falling like a miasmic snow. She gnashed her teeth and spittle flew from her lips with curses spoken in the old tongue.

Then the witch's arms jerked up, her fingers stiffened. She muttered strange incantations and drew icicle daggers, needlelike and deadly, from the air itself. They flashed at Gethen. He hit the ground and rolled then raised his hand, scribing a ward of heat before him, a shield that caught and melted the icicles mere inches from his body. He pushed forth with his fingers and hands, throwing the heat toward her, and was rewarded with her shriek and the stench of burned hair.

The witch prowled back and forth. "Your sun sorcery is weak and your dark sorcery is gone. But I'll take your power and raise Ranith's shadow army." She clapped her hands together and hissed another spell. Gethen had only seconds to move as the moisture from her ruined ice daggers and needles coalesced into two hoarbeasts.

He laughed. "Is that the best you can do?" He raised Halina's sword and summoned the ash that remained adrift upon the air. Around and around it swirled, coalescing silica clouds into which he fed heat. The sword rang, and the witch's hair lifted on end.

Lightning flashed in the room, blue-white and deadly. Gethen captured the bolt with the sword, gritting his teeth as it traveled down the blade, into his hand, and through his body. The heat and pain were excruciating. The power burned his nerves, made him cry out. It stiffened his muscles and stopped his heart for a beat, and then another. But he controlled sunlight, fire, and lightning. He directed the energy through his body, across his nerves, and out his other hand. It struck the closest beast, and the creature shrieked and exploded into flames. A geyser of steam and water collapsed and washed over Gethen's feet.

The other beast lumbered forward, dumb to the death of its partner, and Gethen swung Halina's lightning-touched longsword, an arcing blow that cleaved the head from the hoarbeast even as it reached for him, its nebulous flesh becoming solid, spiked, and deadly. Like its cohort, the creature evaporated into wet ash and steam.

Gethen expected the witch's next strike to follow immediately. But instead of attacking him, like a deranged animal she continued the assault upon her own flesh, gouging the skin from her face and leaving huge, bloodless welts. She screamed and flailed, yanked her hair, then turned and ran straight at the wall. She struck it. Bones cracked and flesh tore, flaked, and fell. She collapsed into a heap on the floor, flipped over, and scuttled toward him, growling and baring her teeth. "You want more, Sun Mage?"

Pain and terror twisted through Gethen. The blood in his veins slowed, his heart and lungs convulsed. His ears rang and his body arched, then he sank to his knees. He couldn't draw breath. He couldn't control his muscles. He couldn't counter this spell. The witch was freezing his blood. He struggled to form the spells that would invoke the sun and its warmth. It sparked enough to keep him from plunging across the Voidline into death, but it didn't break her hold.

She circled him, jeering and sneering. Yet she couldn't crush him either. She stopped suddenly, grunted and growled, "No, no, *no*!" She hissed as inch-by-inch, step-by-step she approached Gethen where, on his knees, he struggled to remain alive. The Rime Witch stopped only inches from him. The smell of thawing, rotten meat wafted off her and turned his stomach.

Gethen's vision tunneled and his ears rang. He pushed back the darkness. He wouldn't succumb to cold and death when he'd only just discovered the sun.

The witch continued her strange, guttural protest as she reached out her shaking left hand as if to touch him. Her fingers were frosted and stiff. Icicles clung to their tips.

Gethen didn't know what compelled her to stray so close to danger, but he didn't hesitate to seize the opportunity. With every bit of strength he could summon, he thrust Halina's sword into the witch's gut.

She laughed and grabbed his hand upon the sword grip. Heat surged through him. He shouted from pain and relief as the witch's spell over him disintegrated. He collapsed in the wet, ashy remains of the hoarbeasts, panting and shaking.

The sword clattered to the ground. He stared at it. Bright red blood slicked the blade.

And then Halina was on her knees before him, shaking and

pressing her hands to her stomach. "That stinking, rotten wench," she said through gritted teeth. Blood oozed past her fingers. It dripped into the ash and water coating the floor.

"Oh, gods, Halina."

"You didn't know."

"Let me help." Gethen reached for her.

She pushed his hands away. "Her first. Then me. She's weak from fighting both of us." She loosened her belt with shaking hands, folded her tunic under it to press against the wound, and then cinched the belt tighter. "I've had worse."

He pulled her to her feet.

She retrieved her longsword, wiped the bloody blade on her trouzes, then shouted at the missing witch: "Get your cold, cowardly arse back here so I can kill you!"

"Red Blade, indeed." If he hadn't been so horrified by what he'd just done Gethen would've laughed. "I see why men fall over themselves and each other to follow you into battle."

"Because they're fools."

"For you." Gethen searched the basilica for the Rime Witch. There was nowhere to hide, yet she'd disappeared. "She's here. Be wary."

Halina met his gaze and smiled like a wolf that had found its dinner. "Let's find her," she said and stalked toward Sulwen's tomb.

The room plunged into darkness, the temperature plummeted, and a choking blizzard wind enveloped them. The witch had waited to attack when they'd moved apart.

With another incantation, Gethen banished the cold and darkness. And revealed the Rime Witch above and behind Halina clinging to the wall like a spider. He shouted a warning as the witch roared, her sound ghostly and wild. He wove a net of fire and magic as he ran.

"Stop this, you damned child!" The militess pivoted, her sword poised to thrust. "You're not wielding power, it's wielding *you*."

The witch obeyed the command and stared down at her. Something crossed Yisun's face and, for a moment, she looked like a confused little girl. Then that moment passed and her expression turned ugly and evil once more. "You are nothing! You have no magic. You are an outcast, despised by your own people. A *woman!*" That last sentence came out as a snarl.

Halina sneered and replied, "Just like you."

The witch laughed, and then hissed another incantation. Halina gasped and doubled over. She went to her knees and dropped her sword. Blood crystalized as it dripped from her nose.

Gethen grabbed her and suffused her body with heat. "No!" The witch was freezing her blood just as she'd tried with him. "Fight it!" But Halina gasped and convulsed. Her lips were blue.

The Rime Witch dropped to the floor and raised her arms, summoning the fallen ash and bones to return to the basilica and cloak her in a hideous form. She was a sightless amalgam of teeth and claws, cinders and soot, jagged bones, malevolence, and spite. She began a low, susurrus spell, and the shadows that flickered and danced upon the distant walls surged forward to surround her.

Halina was shaking and cold. "I won't let you die." Gethen placed his hand against her back and forced his own magic into her. It glowed golden beneath her skin and behind her eyes as he willed her struggling heart to pump, her lungs to work, her blood to thaw, and her wound to heal. "Look at me, Militess," he commanded.

She inhaled and coughed, then her eyes opened. "Stop her," she whispered.

"We'll do it together." He retrieved her sword, stood, and pulled Halina up. She cursed, swayed, and took the blade in shaking hands. Gethen slipped behind her and wrapped his arm around her waist. He pulled her back against his body. She was cold against him as she continued to bleed. Halina hefted her longsword. If she died it would be fighting. Gethen raised his hand.

The Rime Witch had summoned Kharayan's immortal shadow army. "You should have joined us, Gethen of Ranith. You could have led this army." She wore daggered armor fashioned from ice and bones. Her generals — Shemel, Olegário, and Volker — stood behind her, armed with black swords. Her officers were more dark and undead shadow mages, and her soldiers were writhing, demonic shadows. "Instead you'll be crushed by it!"

With a shout, she sent them thundering forward, death and damnation coming from every angle to destroy Gethen and Halina.

"Don't die on me, Militess." He was pushing her past her limits.

"Trying not to, Mage." She planted her feet, raised her sword above her head, and waited for one more chance to kill the witch.

As he had done with the bear, Gethen drew power from Halina. It blazed red and surged from her into him, and set his nerves afire. Magic burned through him, flared and formed a fiery cloak that enrobed him and strengthened her. He raised his hands and channeled the magic of the sun and her sword through them. He formed a glowing orb as heavy and hot as the sun itself, and Gethen hurled it as the first ranks reached for Halina.

The orb exploded in all directions in a flash of white light so bright that no shadows could persist. Its heat and mass obliterated them and slammed the witch into the wall beneath the Sun Mage's window. The stained glass exploded and fractals of jeweled glass rained down across the witch and the floor. Her generals blazed, columns of fire that surged up to the basilica's ceiling, and then collapsed, leaving smoking piles of ash. What remained of the shadows was scorched into the basilica's marble walls.

The Rime Witch staggered, her body burning, false flesh returning to ash and scattering with every step she took toward Gethen and Halina. She raised her blackened, crumbling hands, touched her charred face, and screamed. Then she turned her blind eyes upon them. "We'll have our revenge!" she shouted and lunged at them.

Halina brought her sword down and across, striking the witch's head from her shoulders.

The Rime Witch stumbled, fell, and shattered as she struck Sulwen's golden marble grave. But her powerful spirit didn't disappear. Unleashed, it surged through the room, a storm of daggered hail and screaming wind. It sucked up the power that had been unleashed with the destruction of the shadow mages, shook the foundation of the citadel, and engulfed Halina. The militess screamed as it tore her spirit from her faltering flesh, and then both souls disappeared across the Voidline.

As Gethen caught Halina's collapsing body, Magod appeared in the basilica's doorway, an ax in his hand and blood on his face. "Master, I—"

"Get over here!" Gethen pushed healing warmth into Halina's cooling body and forced her weakening heart to work.

Magod knelt beside the stricken militess. "What can I do?"

Gethen grabbed the man's hands, placed them over her sternum, and showed him how to pump her ribcage to keep her heart beating. "Don't stop until she opens her eyes."

"But—"

"Do it!" Gethen released his soul to cross the Voidline in search of the woman he loved and the witch who would kill her.

He stepped into the Void's silent forest of spindly trees and stared around. It had changed. Glittering black frost and ice coated everything. The cobblestone path was slick and obscured, and the slate gray sky was now black and starless. Strangest of all, the trees had aligned into straight rows, an easy route for the shadow army to follow to the Voidline. Masses of them marched past him. The soldiers he'd just banished were already on the path back to the corporeal world.

But Gethen was still the keeper of the border. His will took the form of a hot, howling wind, and he scrubbed their malevolence from the forest. Like dust motes, they fragmented and swirled into the black sky. But they'd be back if he didn't find and stop the Rime Witch.

The sharp clash of steel on steel drew him further into the woods. He ran toward the sounds of swordplay. Shouts and curses grew louder. He emerged into the clearing where the Void's mausoleum stood. There Halina battled Shemel and Volker.

Gethen swallowed a curse when he saw her spirit. She was solidifying and losing the colorful hues of the living world as her corporeal form weakened. Already a gray hole gaped where her abdominal wound still bled. By contrast, the shadow mages were whole and powerful in the Void. They wielded their dark swords, lunging, thrusting, and parrying, seeking weakness in the militess's defenses. But blood magic protected her. Her armor, her sword, and even her scars glowed red with it. She was the superior swordswoman, and she countered their strikes again and again.

Olegário lay in a crumpled heap at the foot of the black mausoleum. He'd already fallen to Halina's sword, and his spirit was dissipating like snow being lifted by wind.

"Where's the witch?" Gethen called.

"In the mausoleum." Halina replied without looking away from her circling enemies. She lunged toward Volker as she thrust at Shemel. Gethen's master fell into the trap and was skewered through the chest by her longsword. He staggered and went to his knees. Halina called, "Shemel's yours to finish, Sun Mage," as she ducked Volker's sword. She yanked hers free, turned, and barely dodged his next blow. It glanced off the ring Gethen had given her and traveled past her right ear. The thrust carried Volker forward. Halina pivoted into his motion and slammed her elbow into the dead mage's face.

Gethen strode to where his former master knelt and snatched the mage's black sword from his hands, scowling at the taint of necromantic magic on it. A line of chalky white liquid oozed from Shemel's nose and mouth. Like Olegário, his spirit was already disintegrating into the Void, creating a widening hole in his chest. He snarled at Gethen. "Weak! So weak you need a *woman* to protect you!"

"I've had enough of you."

Shemel's snarl became a mad grin. "And I you. Let's see who wins this war."

"I already have." Gethen raised the weapon overhead then thrust it straight down into the spirit's skull. Light glinted dully off the blade where it showed through the hole in Shemel's chest. The Sun Mage smiled as his dead master's rotten soul unraveled like knotted wool, then he turned and strode up the steps of the mausoleum. The Rime Witch was in there, and it was time to end this battle. He paused and looked back.

Halina decapitated Volker. She turned from the disintegrating soul, punted his head out of her path, then joined Gethen on the steps.

He considered her.

"What?"

"That was callous even for you."

She shrugged. "He was a prick."

Gethen smiled. "And that's why I love you."

"Do you?" She seemed pleased and perplexed.

But Gethen's smile faded and he grabbed her hand. She felt almost solid. Her body was nearing death back in the basilica. "I've got to end this before it's too late to bring you home."

Halina suddenly pressed against him. Her voice and expression were intense as she said, "Use everything to do it. Use my strength." She raised her glowing sword. "Use this magic. Whatever it takes."

Gethen kissed her then reached for all the power in the sun, the moon, the fiery stars, and all the strength Halina had for him. It pushed against the seams of his soul, threatening to tear him apart and spin his fragments off into the Void. He pressed down on the power, squeezing it, holding it tight with only his will, and using its potential to fuel his magic. He nodded, and they entered the mausoleum.

Expecting an attack from the raging Rime Witch, Gethen was stopped in his tracks by a slight, raven-haired adolescent. She sat upon the floor in a tattered shift, her knees hugged to her chest. "Yisun," he said. *Is this a trick?*

She looked up, and her eyes were no longer pupil-less orbs. Tears stained her face. She was more child than woman and nothing like a witch. "I can't stop it," she whispered.

"Stop what?" He scanned the dark room. It was empty.

"The storm. The changes in the Void. The march of the army.

"The shadow mages said they'd make me powerful, but they lied. They only freed me because I could work the weather so well. Once they had your power, they wouldn't need me anymore. I'm just a girl, just a thing to be used and thrown away." She looked at Halina and added, "A child who let power wield her."

Halina said nothing, and Yisun continued. "You were right, Red Blade. And you made me think for the first time in ... forever."

"I knew it," Gethen muttered. Louder he said, "Then stop being used. Help me put an end to this storm and get Halina back across the Voidline before her body dies."

The girl stood. "I told you; I can't stop it."

He shook his head. "Not alone. But we can together."

Halina grabbed his hand. Her eyes asked if he was certain or insane.

Yisun's expression brightened. She looked askance at Halina and said, "I'm sorry you were hurt."

"So am I." There was no forgiveness in the militess's tone.

The girl held out her hands, palms facing up. The question of trust filled her eyes. But Halina raised her sword, blocking Yisun's approach. The young sorceress bit her lip then said, "I know it's hard to believe me."

Gethen's gaze went from Halina to Yisun and back. The warm

hues of Halina's skin and hair were fading; the widening gray hole threatened to swallow her heart.

"This is a trap," she said.

"Probably. But you're out of time and I'm out of options. I have to trust her for your sake." He addressed Yisun. "If I have any doubt, the militess will remove your head."

Halina's lips became a thin line as she brought her sword's glowing blade up to rest against Yisun's throat. The girl didn't flinch away from the weapon.

Gethen grasped Yisun's hands, and her soul was bared to him. It was raw from loneliness and betrayal, wounded by the hatred and rage that had clawed at its seams for centuries. This was the thing that he'd sensed in the storm, this fractured spirit. The part of Yisun that was the Rime Witch was barely contained, and Gethen felt the girl's control unraveling.

She tightened her grip on his fingers. "Please destroy me."

Gethen shook his head. "You're just a child."

Halina grabbed his arm. "Sulwen spared her and look what's happened."

"She's right." Yisun's voice trembled. "Don't make my sister's mistake. I can't control the part of me that's horrible. Shemel knew that. Others will come and they'll use me like the shadow mages did."

"I know. *Gods!*" Gethen clenched his teeth then released the hold he had on his own power. "I'm sorry." Heat and light surged forth to collide with the cold hatred that was tearing the child apart.

The walls of the mausoleum groaned and the floor jolted. The doors banged open and the darkness and cold that had plagued the Void poured into the marble building. Sparking blue-white power raced up the walls and across the floors, chased by golden fire. Uncontrolled magic forced open cracks and crevices, obliterated mortar, and turned stone to gravel. Creaking, groaning, squealing pounded their ears. Dust rained down.

A hole appeared at their feet. It widened and filled with the chalky unreflective liquid that had swallowed Gethen's reflection the first time he'd encountered the Rime Witch. This was the blood Shemel had bled, the liquid that Halina had coughed up, the witch's cold, blind malice.

The darkness being sucked into the mausoleum poured into the pool, but the liquid remained white and lifeless.

Halina stumbled toward the doorway, pulling Gethen and Yisun away from the ever-widening hole. But the Dargani girl drew back as they crossed the threshold. "You have to destroy the witch!" she shouted.

Halina gasped and sagged against Gethen. Her spirit was tearing loose from her body just like the mausoleum was tearing loose from its foundation.

But with Halina's collapse Yisun's face morphed from sad and innocent to a frozen mask of blind hatred. She crowed triumphantly, and her voice held the screeching, crackling tone of the Rime Witch. "Too late!" She lunged toward them.

Driven by instinct Gethen scribed a golden shield incantation and hurled it at the witch. It struck and threw her backward into the pool. In a blink the surface froze and hoarfrost raced across it, over the floor, and up the crumbling walls of the marble building. Then everything stopped, and the mausoleum was still for a long, slow moment. The Rime Witch's face appeared beneath the ice, white eyes and pallid skin almost indistinguishable from her liquid prison, her face a frozen rictus of rage and agony.

There was no sign of Yisun in that expression.

With a roar, the mausoleum's ceiling and walls collapsed. But darkness continued to flow into the area, finding cracks in the fallen marble and worming into the pool below. The tomb needed to be sealed or it would tear a hole in the Void.

Gethen kissed Halina. "Stay alive for me." Then the howling wind of his will whipped her across the Voidline and back into her body.

He wove a thick amber net of spells and cast them across the mausoleum's foundation, a cap to seal in the Rime Witch and her evil intentions. "If anything tampers with these wards, I'll know." It was an ugly but effective effort and, with a rueful glance at Yisun's prison and tomb, he crossed the Voidline to rejoin life and his lover.

Gethen cursed at the pain and nausea of the brutal return to his corporeal form as he forced his hunched body to straighten. Beside him Halina lay in a pool of her own blood, her eyes open but sightless. Magod still pumped her chest, but his muscles quivered, and he shook his head.

Gethen gathered his remaining sun magic, placed his hand upon her still chest, and kissed her lips. He breathed life and heat back into her body and mended her mortal wound. Gethen found the spark of her soul and coaxed it to flame, stoked it, fed it with his own ferocity. He straightened. "Halina. Come back."

But the flame died. The spark flickered. Her heart quivered and stopped again.

"No! Gods, no, Halina. Come back!" He pulled her into his arms and sought the spark. He'd sent her soul back. It was still there; it *had* to be. Why wouldn't it ignite? "What am I doing wrong? Tell me," he whispered against her hair.

Magod touched his arm.

Gethen bared his teeth at the man. "I'm not giving up!"

"Master, she lost too much blood."

"What?"

"The militess bled to death."

Gethen stared at his man. "Blood. Her blood." His eyes widened. "Give me her sword!"

Magod blinked but obeyed, holding the weapon out to his master.

"Blood magic." Gethen ran his hand down the blade. "Please work." The red he'd seen in the Void flickered beneath his touch, and he pulled the smallest thread of power from the sword. He mingled it with his own sorcery, pushed the mass of the sun and the power of lightning into it, and placed his hand against her still chest. Gethen pressed his forehead to hers and let the magic fall into her body. "Don't give up, Halina."

There was nothing for an infinitesimal moment.

Nothing.

Gethen's grip tightened on her. "You never give up," he whispered.

And then, the weight of their mingled magic hit the dim ember of her soul. Halina's body jerked as if struck by lightning and, like black powder catching, her spirit exploded outward. She gasped and arched, then curled into a ball and cursed a string of unsavory but widely popular epithets.

Gethen laughed and leaned over her, lifting the hair from her face and tucking it behind her ear as she quieted. "Better?"

She looked at him from the corner of her eye. "Was that your doing, Mage?" she whispered.

"It was, Militess."

"And you're still here?"

"Why wouldn't I be?"

She turned toward him. "Because usually when someone causes me that much pain, I stab them. A lot."

"I never meant to cause you pain, Halina." Gethen kissed her deeply and passionately, his hands in her hair and holding her tight until she said, "Ow."

He pulled back. "Sorry." She was ghostly pale and her lips were bloodless. He lifted her into his arms then stood and strode from the basilica.

"Put me down, you horse's arse. I'm not an invalid," she muttered weakly.

Magod grunted and Gethen replied, "Yes, you are. For a day, maybe two." He turned to his groundsman. "I need hot water and towels for a bath. And take my haversack to my bathing room. There's metheglin and unguent in there for the militess's wound."

He glanced at the man and added, "That cut on your skull needs tending, too."

"Gethen." Halina tugged on his collar. "I need to leave."

She wanted to get away from him and his cursed citadel. He didn't blame her. Ranith hadn't treated her gently. He swallowed a lump of regret. "I'm sorry you've suffered so much here."

She pushed back a little to peer at him, her brow furrowed with annoyance. "Don't be daft. I need to get a message to my father about that damnable death mark."

"Oh. That." Relief flooded him and he smiled. "I'd forgotten." He sat her down on a stool in his bathing room and unbuckled her tabard while Magod gathered the water buckets to take down to the kitchen.

"Well, I haven't." Halina trembled as he began removing her bloody armor. "It'd be an inconvenience to see you killed when I've just begun to enjoy your company. Plus, you come with wolves, a horse, and a skilled groundsman. And there's that sorcery that you do. The value of those things alone makes keeping you alive worthwhile."

Gethen cocked his head. "Very sensible, Your Ladyship."

She captured his hand and added, "And you're quite skilled with stitching, something I often require."

Gethen kissed her palm, her knuckles, and the ring that had redirected Volker's sword. "I'm at your service, Margrave Khara." Then he added, "And I'm grateful for your help with that death mark. Dying right now would be very inconvenient." He kissed her lips and added, "Since I've just begun to enjoy your company, too."

EPILOGUE

Halina carved a small, mealy apple with an eating knife. She pointed the blade at a schematic of Kharaton Castle, a slice of apple pinned beneath her thumb. "This is the better design. The keep can handle the greater height of a single tower."

Gethen slid the slice of fruit from her blade and bit off half of it. "That'll improve the vantage and defenses from all sides without the expense and inconvenience of raising the outer walls." He offered the remainder of the slice to her.

A fortnight had elapsed since the shadow mages' defeat and Yisun's surrender. The cold gripping Khara, the Silver Sea, and the Valmerians had eased. But spring's thaw remained months away, and Khara's second harvest had failed.

Halina opened her mouth and he put the apple on her tongue. "Then we're agreed," she said around the fruit. Parchment rustled as she shifted the schematic to the side. She stopped chewing and scowled. The fruit soured on her tongue. Beneath the drawing was a letter bearing King Vernard's official seal.

Gethen tapped the envelope. "A new demand?"

She swallowed. "Same as the last one, except this came from

Ilker. You're expected at the king's court. Official mage to His Majesty. Vernard's patience won't hold." She turned her knife and buried its tip in the table, pinning letter to wood. "He says nothing of aid for Khara's starving citizens. Offers no thanks for your efforts in battling the witch and mages. Doesn't return my soldiers or send supplies to help defend my hold. Just repeats Vernard's demands and threats."

She looked at the shriveled red fruit then dropped it on the blue plate upon which it had arrived. She'd lost her appetite. She wanted to throw it, but food couldn't be wasted in Khara now. "I expected better from my brother."

Gethen stepped behind her and placed his hands upon her shoulders. "We'll manage, Halina. Somehow."

"We must," she said.

He slid his hands around to cross her chest, pulled her body back against his, and pressed his cheek to her ear. "I'm untroubled by Vernard's idle threats. It requires too much effort and risk to muster an army through frozen and treacherous mountain passes. By spring your father and brother will have forgotten me."

She pressed back against him. His warmth filled her. She closed her eyes, reveling in the power humming into her through him, the unbowed strength of his lean, muscular body, and the honeyed, spiced musk of his skin. She laughed bitterly. "Vernard hates that you accepted his offer."

"With caveats."

"Oh, yes, and he hates those most of all."

"You mean he hates *me* most of all."

"Likely true, but I don't blame him for being suspicious. That shadowy fellow you were was a complete bastard."

Gethen nuzzled her ear. "I'm rather partial to bastards, you know."

The dark blue silk of his surcoat slipped beneath her fingers. "I know." She turned in his arms. "But you've complicated an already complex situation. The problem is I've been promised to Margrave Anatos."

"Anatos?" Gethen laughed. "That's a terrible match. The margrave is too genteel for you." He sneered and added, "You'll discover his shortcomings and crush his spirit."

"How do you know Anatos?"

Gethen waggled a finger at her. "A healer never reveals his patients' maladies or *deficiencies*."

Her eyes widened, then she laughed. "He's a gentleman and has always come to Khara's aid. Something I can't say about that fellow from Ranith."

"Yes, well, we've already established what a coxcomb *he* is."

She laughed again, but her smile quickly thinned.

He pulled back to look at her. "What?"

She opened her mouth then closed it and looked pained and like she was carefully choosing her words. "You and Anatos aren't the only ones."

"Who else?"

"That I know of?" she said slowly. "Ellis, the Duke of Carnes."

"My *cousin*?"

She cringed as she added, "And Crown Prince Waldram of Nalvika."

"Augh." It was Gethen's turn to look like he'd eaten something rotten. "The Nalviks won't be easily dissuaded."

She rolled her eyes. "I know. I've been trying."

He began to reply when a knock at the door interrupted him. He blew out a breath then stepped back from her and composed his features into a threatening glower.

"Enter," Halina called then lowered her voice and asked, "Why do you wear that expression for my aides?"

A messenger opened the study door as Gethen murmured, "Because it increases their awe of Your Ladyship." He widened his eyes at her. "Militess Halina, tamer of dangerous mages and crazed witches."

She turned away from the messenger, pressing her lips together and swallowing a laugh. The man paused in the doorway and bowed. She drew a steadying breath, faced him, and said, "You have a message for me?"

"Yes, Your Ladyship." True to Gethen's claim, the man's focus skipped past her, and his eyes widen at the hawk gaze of the powerful mage behind his liege. Then his attention snapped back to her face. "Beseran troops have been spied making for Kharaton Harbor."

Halina cocked her head and frowned. "Troops? How? The sea is frozen. Who reported this?"

"A group of fishermen. They were cutting holes in the ice for their lines."

"Has anyone confirmed it from the weather tower?"

"Yes, Your Ladyship."

Halina's frown deepened. "Tell Captain Thaksin to meet me there." She looked askance at Gethen. "Is this 'Bring Ursinum to Besera?' Or are they here for you?" He shook his head, his expression grim.

The messenger bowed and disappeared into the hallway as Halina followed, Gethen beside her. The solar was on the wrong side of Kharaton Castle. They went out into the damp morning, crossed the battlements, and climbed to the top of the east-facing weather tower.

Thaksin awaited them. He offered a spyglass to Halina and a cold shoulder to Gethen. "They've stopped outside the harbor walls, Your Ladyship."

The captain was reserved and formal with her now that Gethen had replaced him in her bed. He didn't approve, that was obvious, but he knew better than to openly object. She regretted the loss of his amity; they'd been friends before they became lovers.

She raised the glass to her eye. "How long have they been there?" Fog lay thick upon the harbor, but dark shapes hulked in the brume just beyond the port's narrow opening.

"The better part of an hour," Thaksin replied.

She rounded on him. "And it took so long to inform me because why?"

"I'd hoped to confirm their numbers and armaments, Your Ladyship, so that I could provide a complete report."

"But?"

"The mist is too heavy to get a clear view from here, and waiting for the scouts has taken too long."

Gethen uttered an incantation and swept his hand across his body. The fog billowed and rolled. It lifted and curled back upon itself, revealing the craggy rocks that formed the long arms of the harbor. Just beyond them, sitting upon the ice, were massive, wooden Beseran barges. Two dozen, the length of ten horses each, and each pulled by as many horses. They sat upon carved runners that helped them glide across the Silver Sea's ice. "Those aren't troop barges," the Sun Mage said.

Thaksin stared at him with a mixture of awe, fear, and suspicion. "What are they?"

Halina lowered the frigid copper spyglass. "Assistance."

"Food. Blankets. Fodder." Gethen smiled slowly. "Looks like Zelal's decided to be the Sun Mage's friend."

"That's good enough for me." Halina turned and slapped the spyglass into her captain's hands. "Send a welcoming party. Bid them to enter Kharaton Harbor and tell them I'll greet them upon the wharf."

Thaksin saluted and ran down the stairs.

Halina grabbed Gethen's cloak and pulled him to her for a kiss. He shared her smile as they hastened to her apartment.

A chambermaid was changing the bed linens. She turned and curtsied as they entered.

"Vi, I need to dress for visitors. Fetch my heavy red kirtle and the gray winter surcoat; the one with the cutouts." Halina began pulling at the back laces of her green house kirtle and cursing them beneath her breath.

The chambermaid hesitated like a cornered mouse, uncertain if she should gather the clothes as she'd been told or help her mistress with her laces. Gethen shooed her to the gown room while he deftly unlaced the kirtle. When it was off, Halina sent him to his chamber for his own outside clothing, saying, "You're coming with me."

"Why?"

The maid quickly laced one of the surcoat's heavy sleeves onto its shoulder seam as Halina said, "Because you're King Zelal's brother. And because I'm terrible with the Beseran tongue."

He looked at her for an intense moment then gave her a wolfish grin. "No, you're not." He bowed deeply and said, "The Sun Mage is at your disposal, Your Ladyship."

Ignoring Vi's giggles, Halina curled her lip at him as she buckled on a bejeweled sword-belt and frog. She settled her sword in place on her hip, comforted by its familiar heft and yaw. She was a lady, but she was a militess first. And she'd make sure Zelal didn't forget it.

When Gethen returned, wearing his heavy, fur-lined cloak and his own sword, she said, "This evening I'll compose a response to my father. He can stuff his threats and agreements up his royal arse." She captured his hand. "I won't be releasing my mage to His Majesty's service or marrying anyone else. I won't be a fish dangled before sharks anymore."

Gethen cupped her jaw and kissed her then led her through the halls and down the main stairs to the front of the castle. "This won't make him sell your young sister to the highest bidder, will it?"

Halina laughed. Her soldiers were saddling and mounting as a stable boy brought Remig and Abelard.

"Oh, no. Don't be fooled by Arevik's youthfulness," she replied. "My sister takes after our Beseran mother, and there's magic in her. She knows how to survive the asps and toads of the royal court and twists our father around her finger in ways I never could."

Gethen's brows rose. "That means a bit of magic runs through your veins, too, Your Ladyship."

She tipped forward and kissed him. "Only enough to bewitch a mage."

DEAR READER

Thank you for purchasing and reading *The Shadow and the Sun*. If you enjoyed this book, please consider recommending it to your friends or leaving a brief review with the retail site where you purchased it. Word of mouth is an indie author's best friend and much appreciated. And please take a moment to connect with me via social media. You can find me at the links on the About the Author page. I'd love to hear from you.

Thanks!
Monica

ACKNOWLEDGMENTS

As always I must first acknowledge Scott and Emeline, for their incredible patience and support, and for tolerating the slow decay of my housekeeping abilities as this book progressed. I need to thank my incredible editor, Maia Driver, and my incredible mother, Judith Ross Enderle; you ladies make me look smart and keep me from being lazy. A special thanks goes to Qistina Khalidah for creating the amazing faces of Gethen and Halina; your beautiful artwork inspires me. Thank you to all the readers who've patiently waited and supported me as I've figured out my path, and to my many friends (authors, readers, and others) who are always ready to encourage, answer, and commiserate.

Militess & Mage Series

The Shadow and The Sun

A Castle to Keep

The Bones Beneath

To Give Her Heart (short)

Glass and Iron Series

Girl Under Glass

The Mother Element

A Sad Jar of Atoms (short)

Rust and Ruin (short)

The Apocalyptics Series

Famine

Short Stories

Love Lies Bleeding

Anthologies & Collections

The Dragon Chronicles

Prep For Doom

The Doomsday Chronicles

Once Upon a Time in Gravity City

ABOUT THE AUTHOR

Monica Enderle Pierce and her characters have been kicking the crap out of evil since 2012. She writes fantasy and science fiction and her stories are filled with strong women, smart men, love, adventure, and magic. She has an English literature degree from the University of California, Los Angeles, and she lives in Seattle, Washington, with her husband, their daughter, a neurotic dog, and two crazy tomcats. When she's not sending characters into battle or off on an adventure, she's reading minds, seeing through walls, and reveling in the glorious Pacific Northwest rain.

How to reach me:
monicaenderlepierce.com
monicaenderlepierce@gmail.com